D0057637

THE GRINDER

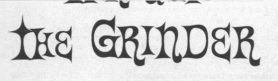

CLEO COYLE

BERKLEY PRIME CRIME, NEW YORK

THE BERKLEY PUBLISHING GROUP
Published by the Penguin Group
Penguin Group (USA) Inc.
375 Hudson Street, New York, New York 10014, USA

USA | Canada | UK | Ireland | Australia | New Zealand | India | South Africa | China

Penguin Books Ltd., Registered Offices: 80 Strand, London WC2R 0RL, England
For more information about the Penguin Group, visit penguin.com.

THROUGH THE GRINDER

A Berkley Prime Crime Book / published by arrangement with the author

Berkley Prime Crime Books are published by The Berkley Publishing Group.
BERKLEY® PRIME CRIME and the PRIME CRIME logo are
trademarks of Penguin Group (USA) Inc.
A COFFEEHOUSE MYSTERY is a registered trademark of Penguin Group (USA) Inc.

For information, address: The Berkley Publishing Group,
a division of Penguin Group (USA) Inc.,
375 Hudson Street, New York, New York 10014.

ISBN: 978-0-425-19714-1

PUBLISHING HISTORY
Berkley Prime Crime mass-market edition / October 2004

PRINTED IN THE UNITED STATES OF AMERICA

24 23 22 21 20 19 18 17 16 15

Cover illustration by Catherine Gendron.
Cover design and logo by Rita Frangie.
Interior text design by Kristin del Rosario.

ALWAYS LEARNING   PEARSON

*Once again to Martha Bushko and John Talbot—
with whipped cream and caramel syrup on top!*

When you are worried, have trouble of one sort
or another—to the coffee house! . . .
You could not find a mate to suit you—coffee house!
You feel like committing suicide—coffee house!
You hate and despise human beings, and at the same time
you can not be happy without them—coffee house!

—"To the Coffee House!"
Viennese poet Peter Altenberg

PROLOGUE

~~~~~~

SHE had to die.

The Genius knew this and was absolutely fine with it. The problem, of course, was how.

In the Genius's view, almost any problem could be solved through study. So it was no surprise when the study of Valerie Lathem's life yielded the solution to her death.

The air on that pale November morning displayed an especially cruel bite, stabbing at cheeks, chins, and all other areas of exposed human flesh. Still, the Genius stood with the usual patience at the usual bus stop, pretending to wait for the usual bus. Reading the paper was usual enough, too, but the Times articles felt incomprehensible today, and the wait became interminable.

When the twenty-seven-year-old woman finally emerged from her dingy brick apartment building, the Genius followed the pert face and slender figure, the shoulder-length retro flip hair the color of rancid butter, the black boots *with heels too high, green cargos a size too small, and that cheap red leather jacket she'd purchased at SoHo Jeans the day before.*

With brisk steps, the woman followed Bleecker across Sixth Avenue, the wide, high-traffic chasm dividing modern Manhattan from the year 1811, when city fathers and their Euclidean plans for perpendicular streets were defied by village residents who refused to have their district's twisted lanes made straight.

For two hundred years, this winding web of cobblestone streets, narrow alleys, and secluded pathways has obeyed no logical pattern. The frosty air has been tinged with the acrid smell of logs burning on nineteenth century hearths. Gas lamps have been flickering near gated mews, hidden gardens, or sedate churchyards. And the sidewalks have edged not skyscrapers arranged in uniform grids, but a low-lying landscape of three- and four-story row houses, many now lodging offbeat boutiques, pricey bistros, and the occasional dark-paneled pub—all closed for business at this early hour.

A corner on Hudson was the woman's first stop, the site of a four-story Federal-style townhouse occupied for the last ten decades by the Village Blend coffeehouse. As she reached for the old brass handle, the beveled glass door swung wide, vomiting out three pubescent NYU students with a gust of roasting coffee.

"Ah, yes," whispered the genius, "that heavenly smell . . ."

The earthy aroma drifted across the cobblestones on the crisp, fall air—a siren's call of freshly frothed cappuccinos, warm pastries, anise biscotti, and bracing espressos. But entering the Blend was not an option. Not for the Genius. Not until the objective was achieved.

"One push. Timed just right. One simple push."

Until then, there would be no cozy fireplace, no foamed milk, no buttery croissant. Across the street, the Genius shifted from foot to foot on the cold sidewalk, eyes peering through the Blend's twelve-foot-tall front windows.

Like trendy cattle, a dozen customers milled around the coffee bar counter. The woman placed her order with a lanky young man, waited a few minutes, then collected a paper cup from a petite brunette.

At last, the door swung wide again. An enviable puff of aromatic steam rose from the cup when it hit the cold air. For a moment, Valerie Lathem's snug green cargo pants paused on the sidewalk to touch her full lips to the edge of the lid. A shiver of delight followed, and the Genius struggled against a sharp memory of another place the woman's lips had touched . . . that place on him . . .

And on other men.

For a moment, the Genius had trouble breathing. "One push. Timed just right . . ."

Then the Slut continued her journey, hiking north and east, to Fourteenth and Broadway, where a wide public area of grass, tress, and benches formed Union Square Park.

On Tuesdays, Thursdays, and Sundays, the wide concrete border to the west of the park was reserved for metered parking. On Mondays, Wednesdays, Fridays, and Saturdays, however, cars were banned and an open-air farmer's market appeared.

Regional growers from New Jersey, Long Island, and upstate New York packed the white-tented stands with produce. The Genius trailed the Slut as she visited table after table, purchasing organically grown apples and carrots, three kinds of homemade jams, a jar of natural honey, and finally a fresh-baked loaf of whole wheat bread. These were intended for the Slut's elderly grandmother, whom she visited uptown every Saturday—most likely in an effort to cinch some share of inheritance.

The R train had been the Slut's transport of choice for the last two Saturdays, and when she headed toward the subway stairs again today, the Genius allowed a small exhale of relief.

Below ground, the northwest entrance provided a bank of Metrocard machines and a "token booth"—which hadn't sold tokens since 2003. The Slut had already purchased her Metrocard, so she strode across the black spotted concrete floor, past the vending machines to the turnstiles, and swiped the bright yellow rectangle through the silver slot.

An almost imperceptible click sounded as the machine deducted the cost of the ride from the card. Then, with a ker-chunk, ker-chank, the Slut pushed through the metal spider and strode toward the stairwell on the left, leading down another level to the Broadway line's Uptown platform.

After waiting thirty seconds, the Genius swiped a pre-purchased Metrocard, just as the Slut had. But there was no click. The little screen embedded in the silver turnstile arm read STOP: PLEASE SWIPE YOUR CARD AGAIN AT THIS TURNSTILE.

The Genius swiped.

The STOP remained.

On a weekday at such an early hour, this station would be packed with office workers and college students, but on a Saturday, riders were scarce. Two turnstiles away, the only other riders at this entrance—a middle-aged woman and two little girls—laughed and giggled as they swept through and away, toward the Downtown stairwell to the right.

The Genius stared straight, trying not to call attention. Sweaty palms made the plastic moist. Slowly came a distant rumbling.

A train was coming. Uptown or down? Unable to tell, the Genius brushed the card across a coat sleeve, and swiped again.

The green GO appeared.

Go! Go! Go!

The Genius bolted through the spider arms then flowed down the stairs like liquid. Feet on the platform, the Genius leaned over the tracks. At the far end, near the mouth of the tunnel, the reflection of a headlight beam stretched along the tiled wall like the advancing movement of a pointing finger.

The train was coming—an uptown train.

Uptown, uptown! Now, now, now!

The Genius swiftly snaked around the edge of the staircase. Here the narrow concrete platform measured no more than the length of two subway cars. At one end was a wall, at the other, the back of the staircase the Genius had just descended. Only commuters who wished to ride in the first two cars would wait here—riders like Valerie. She stood alone behind the staircase, hidden from the few other riders on the platform's south end.

The track curved a bit at this particular station, and the train could not be seen approaching unless the commuter leaned forward, peeking around the row of dull green vertical support beams. The Slut was doing just that—leaning a bit over the edge of the platform, watching the approach of her train. One hand held her bag of farmers market produce, the other her double tall cup of Village Blend coffee. No hand free—not to fight, not even to balance herself.

The Genius stepped carefully behind the Slut, the mechanical junk-rumble of the coming train, like spare parts in a washing machine, drowning out any footsteps. This station was one of the loudest in the city—the decibel level making it impossible to hear conversation, maybe even screams. In another three seconds, the Genius would know for sure.

One push. Timed just right. One simple push.

As the red leather coat fell forward into the empty air,

then down, toward the grimy tracks, the Genius did hear a scream. And finally there was red on the tracks. First one way. Then another.

As the shriek of the victim was drowned out by the shriek of the R train's brakes, the Genius backed into the shadows of the staircase, snaked around the corner, wandered back up, then through the turnstiles, and up once more, ascending into the invigorating chill of this brand new day.

Finally, finally, that feeling of accomplishment. Objective achieved . . . and . . . time for that cappuccino!

One

~~~~~~

"...**And** he called to tell me it's on the covers of both the *Post* and the *Daily News*. The cover story, Clare!"

Sitting up in bed, I rubbed my eyes, trying to concentrate on the monologue percolating against my ear. But for a good two minutes (5:02 to 5:04 A.M. Eastern Standard Time to be precise), the only thing my mind clung to was the image of something dark, powerful, rich, and warm.

No, this something did not have bedroom eyes, a Swiss bank account, and a heavy, sinewy frame depressing the other side of my mattress. As a perpetual single mother, I'd had nothing remotely like that on the other side of my mattress for years—sinewy or otherwise—just clean cotton sheets and a sour female cat.

In point of fact, that dark, powerful, rich, and warm *something* I yearned for was a cup of Guatemala Antigua— one of those smooth, tangy coffees, like Costa Rican and Colombian, which would awaken my yawning palette with a full-bodied, slightly spicy flavor and bracing, rich acidity. ("Acidity" being the pleasant sharpness as the flavor finishes in the mouth, not to be confused with "bitterness," but I'll get to that later.)

I sighed, almost smelling the earthy aroma of that first morning cup, tasting its nutty essence, feeling the shudder of radiant pleasure as the jolt of heat and caffeine seemed to flow directly into my veins.

God I loved the morning ritual.

My ex-husband, Matteo Allegro, used to say that abandoning the peace of sleep was only tolerable if a fresh pot of coffee were waiting. He and I never agreed on much. But we agreed on that.

"It's very upsetting, Clare. Not the image we want for the Blend. Don't you agree?"

The bright voice (displaying more than trace amounts acidity) on the other end of the phone line was finally penetrating my wake-up fog.

"Madame, slow down," I said, rising from a half-reclined to a fully upright and locked position. The bedroom's silk drapes were pulled shut, but it being November, no light would be forthcoming even if they had been open. The break of dawn was over an hour away.

"What is on the cover exactly?" I asked Madame through a yawn.

"The Village Blend," repeated Madame. "It's been mentioned in connection to—"

I yawned again.

"Clare, dear, did my call *wake* you? Why are you sleeping in?"

I rubbed my eyes and glanced at the digital alarm clock. "I'm not sleeping in. I usually sleep until five *thirty*."

"With your bakery delivery at six?"

Madame's censuring tone was abundantly perceptible. But, because of my enormous respect for my eighty-year-old, French-born ex-mother-in-law, I remained only mildly irritated.

It didn't matter to me if the bakery delivery occurred at six every morning. All I had to do was roll out of bed, shower, throw on jeans and a sweater, and descend three floors. It wasn't as if the coffeehouse was fifty miles away. The delivery would be made literally at my back door.

Granted, that hadn't always been my situation. . . .

Just a few months ago, I'd been raising my daughter in New Jersey, writing the occasional article for coffee trade magazines, a regular cooking tips column for a local paper, and working odd catering and child day care jobs to make ends meet when one morning Madame had called. She'd begged me to come back to the city and manage the Blend for her again as I'd done years before—when I'd been her daughter-in-law.

I'd agreed, *partly* because my now grown daughter had just enrolled in a SoHo culinary school and managing the Blend meant I'd be in the next neighborhood instead of the next state. And *partly* because Madame's generous contract afforded me increasing ownership of the Blend as time went on, which included the incredible duplex apartment above the two-floor coffeehouse itself.

Who wouldn't jump at the chance to one day own a historic townhouse, complete with a duplex filled with antique furnishings, Persian prayer rugs, framed Hoppers, and working fireplaces, in one of the most in-demand areas in Manhattan? Certainly not *moi*.

"I've never missed a bakery delivery in all the years I've managed the place for you," I assured her flatly, "and I'm not about to start this morning."

"I'm sorry, dear," she said. "Of course, you have it in hand. It's just that never in my life could I bathe and primp in mere minutes. Your morning routine must resemble something not found outside of sports locker rooms."

O-kay, it's going to be one of those days.

I cleared my throat, silently reminding myself that this was just Madame being . . . Madame. After all, the woman certainly had a right to say anything she liked about running the Blend—and not just because she owned it.

Madame Blanche Dreyfus Allegro Dubois, an immigrant refugee of World War Two Paris, had managed the Blend herself for decades, personally pouring cups o' joe for some of the twentieth century's most renowned artists, actors, playwrights, poets, and musicians. Mention Dylan Thomas, Jackson Pollock, Marlon Brando, Ella Fitzgerald, Frank Sinatra, Miles Davis, Jack Kerouac, Barbra Streisand, Paddy Chayefsky, Robert DeNiro, Sam Shepard, or Edward Albee— and she'd share a personal anecdote.

So, the way I looked at it, if anyone had earned the right to be a pain in the ass when it came to running the Blend, she did.

Still . . . it was five in the A.M.

"Madame, tell me again *why* you called?"

"The Blend has been mentioned in the papers, dear, all of them."

"In connection to what?"

"A suicide."

"WHAT is it with *New York 1,* running the same stories, like, twenty-four times in twenty-four hours?"

My Jersey Girl daughter, Joy, was still adjusting to the array of trivialities that characterized Manhattan life. Just before eleven o'clock, she crossed the Blend's sun-washed, wood-plank floor on her stacked black boots and ordered her usual double tall vanilla latte.

Current conversation topic at the coffeehouse counter—Basic Cable's Channel 1.

I must have heard thousands of these discussions in my time managing the coffeehouse—the eccentricities of cabbies, bad Broadway shows, sucky bands at CBGB, *Time Out*'s cover stories, film crews that close down entire blocks, trying to sleep through relentless ambulance sirens, kicking cars that block pedestrian crosswalks, the best slice below Fourteenth, Barney's warehouse sales, the end of porno on Forty-Second, kamikaze bike messengers, the real meaning of some Yiddish word, the difference—if any—among the Indian restaurants lining East Sixth, the *New York Post*'s Page Six, the precise contents of an egg cream. And, of course, rents, rents, apartments, and rents.

One of my best baristas and assistant managers, Tucker Burton, a lanky, floppy haired, gay playwright and actor, who also happened to believe he was the illegitimate son of Richard Burton, slid Joy's drink across the slab of blueberry marble.

"Sweetie, don't knock *New York 1*. What other town's got a cable channel devoted to twenty-four hours of local coverage? Okay, so the stories repeat a lot, but you haven't yawned till you've heard the fisherman's weather in rural Louisiana. Lemme tell ya, swamp humidity levels aren't pretty—or in the least interesting. Give me a 'Subway Surfer Falls to His Death' story repeated ten times any day."

"That's sort of morbid, Tucker," I pointed out behind the coffee bar's efficient, low-slung silver espresso machine.

(We actually had a three-foot-tall, bullet-shaped La Victoria Arduino espresso machine behind the counter, too. Strewn with dials and valves, the thing had been imported from Italy in the 1920s; but, like the eclectic array of coffee antiques decorating the shelves and fireplace mantel—

including a cast iron two-wheeled grinding mill, copper English coffee pots, side-handled Turkish *ibriks*, a Russian samovar, and a French lacquered coffee urn—it was for show only.)

"Get over it, Clare," said Kira Kirk, the eight-pound Sunday edition of the *New York Times* cradled in her slender arm like a newsprint infant. "What do you expect from a city of aberrant people?"

"Aberrant?" said Joy.

"Devious. Wayward. Offending. Sinning—if you will." Kira was a crossword puzzle freak. "Where else would goofball kids think surfing on top of a subway car is something to do for kicks? If you ask me, they deserve to get squashed like bugs."

As a coffeehouse manager, I'd seen many flavors of urban humanity pour through our front door. Kira was one of that group who embodied those lines from the poem "To the Coffeehouse":

"You hate and despise human beings, and at the same time you can not be happy without them . . ."

A consultant of some sort, Kira was recently divorced, living alone, and approaching fifty. She'd started coming by the Blend pretty frequently about six weeks ago. When I first saw her, I thought she was a striking woman with refined features, beautiful cheekbones, and an admirable head of long dark hair. Lately, however, I noticed she'd started letting herself go. Her usually creamy skin looked blotchy and wind burned, her body looked far too thin, like she wasn't eating enough, and she'd even stopped dyeing her hair. It now hung in a long gray braid down her oversized blue sweater.

Kira's usual Sunday ritual was the *Travel and Leisure* section, then the crossword puzzle, accompanied by a grande cappuccino and a butter croissant. As a regular, she didn't need to tell me her order. She just needed to appear.

I half-filled the stainless steel pitcher with whole milk, then opened the valve on the steam wand, warming the milk on the bottom and foaming it on top. Then I set aside the pitcher, ran the ravishingly oily espresso roast beans through the grinder, dosed the ground coffee into the portafilter cup, tamped it tightly down, and, after sweeping excess grinds from the rim, clamped its handle into place.

With the start of the extraction process, I checked the espresso's viscosity, making sure it was oozing out of the machine (yes, it should ooze like warm honey—if it gushes out, the machine's temperature and pressure is off, and it's not espresso but a brewed beverage).

Our machine is semi-automatic, which means the barista (that's me) must manually stop the water flow between eighteen and twenty-four seconds. Any longer and the beverage is over-extracted (bitter and burnt-tasting because the sugars have deteriorated). Any shorter and its under-extracted (weak, insipid, and completely uninspiring). Like a lot of things in life, making a great espresso depended on a number of variables—and timing was certainly one of them.

"It's not a real channel anyway, is it—*New York 1*?" asked Joy. "I mean, it's one of those community service deals, right?"

"Right. A tax write-off for Time Warner," said one of my part-timers, Esther Best (shortened from Bestovasky by her grandfather), an NYU student with wild dark hair currently stuffed into a backward baseball cap. She was swabbing one of the few empty coral-colored marble tables with a wet towel. "I've got a friend whose sister works there. Apparently, they have a saying in the newsroom— you can get on *New York 1,* but you can't get off."

"What does that mean?" asked Joy.

Esther shrugged. "It's because they run the stories so often. But you can't blame them. Because of their budget, their staff is, like, miniscule, I mean compared to an outfit like CNN."

Joy shrugged. "All I know is, my favorite segment is that one they repeat every hour in the morning, the one where they read you the headlines. It really rocks."

"True," said Esther. "I myself can't get out of bed in the morning till I hear Weather on the Ones, and that hottie anchor Pat Kiernan reads me the headlines from all the New York papers."

"Word," said Joy.

(Eavesdropping on the college crowd, I'd long ago assumed, contextually, that *word* was vernacular hip-hop for "right on" or "and how"—or something along those lines.)

Tucker made a sour face. "You ladies think Kiernan's a hottie? With that baby face and those insurance salesmen suits?"

"Sure," said Joy. "He's nerd hot."

"Yeah, like Clark Kent or something," agreed Esther, adjusting her trendy black-framed glasses.

My eyebrow rose. Joy's last boyfriend was anything but "nerd hot." With his long dark ponytail, olive complexion, barbed-wire tattoo, and flashing arrogant eyes, Mario Forte looked more like Antonio Banderas's younger brother. My ex-husband, who shared many of these features, had hated him on sight.

So what happened to Mario? I was dying to ask my daughter. But I'd already read *The 101 Ways to Embarrass Your Daughter and Piss Her Off for Decades* handbook—and I figured it was better left unasked . . . for now.

Instead, I poured Kira's freshly drawn espresso shots into a grande-size cup, slid in the steamed milk, topped it with foamed milk—and changed the subject. "So did Clark Kent Kiernan cover that suicide story this morning?"

"Are you kidding?" said Esther. "He was totally all over it. Pat doesn't usually do the weekend anchor thing. He's the weekday guy, but I got lucky this morning. And lemme tell you, my pulse was on overdrive. It felt like he was talking about *me*."

"Excuse me, Miss Six Feet Under," said Tucker, "but since when do you identify yourself as a corpse on the tracks of the Union Square R train?"

"Excuse *me,* Mr. Queer Eye," Esther snapped right back. "I meant the Village Blend part. I work at the Blend. He talked about the Blend. Hello? Get it?"

"Yes, sugar-lumps, I got it."

"Good."

"Here you go," I told Kira, handing her the steaming cappuccino and a small plate with a warm croissant.

"Thanks, Clare. You know, I've got all the papers this morning if you haven't seen them yet." Kira held up a big Lands End canvas carryall. Inside was enough newsprint to wrap dead fish through a nuclear winter.

I hesitated a moment. Since Madame's predawn phone call, I'd tried to put the gruesome news out of my mind and just focus on serving the rush of regulars that came in on Sunday, which was much different than the weekend crush of office workers and commuters.

Today we'd see mostly dog-walking residents, straight and gay couples sharing fat editions of the Sunday *Times,* and well-dressed worshipers from the many nearby churches. Interns and staff from St. Vincent's Hospital would come in around noon, and NYU students would take over most of the tables after that, with their laptops and cell phones.

"Mom, we should probably take a look," said Joy.

I nodded and poured myself a cup of the house blend— a unique mix of beans that changed annually, depending on my ex-husband's recommendations.

Matteo Allegro, apart from being Madame's son—and my ex—was an astute coffee broker, the Blend's coffee buyer, and the descendant of Antonio Vespasian Allegro, the man who'd originally opened the Blend. He was also a pain in my ass—and, thank goodness, currently in East Africa, chasing a primo crop of Sidamo, if not shapely legs and long-lashed eyes, which was why I'd applied the prefix "ex" to my husband in the first place.

"What's wrong?" asked Joy as she watched me bolt half the cup of java.

I shrugged, pouring more and moving around the counter. "Death isn't something a person should face without a fortifying hit of caffeine."

Two

I didn't notice when he'd arrived. Not right away. Which was very unusual. Because ever since he'd first walked through the Blend's front door a few months back, I'd *always* noticed.

Today, however, I'd been especially distracted. So when I finally did realize that Detective Mike Quinn of the Sixth Precinct's detective squad had entered the coffeehouse, crossed the sun-washed room, and wandered up behind the huddling group of us, I was caught by surprise and actually became a little flustered.

The main floor of the coffeehouse was rectangular in shape, with a row of tall, white French doors lining one side. In summer, these were thrown open for sidewalk seating, but on this chilly autumn day they were shut tight. At the room's far end was an exposed brick wall, a working fireplace, and a wrought iron spiral staircase leading to the cozy second floor. (This staircase was for customers. The staff used the service stairs near the back door behind the pantry.)

At the moment, the Sunday papers were spread out across one of the circa 1919 coral-colored marble-topped tables near the coffee bar. The *Times,* with their usually restrained reportage, had tucked the story of Valerie Lathem's suicide on the inside of the Metro section. The *Daily News* and *New York Post*, however, had splashed lurid leads across their tabloid fronts.

"Final Cup of Coffee" and "Jumpin' with Joe" headlines were accompanied with nearly identical front-page photos of a Village Blend cup lying in the middle of grimy subway tracks. Because of the subway train's height, the paper cup had been left eerily unmolested between the rails—unlike Valerie herself, whose blood had been splattered everywhere. This bizarre contrast had clearly piqued the morbid interest of the photographers.

A color photo of the pretty young woman had been inset next to the stories on her suicide. Apparently, reporters had borrowed the picture from her grandmother, whom they'd visited for quotes before filing.

"Any of you know Ms. Lathem?" the Detective abruptly bit out.

Even on good days Mike Quinn's manner wasn't the warmest. On days like this, however, days after a particularly tragic death, the man had a voice like stale coffee—wrung out and bitter.

I turned to find his twilight blue eyes on me, his square jaw sprouting the shadowy stubble of a beard. His clothes were relatives of the family Beige: brown pants, a gold printed tie hanging from a loose knot, and a winter coat the color of a cinnamon roast bean. From experience, I knew that beneath that coat, strapped across muscular shoulders, was a brown leather holster that held a gun the size of a howitzer.

Under his bloodshot eyes, I noticed shadowy crescents. He'd probably been up half the night.

"Let me get your usual," I told him.

He nodded, and I noticed his dark blonde hair, which was usually trimmed fairly short, was looking a little shaggy.

The conversation around the table continued as I pulled the fresh espresso shots and steamed the milk for Quinn's latte.

"I've seen her come in here," Esther Best told Quinn. "But I didn't know her."

Tucker, Joy, and Kira all concurred. Each had recognized Valerie Lathem as a regular customer, but that was it.

"The typical Manhattan existence," said Tucker. "Many recognize you, but no one knows you."

"It's awful," I said, when Quinn moved to the coffee bar to take his latte. "She was so young."

"Twenty-seven," said Quinn, leaning on the blue marble counter. He took a sip from the paper cup and closed his eyes. For the briefest moment, his features relaxed and his load seemed to lighten.

When I'd met the detective a few months back, he'd been on a steady diet of stale Robusta bean crap, poured from a stained carafe at a Sixth Avenue bodega. I'd converted him into a regular with one good mug of Arabica house blend, followed by a freshly drawn latte. Ever since, I'd been savoring these brief flashes of surrender that would cross his routinely haggard face.

My ex-husband seemed to think Quinn's interest in me went beyond my ability to mix perfect Italian coffee drinks.

I begged to differ.

Quinn was a married man and our conversations rarely went beyond the level of a coffee barista bantering with her customer. On the other hand, if this truly was the only time the detective allowed himself to surrender to pleasure in the course of his day—I really did wonder what that said about our relationship.

"Do you remember what she ordered?" Quinn asked me, suddenly opening his eyes. "As her final cup?"

"What you're having," I said. "A double tall latte."

Quinn nodded.

"It's our most popular drink—which isn't surprising. It's the most popular drink at most specialty coffeehouses in America."

Quinn raised a questioning eyebrow.

"Part of my research for an article I did last year for *Cupping* magazine," I explained.

He nodded.

Behind the coffee bar, I prepped the espresso machine for its next shot, unclamping the portafilter handle and dumping the packed black grounds, knocking the cake-shaped debris into the under-counter garbage can.

"So, Valerie Lathem's death was a suicide then?" I asked. "I mean, according to the newspaper reports, the transit police are calling it a suicide. You're not involved in the investigation, are you?"

"It's transit's case. But Ms. Lathem was a Village resident, so my partner and I have been assigned to *assist* my transit *brethren*," he said. "Search her apartment and such."

The caustic tone was subtle. Although you could never be sure with Quinn, I assumed he was not entirely happy with the course of the investigation.

"You searched her apartment?" I repeated softly, pausing before I rinsed out the filter.

Quinn nodded.

"What do you think?"

Quinn took another sip of his latte.

Before he could say more—and, knowing Quinn, he certainly wouldn't have said much more anyway—he was distracted by the increasing volume of the conversation at the table I'd just left.

". . . and the *Post* reports at the end of the article that she was just promoted," said Tucker.

"Where did she work?" asked Joy.

"According to the *Post* . . . Triumph Travel," said Tucker, examining the page.

"Triumph has a lot of contracts around the city," noted Kira. "They specialize in booking business trips for CEO-level execs."

"Really?" said Tucker, skimming the page, then looking at another paper. "How do you know that, Kira? Nobody mentions it."

Kira shrugged. "Easy, Tucker. I'm a genius."

"Why would she kill herself, do you think?" asked Joy.

"Why does anybody kill themselves," said Esther with a shrug. "Love."

"Love?" said Tucker. "And this from *you,* our Goddess of the Jaded?"

"It's only, like, monumentally embedded in our literary history," Esther said. "Don't you know that?"

Tucker rolled his eyes, then loudly cleared his throat and clapped his hands. "People! People! I have a question—"

I tensed as the entire coffeehouse of customers looked up.

Esther should have known better. As an NYU English major, she liked to display her literary attitude on her sleeve (such as her frequently announced reason for working here—Voltaire and Balzac both supposedly drank over forty cups of Joe a day). But to imply that Tucker, a playwright and actor, wasn't acutely aware of the myriad causes of human angst was practically daring him to make a scene.

"Show of hands please!" shouted Tucker. "Who in this room can trace their pain to (A) their parents? (B) Events that happened in the school or peer arena? (C) Genetics?"

The customers blinked and stared.

"I trace my pain to my bad mattress."

The place erupted in peels of laughter.

Tucker turned and gave a little bow to the woman who'd made the quip—a strikingly elegant brunette standing by the front door in a gorgeous floor-length shearling.

Like Valerie Lathem, I'd seen Shearling Lady a few times before, but I'd never gotten to know her by name. Tucker took her order as she approached the counter.

"I don't care what you think," Esther called to Tucker. "I still say it was love."

"Word," said Joy. "Someone might have broken her heart."

Oh god. My daughter had finally mentioned the subject of broken hearts.

"A guy just dumped me," Joy told Esther rather matter-of-factly.

Now I was really tensing.

"If I had loved him, I think it would have been really devastating."

I sighed with extreme relief, grateful to hear that Mario Forte hadn't caused my girl any real pain.

With her cute heart-shaped face, bouncy chestnut hair, and equally bouncy personality, my daughter had gone on her share of dates in high school, but she had yet to fall— really fall—in love.

As a woman, I certainly did want Joy to experience the exhilaration Juliet felt for Romeo. But as a mother and ex-wife, I was acutely aware of that character's completely screwed position at curtain's close—so you'll have to excuse my being profoundly happy that my daughter had just announced she had not in fact experienced the L word.

"What if it was a lack of love—lovelessness," suggested Tucker as he coated the bottom of a cup with chocolate syrup for Shearling Lady's Café Mocha.

"What are you implying?" I asked. "That Valerie Lathem was so lonely she leaped in front of the Broadway line?"

"Not having a man is a pretty common issue for women in this town, you must admit," said Tucker. He added a shot of espresso, splashed in steamed milk, then stirred the liquid to bring the chocolate syrup up.

I frowned.

"He's right," said Shearling Lady. "According to the latest Census figures, there are four hundred thousand single women in New York City between thirty-five and forty-four, compared to three hundred thousand in a traditional marriage. And there are three times as many divorced women in the city as men."

"I have more bad news," said Tucker. "*Désolé*. Not all of those men are straight."

Shearling Lady's perfectly shaped raven eyebrow rose. "Neither are all the women."

I took a closer look at Shearling Lady, wondering whether she were gay, too. Mid-forties was my guess. Her short raven hair, a rich black color with reddish highlights, was cut in the kind of trendy, feathery style I'd only seen on models. Her makeup was flawless. I was dying to ask where she'd gotten the coppery lipstick with a matte finish that perfectly set off the cream of her complexion—but I didn't bother. I could tell by the coat and the hair that I probably wouldn't be able to afford it, anyway.

"What are you? A Census taker?" Tucker asked the woman.

Shearling Lady smiled and shook her head. "Just a lawyer with a good head for stats. And recently divorced myself."

That explained the money. Obviously, she was a highly successful lawyer. It also explained why she'd moved to the Village. Same reason as me—to start over, whether with a man or a woman. For my part, there was no wondering. Men were my cup o' tea . . . as long as they were coffee lovers.

"I'm Clare Cosi," I said, extending my hand. "Thanks for patronizing us."

"Winslet's the name," said the woman. "Just call me Winnie."

"You know what I think?" said Kira from her table. "A good cup of coffee is better than any man . . . it's warm, satisfying, and stimulating. And it won't cheat on you."

"Amen," said Winnie.

Tucker finished the Café Mocha with a dollop of whipped cream, shaved chocolate, and cocoa powder.

"Girls," he said, handing Winnie her drink. "You've got it all wrong. A good man may be hard to find, but a hard man is definitely the best find of all."

I smiled. Detective Quinn didn't.

"Clare," he said, quietly motioning me over as the coffeehouse conversations continued.

"Another?" I asked, seeing him hold up his nearly empty cup.

"Do you have anything stronger?"

I smiled. "You want a Speed Ball?"

Quinn choked on his last sip of latte. "You got heroin back there?"

I laughed. "Our Speed Ball is a grande house blend with two shots of espresso. It's like a Boilermaker with coffee instead of beer and whiskey."

"Speed Ball," he muttered. "And I thought I'd encountered every street drug alias there was back when I was in uniform."

"You want?" I asked.

"Set it up," he said, and I did.

"You know, the same basic mix is called a Red Eye in L.A.," I told him as I pulled the espressos. "I've also heard it called a Depth Charge, a Shot in the Dark, and a Café M.F."

"Thanks for the street-slang briefing, Captain."

"No sweat, Detective. And don't forget"—I handed him the Speed Ball—"this drug's legal."

He took a healthy hit and his eyes widened. "Maybe it shouldn't be."

"I'm warning you, Quinn. Don't mess with my fix."

He smiled—for the first time since he'd walked in, and I wanted to keep it there.

"I'll bet you didn't know that Germany's King Frederick once hired a special coffee police force known as Kaffee Schnufflers," I told him.

"*Coffee* police?"

I tried my best to affect a cheesy Gestapo accent. "Yavolt. To sniff out unauthorized coffee roasters. He didn't think coffee-drinking soldiers could be depended upon . . . Fortunately for the Germans, he failed."

Quinn shook his head, but I was happy to see the smile remain.

"So, Miss Census," said Tucker, still conversing with Winnie Winslet. "I'm curious. Now that you're divorced, are *you* having trouble finding a man?"

"Me?" She laughed. "I don't find men, darling, men find me. But the truth is, the signature on my divorce papers isn't even dry yet, so I'm not actually interested in being found. Not yet anyway."

"Well, when you're ready, you should look into our Cappuccino Connection night," said Tucker.

"And that is?"

"A local church group puts it on twice a month on our second floor. You just sign up and show up."

"Which church?" asked Winnie skeptically.

"It's nondenominational," said Tucker. "Just a way for single straights to meet. They even do that 'Power Meet' thing so you'll meet a lot of men in one night."

Winnie shook her head. "No thanks. If I were actively

looking, which I'm not, I'd probably go with the e-dating thing."

"Ohmygod!" cried a new voice. Inga Berg walked up to the counter. "I totally don't know how I met men before the on-line thing."

An assistant buyer for Macy's, Inga had just been promoted to buyer—and the raise had given her the income to move out of her rental share off Seventh Avenue and purchase a condo in one of those new buildings overlooking the Hudson River.

"Inga, you can't tell me you ever had trouble meeting men," I said. She was a bubbly woman with a curvy figure, nearly waist-length golden hair, and dark eyes, so frankly it was hard for me to imagine.

"Oh, Clare, you just don't get it. The on-line thing opens up a whole new world. I mean, it let's you brrrrrrr-owse."

Now she sounded like Catwoman.

"Inga," I said, "you make it sound like a shopping spree."

"Exactly! And you know shopping is totally my life!"

O-kay. "So what can I get you this morning?"

Inga was a regular but she didn't have a "usual." She ordered something different almost every time she came into the Blend—which, now that I'd heard her approach to dating, helped me understand her ordering philosophy in a whole new way.

"Hmmmm . . . let me see . . . what do I *feel* like . . . how about a Café Nocciuola?

"Coming right up."

Nocciuola, which is Italian for hazelnut, was basically a latte with the addition of hazelnut-flavored syrup.

(We didn't have a liquor license, but I did keep a bottle of Frangelico, a lovely Italian hazelnut liqueur, hidden under the counter for the occasional spike—for a few very special customers upon request. When Matteo was around, he preferred to mix his own cheeky version, which he called a "Coffee-Hazelnut Cocktail," a combination of Kahlúa, Frangelico, and vodka—hold the espresso. He especially liked to whip these up for the staff after closing on Saturday nights.)

"You know, I've been thinking of trying the on-line thing out," said my daughter, approaching the counter. She turned to Winnie and Inga. "Can you recommend any sites?"

I tensed.

The last thing I wanted to hear was my daughter, my innocent Joy, inquiring about signing herself up for the shop-and-drop grinder of this city's computer dating scene. Not that I knew about it firsthand—but I'd heard quite enough war stories from the front lines.

Still, what could I say? The last thing my daughter wanted to hear was advice from her mother, telling her to stop before she'd started. *So zip it, Clare,* I counseled myself. *Joy doesn't want your advice . . . She doesn't want it . . . She doesn't—*

"Joy, aren't you busy with your culinary classes?" I blurted out. "I mean, computer dating doesn't sound like something you'd have a lot of time for."

Joy gave me a look I can only assume was also used on heretics during the Spanish Inquisition.

"I'd really like to know," my daughter told Winnie, ignoring me completely.

"Um . . . I don't know," said Winnie, glancing uneasily from Joy to me and back again.

"SinglesNYC.com," said Inga without hesitation. "I'm on it, like, 24/7, you know, to check out the new guys."

"Thanks," said Joy. "I'll register this afternoon."

God, Joy, sometimes you're as stubborn as your damned father!

"You know what," I said. "I'm going to register this afternoon, too."

"You!" cried Tucker.

"You?" cried Esther.

Then everyone stared.

"Why not?" I said.

"Because . . ." said Tucker, "for one thing, you've never even attended the Cappuccino Connection."

"And that goes on right upstairs!" added Esther.

"True. But I feel differently all of a sudden." I threw a pointed glance at Joy. "Like computer dating might be worth a try."

Joy rolled her eyes. "Okay, Mom, first of all, it's called on-line dating. Not computer dating. 'Computer dating' was like something somebody did with punch cards in the stone age. But, you know what, go ahead. You register, too. In fact, I'll help you with the profile. Maybe you'll finally see there's nobody better than Daddy out there."

"I sincerely doubt that," I told her.

I also sincerely doubted I'd actually meet *anyone* of romantic consequence. But, for my daughter's sake—or maybe my own peace of mind where my daughter was concerned—I was going to make sure any service she used was legit.

A few minutes later, a crew from St. Vincent's Hospital came in looking for their caffeine hits, and Tucker and I were swamped.

"Got that lat?"

"Got it!"

"Skinny cap with wings!"

Cappuccino with skim milk, extra foam.

"Dopey X!"

Doppio—aka "double"—espresso.

"Caffé Carm!"

Caffé Caramella—a latte with caramel syrup, sweetened whipped cream, and a drizzle of warm caramel topping.

"Americano!"

Espresso diluted with hot water.

"Grande skinny!"

Latte with skim milk.

"XXX!"

Triple espresso.

"Cap, get the lead out!"

Cappuccino with decaf. I shuddered—decaf drinkers truly gave me the creeps.

"Clare," called Detective Quinn, approaching me behind the counter. "I have a question for you before I go."

With his grim expression back, I expected a query concerning Valerie Lathem . . . or at the very least one about the list of coffee drinks that seemed to constantly perplex him. But to my stunned surprise, he didn't mention either one.

"Are you free for dinner Thursday?"

THREE

∾∾∾∾∾∾∾∾∾∾∾∾∾∾∾∾∾∾∾∾∾∾∾∾∾∾∾

SHE lived in one of those high-priced new buildings they'd put up near the river with rooftop parking and a view of the Jersey swamps.

HUDSON VIEW read the white metal sign bolted to the red brick building. "CONDOS AVAILABLE, INQUIRE IN-SIDE."

The bricks were new, the cheap chrome light fixtures shiny as a drawer full of QVC cubic zirconias, but the building had no style, no character, and no history. A nearly featureless rectangle, which, in the Genius's view, would succinctly describe the woman inside—if you added a pair of pathetically second-rate breasts.

Her SinglesNYC.com profile had lied, of course.

"All of them lie," whispered the Genius. "All of them . . ."

From the building across the street, the Genius watched the woman prepare for her Thursday night date. With her drapes left wide open, the blonde probably assumed no one was peeping. An easy mistake, since she was fifteen floors up, the office building directly across from her condo was only half leased, and the space where the Genius now stood appeared unlit and uninhabited.

Through the dark window, the Genius watched the woman drop her white towel and step into a lacey pair of black panties.

"Well, well, well, I see our hair color's a dye job . . ."

Next came the bra—a push-up lace number that matched the black panties.

"That's it, honey, work what you've got," whispered the Genius, disgusted by the woman's attempt to disguise her second-rate breasts.

Then came the little black dress, the shoes, the jewelry, the makeup. And . . . what's this? The Genius peered through a pair of binoculars to find the woman moving toward her laptop. After punching up the SinglesNYC Web site, the woman stared at the photo, reread the profile.

"Yes, and what do you think of tonight's date? Quite a catch isn't he?"

Inside her apartment, the woman strode confidently to the mirror to survey herself. Then, giving herself a dirty little smile, she reached up beneath her skirt and slowly pulled off her panties.

"No panties for the big date? Hmmmm . . . another bad girl."

"So what's bothering you about it?" I asked Mike Quinn that Thursday evening.

"Something doesn't sit right," he said. "I mean apart from the fact that the transit boys let the news vultures snap away before the blood was swabbed up."

"Those front page photos were . . . unfortunate," I said. "I can't imagine how Valerie Lathem's poor grandmother felt, seeing her granddaughter's blood on the tracks like that. Splashed all over the newspapers."

"You got it," said Quinn on an exhale of disgust. "You got it."

I put down the salad bowl of fresh mesclun, raddiccio, and grape tomatoes, glistening in a dressing of olive oil, aged balsamic, and freshly ground sea salt, the shaved Pecorino Romano cresting over it all in creamy curling waves. Then I sat next to the detective in the cozy dining room of my duplex, which was located in the two floors above the Village Blend.

I'd set the antique Chippendale table with care, using the handmade lace cloth Madame had purchased in Florence and the candleholders of blown Venetian glass. Before Quinn arrived, I'd lit the candles and lowered the chandelier's wattage, so the flickering glow of candlelight would reflect itself in the polished wood sideboard and bring a feeling of warmth to the room.

Earlier in the day, Quinn had offered to take me out to a nearby restaurant, but I told him it was a better idea for me to cook dinner for him at my place. No mental slouch, he understood.

Quinn was a married man. A lot of people knew us in this neighborhood. Since I had nothing prurient in mind—and I sincerely doubted he did, either—I didn't think we should take the chance of giving the wrong impression to some passing acquaintance. Ours, or worse, his wife's.

Better, I thought, to keep our private friendship just that—private.

"Wine?" I asked.

He'd thoughtfully brought a bottle of Pinot Grigio, and I'd been letting it breathe on Madame's Florentine tablecloth for the last ten minutes.

"Let me," he said and poured for us both.

I was relieved to see him take a glass because, from the moment he'd entered the apartment, he seemed tense, making me wonder if I really had made the right decision to entertain him privately.

Maybe the wine would relax him.

"So is that why you were unhappy with the transit police?" I asked. "Because of the news photos?"

"Something doesn't sit right," he repeated.

I studied Quinn's face, all freshly shaved angles, shadows still present under winter blue eyes. As usual, his expression was unreadable.

We sat in silence a few moments.

Like most men, Quinn was the Twenty Questions type. "Something doesn't sit right with . . . the search you made of her apartment?" I prompted.

The detective nodded as he took a sip of wine. "And with the suicide."

I could think of a dozen more questions, but it wasn't my business to grill him. It was police business. And Valerie Lathem's family's business. And none of mine. So I dished the mesclun into the Spode Imperialware "Blue Italian" pattern salad bowls. (It wasn't Madame's best china, but it was my favorite. The homey blue scenes of Northern Italy set against the white earthenware reminded me of an especially carefree summer when I was Joy's age.)

"Clare, do you recall ever seeing Ms. Lathem come into the Blend with a companion?"

"Companion?"

"Friend or lover? Male or female?"

For a moment, I tried to recall her visits—anything unique about them, but it was so difficult to even remember her face. "It's difficult . . . we serve hundreds of people a day. I try to get to know the regulars . . . but when we get busy . . . well, you've seen how crazy it can get . . ."

Quinn nodded.

"I can only recall her coming during the morning rushes. Alone."

We ate in silence for a full minute.

"Did she leave a note?" I asked, too curious not to. "You know, a suicide note. Explaining why . . ."

"No note. No nothing," said Quinn. "No drugs, no alcohol, no record of mental instability, or strained relationships. Everybody loved her. That's what doesn't sit right. There are usually some signs of problems. Issues. But my search and interviews have turned up a young woman who had everything to live for."

"Was it possible she didn't kill herself? That she just . . . I don't know, slipped off the platform?"

Quinn shook his head. "The motorman said she *flew* right out in front of him. Flew. She didn't drop down partially. She projected forward . . . and yet . . ."

"What?"

"She'd bought a bag of groceries at the Green Market. Who the hell buys groceries ten minutes before they off themselves?"

"You think she could have been pushed?"

Quinn's thumb and forefinger caressed the stem of Madame's Waterford crystal wine glass. "No witnesses. The platform's security camera was mounted right above the woman's head—so we've got no usable pictures. And the motorman claims he didn't see anyone—but with the way that station slightly curves, and the place on the platform where the victim had been waiting, the pusher could have remained invisible behind a staircase."

"So you think there was a . . . 'pusher.' "

"Can't prove it."

I nodded, having been down this road with Quinn before. From past experience, I'd learned that New York City detectives didn't just investigate shootings, stabbings, and stranglings, but any suspicious death or accident that appeared might result in death.

According to Quinn, his department was routinely

swamped and his superiors wanted what he called a "high case clearance" rate. They had no patience with Quinn's marking time on cases that wouldn't make an Assistant D.A.'s pulse race.

Quinn explained to me that the transit police statements to the press had played the death as a suicide in the public's eye. So any other theory Quinn might wish to introduce would now be met with a great deal of political resistance within his own department—especially a theory with little evidentiary support. Even his partner on the case wanted them to close it out as a suicide.

After we finished our salads, I moved our bowls to the sideboard, ducked into the kitchen to retrieve the main dish, then set the platter of Chicken Francese down on the table between us.

"It smells delicious," he said.

I served it up, and he began to eat.

"Save room," I told him. "I've got a killer desert."

Quinn closed his eyes, like he did every day when he took that first sip of my latte—but this time his mouth was chewing instead of sipping.

"Clare," he finally said, "this is amazing."

"It's a crime how easy Chicken Francese is to make," I told him between bites, "so if I were you, I wouldn't be too impressed."

"I don't know," he said, opening his eyes. "If I were you, I'd be careful with your confessions to crimes around me."

I smiled. "And why is that?"

He took another sip of wine, a long one, and I'd swear that frosty blue gaze of his was drinking me in, too. "I've got cuffs, babe. And I know how to use 'em."

I think I managed not to drop my fork—my jaw, I couldn't account for. "I can't believe you said that."

Quinn's dark blonde eyebrows rose, and he gave me one of those looks landscape surveyors reserve for choice pieces. He started at the top of my wavy, shoulder-length, Italian-roast brown hair, running down my heart-shaped face and lavender V-neck sweater, pausing just long enough on my C-cups to make me break a sweat.

Then he raised an eyebrow, tilted his head a bit, made a little sighing sound, and turned his attention back to his meal.

Taciturn bastard.

It wasn't the first time we'd flirted, and I assumed it wouldn't be the last. But I knew it wouldn't go anywhere. Unlike my impulsive, outspoken, adventurous—and ultimately shameless—ex-husband, I could never consent to an extra-marital affair. And I sincerely doubted Quinn could, either.

On my part, I was raised a strict Roman Catholic. Even though I had lapsed in many ways, the sense of right and wrong (and guilt) had long ago been sewn into the lining of my clothing by the immigrant grandmother who raised me.

Still, unlike the St. Joseph medal affixed to the dashboard of my car, I wasn't made of plastic. Testosterone wasn't going to stop turning me on, and neither was Detective Michael Ryan Francis Quinn.

I'm sure I would have seemed far more sophisticated and mysterious if I had just sat there all enigmatic and silent like him. But I wasn't a twenty-year veteran of poker-faced interrogations, and I suddenly couldn't stop myself from babbling the entire contents of one of my old "In the Kitchen with Clare" columns from my Jersey days.

"You know, a lot people get frustrated trying to find the recipe for Chicken Francese in Italian cookbooks," I yammered, "but they're looking in all the wrong places. I mean, the recipe has antecedents, mostly in Italian-language Neapolitan cookbooks, but it's really a New York dish. Francese, of course, means 'in the French manner,' but what you've actually got here is a basic chicken cutlet pounded out and dipped in flour and egg and more flour, then fried in olive oil, then dressed with fresh lemon juice. And since it's best made in single portions, it seemed the perfect dish tonight for just the two of us . . ."

Just the two of us? Oh god. That came out all wrong!

"What I mean is, I'm sure your *wife* could make it for you—or for more people. All she'd have to do is undercook the first batch, that way she can keep it warm in the oven without drying out the chicken while she's cooking the additional batches. You see?"

"Clare." Quinn put down his fork, and looked straight into my eyes. "There's a personal reason I came here tonight."

"Personal?"

"I wanted some advice . . . marital advice."

FOUR

~~~~~~

GETTING *in was easy.*

This being a new building, few of the tenants would know each other by face—given the typical all-hours comings and goings of Manhattan life—and even fewer would know each other by name.

The Genius simply waited.

Within minutes, a well-dressed man and woman came out the door, arguing about directions to a nightclub. The Genius stood just outside the door, pretending to fumble with a wallet—and, presumably, the pass card. As the couple stepped out, the man politely held the door open.

And, just like that, the Genius was in.

The cheap chrome light fixtures that illuminated the building's exterior were tediously present in its interior, as well, throughout the featureless space that formed the small lobby and down the short hall leading to the elevators.

The Genius pushed the UP button and waited.

"Just another slut," whispered the Genius. "Like all of them . . ."

The Genius had followed the woman to the restaurant. Watched her dine with her new e-date. An expensive meal. A second bottle of wine. Finally, dessert. The woman had placed her manicured hand on her date's, lifted it off the table, and brought it down underneath.

Surprise had registered on the man's features as she'd made him feel what was there beneath her little black dress—and what wasn't.

To the other diners, nothing had looked amiss. But the Genius had known what was happening beneath that table-cloth, and what would come next. A hastily requested check, the flagging of a cab. Fumbling in the back seat on the ride back to her building—and then the quick and feral mating.

An invitation had followed, of course, but the man had declined. His departure in a hired car had been expected . . . a signal for the Genius to act.

The mechanical bing of the elevator sounded, and the doors opened on the fifteenth floor.

With gloved hands, the Genius pulled the note from a pocket, opened it, and glanced at the first few lines.

Inga,
I saw you at the restaurant with him.
It drove me wild.
Meet me by your car right now, bring this note
    with you.
You can exchange it for a special surprise. . . .

After folding the note once more, the Genius slipped it beneath the front door of Inga's condo, knocked twice, then quickly strode to the stairwell.

When she read it, she'd come. The Genius knew this. For him, the Slut would do anything.

"**M**ARITAL advice?" I asked, repeating Quinn's words more out of shock than premature deafness.

Next to me at the dinner table, Quinn shifted uneasily in his Chippendale chair. Elbows went off the table then on again, and suddenly he was acting as though he'd grown too big for the small dining room.

Okay, this was serious. Quinn had never before acted this awkward around me. The man was cooler than arctic ice—and his tall, broad-shouldered form usually moved with the intense ease and confidence of an Alaskan wolf.

I tried to guess what was coming, but didn't dare. Over the last few months, we mostly spoke about his work, or New York trivia, or the coffeehouse. Occasionally, he'd bring up his children—Molly, a six-year-old girl, and Jeremy, an eight-year-old boy—both of whom he always talked about in glowing terms. His wife he seldom mentioned, and whenever I'd open the topic of his spouse, he'd close it fast, usually with a negative quip along the lines of (on a good day) "they say marriage is a challenge, but I'm fairly sure ascending Everest would have been less effort," and (on a bad day) "let's just say my wife is an entrée that seemed promising on the menu but came to the table cold."

"Maybe that didn't come out right," said Quinn, rubbing the back of his neck. "What I'm trying to say is . . . or rather ask is . . . when did you know it was time to . . . give up?"

"Whoa . . ." This was a little more than I'd expected to deal with tonight. I took a deep breath, reached for my wine glass, and considered it a notable accomplishment to have stopped myself from chugalugging the entire bottle of Pinot.

"I'm sorry," he said. "I'm putting you on the spot—"

"No, no. It's fine . . . I was about to tell you, 'I know what you're going through,' but the truth is, I don't. Have you ever heard John Bradshaw talk about how every happy family is happy in the same way—but every unhappy family is unhappy in its own unique way?"

"No."

"Well, he's the dysfunctional family expert—and I believe that idea applies to marriage, too."

"I'm not sure I follow . . ."

"Every couple's marriage plays out very similar chords, but it's own unique discords. You see?"

Quinn shook his head. "I'm not sure."

"Well . . . take my own marriage. Matteo and I hadn't stopped loving each other. We just needed to stop hurting each other. It might be the same for you—or it might be something else entirely. That's why I'm not sure if my experience is even valid. Do you want to tell me more about your own marriage?"

"No," he said flatly. "Not really."

"Oh." *O-kay,* I told myself. "So how about those Jets?" I said with enough forced perkiness to sweeten a Mafia wedding cake.

Quinn raised an eyebrow. "You follow pro football?"

"Not since Terry Bradshaw was a Steelers quarterback," I said. (I'd followed football back then primarily because dear old Dad ran a bookie operation in the rear of my grandmother's grocery back in western Pennsylvania.) "But if you don't want to talk about your marriage problems, now that you've told me you have them . . ." I shrugged. "It's pro teams, the weather . . . or I could give you the culinary history of penne alla vodka. What do you think?"

Quinn sighed and smiled. He actually smiled. "Sorry," he said. "Shutting down is a knee-jerk reaction of mine, in case you haven't noticed . . ."

In case I haven't noticed? I stared at the man. "You're kidding, right?"

"I don't want to be rude, Clare. Especially to you."

I shook my head. "It's okay. We really don't have to talk about it if you've changed your mind. It's your business."

"I'm just not good at this."

"At . . . what . . . exactly?"

Quinn began fidgeting again, this time like a teenage boy, playing with this silverware, then awkwardly scratching his square, freshly shaved jaw. "At asking for personal advice . . ."

"It's okay. I understand."

"Do you?"

"When Matteo was cheating on me . . ." I began. Then I stopped, stared, and took another sip of wine—a long one.

All of a sudden, I felt a little more forgiving of Quinn's reluctance to talk. When you spend most of your adult waking hours trying to look dependable, responsible, and together, the last thing you want to do is admit to anyone, let alone yourself, that your personal life had once gone totally to shit.

I put down the wine glass. "When I found out he was sleeping around," I continued, "I was so ashamed. I couldn't tell anyone. For a long time, I just pretended it wasn't happening. At first, I blamed the work, all the traveling that went with his job . . . and then I blamed the cocaine. I tried to tell myself he wasn't really himself . . . he wasn't really responsible. The thing is . . . I loved him so much, and I knew he loved me. And there was Joy to consider."

"Yeah, that's my main concern . . . Molly and Jeremy."

"I know."

"So . . ." said Quinn slowly. "What made you finally decide to . . . ?"

"To give up?" I said.

"Yeah."

"Well . . ." I began. "It wasn't easy. I didn't just love

Matt, you know? I was in love with him. So much in love, I even thought for a little while that I should try to make it work the way he wanted. An open marriage—at least for him because I could never cheat and live with myself . . . but then, a little at a time, I shut myself down emotionally. And the more I shut down, the more he turned away, until finally I decided I couldn't live that way anymore."

"Was there any one thing that happened or did you just . . . ?" Quinn shrugged.

"One morning I was preparing an urn of our Breakfast Blend, and I just broke down. It sounds silly, but I was grinding this beautiful freshly roasted batch, and it just hit me that my marriage was doing to me what that grinder was doing to those beans. On the outside I held it together, but on the inside, I was being ground up into unrecognizable pieces." I shrugged. "That's when I realized the truth."

"You wanted a divorce?"

"No . . . that it was impossible for me to fit myself in a filter, pour steaming water over myself, and serve myself in cups to customers."

Quinn stared at me for a second.

"It's a joke," I said.

We both burst out laughing.

It was good to hear him laugh.

Quinn exhaled, and the tension he'd carried since he'd arrived seemed to leave his entire body. (And here I had thought he'd been uptight because of his caseload.)

Then his eyes met mine, and he stopped laughing.

"She's had affairs for years, Clare." His voice was eerily cold. Unemotional. Dead. "With men. And, lately, with a woman. She's shredded our marriage vows into worthless rags. Lied to me more times than I can count."

I took a deep breath. "Then the real question is whether you've come to the point where you can live without her."

With his free hand, Quinn reached for the wine glass

again, but only to finger the stem. His eyes wouldn't meet mine now. They focused on the fine Waterford crystal, its facets reflecting the flickering candlelight.

I waited for him to continue—because I thought we had all evening, and I had plenty of time to hear more about his marriage, about any attempts he might have made at marriage counseling, and generally to witness this rare occasion of his finally opening up. But then Quinn's cell rang. The second he heard the voice on the other end, that glacier curtain came down. Work, of course. Something had come up and they needed to call him in.

"Are you going to a crime scene?" I asked after he flipped closed his cell and slipped it into his jacket pocket.

"Yeah."

"Tucker's managing downstairs tonight," I told him. "Stop in and ask for a tray of lattes to go. On the house."

He thanked me, and I walked him to my duplex's door. Then, on the landing above the service staircase, he stopped.

"Mike? Did you need something else?"

He just stood there, looking down, as if considering his answer. "Thanks," he said, then without another word, he was gone.

Hiding in the crowd of tenants, the Genius watched the tall, broad-shouldered detective in the dark brown coat case the crime scene.

"Sorry, Mike. Sorry to pull you in."

"It's all right. What have you got?"

"Jumper."

Uniformed police had already cordoned off the area around the body and were scanning it for evidence. But it was a waste of effort. They'd quickly come to the same conclusion as the other cops at the other crime scenes—suicide.

Ms. Inga Berg, they would assume, had said goodnight to her big date earlier than expected . . . because taking off one's panties may get you sex, but it doesn't guarantee a long night of lovemaking by any stretch. After retiring for the evening, Inga had decided to take the elevator to the rooftop parking area, walk to the edge, and somersault over the banister.

Inga Berg, they would conclude, had leaped to her death.

"Objective achieved," whispered the Genius.

Slipping away was the last task left, before the police began to question the tenants. This being a new building, few of the tenants would know each other. These people would naturally assume the Genius to be just another tenant, or friend of a tenant. So departing would be easy.

But the Genius couldn't leave just yet. It was too good a feeling, seeing the handiwork appreciated for the first time. The tape being put up, the police photographer snapping photos, the chalk being drawn, the detective staring up into the cold, black night, estimating the trajectory of the body's fall, then snapping on latex gloves to gently examine the woman's smashed body.

She looked a bit like she was sleeping actually, except for the splattering of blood and brain matter.

Inga Berg's white shoes had been torn off in the fall, but she was still clothed in the white fur-trimmed parka, beneath it, the cream silk negligee with lace trim, her long, dyed hair a blonde mop across her face.

The Genius watched the detective crouch down, tenderly push the long blonde hair away, to reveal staring brown eyes, a mouth frozen open forever.

This was just too good. Seeing the accomplishment like this.

The Genius almost didn't notice the detective rising, turning, scanning the crowd.

Time to slip away, the Genius decided. Slip away . . . slip away . . . And after slithering slowly backward through the heart of the crowd, that's exactly what the Genius did.

FIVE

~~~~~~~~~~~~~~~~~~~~~~~~~~~~~~~~~~

Not pretty.

Not a disaster by any means. But definitely not a thing of beauty.

My first official "date" of the last two years had started out badly and went downhill from there.

Frankly, the last thing I expected to be doing exactly one week after "My Dinner with Quinn" (as I now thought of it) was sitting across from a guy who looked like he'd stepped off the cover of the Metrosexual's Handbook.

Yet here I was, sitting in the Union Square Coffee Shop, which, despite its name, was not, in fact, a coffee shop, but a trendy restaurant made to look like a 1960s-style coffee shop/diner, with the addition of mood lighting, loud music, a slick crowd, and a Brazilian-American menu.

Later, when I was happily back at the Blend, Tucker

would inform me that the waitresses there were employed by a major modeling agency—which owned this restaurant, as well as another, called (appropriately enough) Live Bait. And I would consider myself a heel (in retrospect) for consenting to eat at a place where a twenty-two-year-old reed-thin underwear model with long blonde hair asked my date, "What would you like?"

This man had e-mailed me as a result of the profile Joy had helped me post on SinglesNYC.com—and the only reason I'd even posted in the first place was to check out the dating service my daughter intended to use.

"What would you like?" Paris Hilton asked again.

Ensconced in the vinyl booth, I'd already ordered the churrasquino carioca; however, my date, a forty-something with curly black hair, refined features, watery hazel eyes, and a profile that listed his occupation as "Director of Fundraising," seemed to be having an issue with the menu.

"I thought you had vegetarian fare?" he asked unhappily.

"We have a veggie burger and a ton of fish dishes," suggested the waitress.

"I'm a vegan. No animal products, which includes the swimming animals."

A vegan? I thought. His profile hadn't mentioned that. I could have sworn it said nonsmoking gourmet food lover. *O-kay.*

"Veggie burger?" asked the model-slash-waitress hopefully.

Brooks Newman sighed the sigh of a martyr. "I suppose."

"Cheese?"

"Yes."

"You know cheese is an animal product," I pointed out. "I mean if you're a vegan."

"Oh, yes," said Brooks. "Of course. It's only been three days."

"Three days vegan?" I asked. "Is that like three days sober?"

Brooks wasn't amused. He gave me a little squint. "No cheese," he told the waitress.

"Anything else, sir?"

"Yes," said Brooks. He snapped the menu shut. "And another martini. Dry. Got that? D-R-Y."

"Yes, sir."

The Hilton look-alike spun on her go-go boot heel and left.

"I hate it when girls that age call me 'sir,'" said Brooks, his eyes glued to the waitress's retreating ass. "Makes me feel old."

"Well . . ." I said. *No reason for that. After all, you're acting like a child.*

"You, uh, don't look forty."

"Thanks. I know. It's the botanicals."

"Botanicals?"

"Yes, in the facial products. I find a weekly spa visit to be vital for people our age. You should try it. Really."

Oh, for pity's sake.

"Renu Spa," he said, draining the last of his not-dry-enough martini. "Park Avenue, by the W Hotel."

"Renu, eh? Funny . . ."

"What's funny?" he asked.

"Renew! Renew! Renew!" I said. "You know, *Logan's Run*? Do they have a 'Carousel' treatment for clients over thirty?"

Brooks made his little squinty face again. "Why would they have a merry-go-round in a spa?"

I shook my head. "Not merry-go-round. Carousel. Don't you remember *Logan's Run*? That sci-fi movie from the mid seventies?"

"Sure, I remember it. Farrah Fawcett, right?"

"Right. Well, the entire premise is based on the idea

that it's the twenty-third century and Big Brother takes care of everything for you. Your whole life is spent in the pursuit of pleasure. The only catch is when you turn thirty, the red crystal embedded in your palm begins to blink. So you have to report to this ritual they call 'Carousel,' where you're supposedly 'Renewed.' But in reality they zap you with enough volts of electricity to light up Detroit."

"I don't know what you're talking about."

" 'Run, Runner!' doesn't ring any bells?"

"No."

"Forget it." I sighed and found myself thinking, *Quinn would have laughed.*

Brooks adjusted his pale yellow Armani sweater and looked around the room, his eyes snagging on the tight clothing of the model slash waitresses more frequently than my cat Java's claws on my goose down duvet.

"So . . ." said Brooks. "What's it like managing these . . . I mean, this place?"

"This place? I don't manage this place," I told him.

Brooks frowned. "Your SinglesNYC profile said you managed Coffee Shop."

"Coffee*house.* I manage a coffeehouse. Of course, I didn't put the name of it in my profile. The site instructions said not to put down any information on the public profiles that would give away your identity."

"Your profile said you managed Coffee Shop."

"I don't see why it would say that. Does Singles NYC.com change the profiles of people?"

"No . . . but there's an automatic spell check after you send. Didn't you review the profile once it was posted?"

"Not really."

"I see." Brooks now made a show of looking around the room. "So you don't manage any of these girls."

"No."

The atmosphere got even chillier after that. I politely asked about his work, and he talked about directing the fundraising campaigns for various charities.

"There are myriad techniques," he said, "depending on the not-for-profit's history. Donation patterns can grow stale over time. So I can direct anything from phone solicitation blitzes and letter writing campaigns to gala benefits."

"Interesting."

"It can be."

Not to me. Not then. I couldn't stop thinking about Detective Quinn. Since last week's Chicken Francese dinner, he hadn't been by the Blend. Not for his usual latte, not even to bolt an espresso. For a full week he'd avoided the coffeehouse entirely. I tried to tell myself it was his work, or his marital issues, which appeared to be as emotionally straining as mine and Matt's had been.

Still, I couldn't help suspecting that he was intentionally avoiding me. Maybe he'd regretted opening up. Maybe he felt embarrassed on some level and was worried I'd put him on the spot the next time I saw him. I didn't have a clue—but I refused to let it tear at me, which was another reason I'd gone out tonight after getting Brooks's call. I needed to get my mind off the police detective. The *still married* police detective.

After the food was served, Brooks bit into his vegetarian burger. He chewed, swallowed, and made that squinty face again.

"What is that you ordered?" he asked, eyeing my platter.

"The churrasquino carioca," I told him.

"And that is . . . ?"

"A Brazilian-style grilled steak sandwich."

"Steak?"

"Yes. Steak. Beef. Cow," I said, around a mouth of deliciously marinated meat. "Listen, Brooks, my profile never said I wasn't a meat eater. There's no spell check I know that would change 'gourmet food lover' to 'vegetarian.' "

"No, I know," he admitted, his tone less chilly. "But I have found that everyone lies about something on these sites. One girl had this dominatrix vibe to her profile, but when we went out she mainly talked about her pain-in-the-ass parents, the sex was vanilla, and afterward she just wanted to play Scrabble."

"Brooks, let me be honest with you so we can both digest our food. The only reason I'm here is to see what this on-line dating thing is like. My daughter insisted on signing up, and I wanted to check out the site, see how it worked. I'm really not interested in . . . hooking up . . . or anything."

"Oh." The man leaned back in his chair. "Oh."

"Honestly, you're not interested in me, right?"

He took a sip of his martini and made an unsatisfied face. "I usually go out with women much younger than you. But for thirty-nine . . . you actually look okay. I dislike what you're wearing, that sweater is too big for you and I don't like women in pants, but you have a very pretty face . . . In fact . . ." He took a closer look. "You *are* kinda cute."

"Thanks." *Creep.*

"And you look a little familiar for some reason."

"Ever been in the Village Blend coffeehouse—on Hudson?"

"That's the coffeehouse you manage? Oh, sure. I've been in there. Good cappuccinos."

"Thanks." *Okay, maybe not a total creep.*

"To be honest with you, I thought this could be more of a networking thing than a date," he said. "I've arranged a new approach to fundraising that's going to involve the sort of beautiful young women who work here. And I thought if you managed this place, then you might be able to help me secure the donation of services."

"Services?"

Brooks nodded. "A lingerie show at the Puck building. And, after the show, the girls will serve drinks."

"While still in their underwear?"

"Brilliant, isn't it?" Brooks said with a grin. "I am such the Genius. The big spenders will love it, and I'll certainly be reeling in some new whales, too. As far as the models, I'm sure, if they're forced to work here, then they're between gigs anyway—and they already know how to serve drinks."

"But why would they do it for free?"

"Because, given the type of spenders we've already invited to the event—media and ad execs and the like—it will be good exposure for them."

"Good exposure. Right." (Serving drinks in flimsy underwear would do that for a girl.)

"And it's also for a good cause," he added.

"What cause would that be?"

"M.N.M. I'm in charge of their national fundraising drives for the next six months."

"M.N.M.? Oh, right, I've heard of them. Meat No More—the vegan activist organization? So that's why you've only been a vegan for three days?"

Brooks shrugged. "Let's just say after two weeks on the job, they encouraged me to give the lifestyle a try." He sighed, dejected. "It was just one take-out order of Chinese spare ribs delivered to their offices. You'd think I killed the damn pig myself."

I took another bite of my delicious Brazilian steak sandwich. He frowned at his veggie burger. Then he looked around the restaurant and whispered, "Can I have half of that?"

I smiled. "Sure."

The meat seemed to restore him. He actually smiled, too. "You know, you are really cute. I don't see why we can't hook up . . . you know, just for the night."

"Sorry, but, uh . . . I do." I almost added, "nothing personal," but stopped myself. Of course, it was personal.

He frowned. "Oh, well . . . worth a shot." He shrugged.

"So, what do you think of the SinglesNYC site? I mean, for my daughter?"

"Your daughter, huh? That's an interesting idea." He took a drink of his martini and gave me a leer. "Does she look like a younger version of you? And if she does, what's she doing tonight?"

I pictured Brooks coming in for a cappuccino—and me pointing the steam valve at his face.

"You're too old for her," I said with great relish.

He shrugged. "Can't blame a guy for trying."

Yes I can.

"Look, SinglesNYC is a pretty edgy site. Most of the people go there to widen their sexual circle."

I nearly choked on my marinated cow. "Widen their what?"

"Their sexual circle. How old is she?"

"Nineteen. She turns twenty very soon."

Brooks nodded. "Tell her not to go out with anyone over twenty-five. That should help cut down on the guys who might be married. And here's a warning label: get the guy's home number, home address, and work number. Because if he's reluctant to give any of those out, he could be married or already have a girlfriend."

A pained sigh escaped me.

My e-date leaned forward. "Hey, look . . ." He pulled out his business card, flipped it, and wrote something down. "If I had a daughter, I'd want her to be on one of these two sites instead. They're total duds as far as I'm concerned—people who want, you know, 'meaningful relationships,' and talk about things like 'favorite hobbies.' A lot tamer than SinglesNYC."

"Thanks," I said, and meant it.

We finished our meal and contemplated the desert selection. Both of us ordered the flan, then I asked the waitress for a cappuccino.

"I'll have one, too," said Brooks.

I was just about to conclude the guy was okay when he
opened his mouth one more time and said the one thing
that absolutely put an end to even the remotest possibility
of a relationship with me—

"Just make sure mine's a decaf."

SIX

~~~~~~

Almost time.

The air was crisp tonight, polluted with the occasional acrid fumes from the historic district's wood-burning fireplaces, but there was little wind off the nearby river, and the Genius found tonight's mission almost tolerable.

For one thing, the sorry parade of single men and women brought the Genius a mild degree of amusement.

Saturday night in the Village was always loud and crowded, but each Single seemed to file down this dark street in a particularly pathetic way. There was something pensive and a little desperate about them as they negotiated the clutching couples and raucous revelers. Hands in pockets, eyes cast down.

Standing in the shadowy recesses of an alley across the busy street, the Genius found the perfect vantage from which to watch them file past the faux gas lamp and trudge into the coffeehouse.

*Through the Blend's tall, brightly lit windows, the Ge-
nius studied them as they bumped and squeezed their way
around the crowded tables, then adjusted their clothing before climbing up the wrought iron spiral staircase to arrive
on the second floor, their false courage now in place—
hands out of pockets, eyes lifted up, plastic smiles applied
like last-minute lipstick.*

There was a bald guy in his fifties with a slight limp.

Two women in their thirties, laughing a little too hard.

*An over-dressed fortyish man with enough grease in his
hair to qualify as a Mafia don.*

A brunette with tight clothing and too much makeup.

A geeky twentysomething.

A geeky thirtysomething.

Three Goth girls.

*A forty-plus woman with spike-heeled boots and a
trendy leather coat meant for someone twenty years
younger.*

And they just kept coming . . .

*This Cappuccino Connection thing certainly brought
out the losers. Oh, there were a few somewhat attractive
women in the mix, but nothing special.*

*The Genius was actually surprised it had come to this
for him.*

But SinglesNYC.com really had become a bust.

*The last match had taken place at a nearby restaurant.
She'd been too old for his taste, which might not have mat-
tered, but there was no chemistry. Nothing about the
woman seemed to turn him on. She'd been a bore.*

*As usual, the SinglesNYC profile didn't match the real-
ity. Everything from her photo to her occupation had
seemed better in the on-line profile than it had been in person. A big yawn for him.*

*The Genius hadn't been all that surprised. The only
question had been, "What next?"*

Cruising more SinglesNYC profiles was an option. Giving up was an option, too. But then, of course, so was this . . .

The Genius emerged from the shadows and crossed the street, heading into the Blend.

"Ah, well," murmured the Genius, "at least I'll get an excellent cappuccino out of the evening."

"Clare, I have one word for you," whispered Tucker as he offered me a French café cup of cappuccino from his half-empty cork-bottomed tray.

Cradling the heat in my cold hands, I sipped at the warm froth, then peered over the cup's rim, apprehensively taking in the crowd of milling bodies filling up the Blend's second floor.

"One word?" I asked Tucker.

"Tadpoling."

"Excuse me?"

"That's what they call it when an older woman dates a younger guy."

"Tadpoling. Right. I see. Thanks for clearing that up, Tuck. And I thought you were having a bayou flashback."

"No, seriously, sweetie. I know you probably wouldn't look twice at a guy who was like ten or twelve years younger than you."

"Tucker . . ."

"But tadpoling is the hottest trend around."

"Older women and younger men?" I asked. "In what universe?"

"Uh, honey, don't you know? It's totally *all that.* Demi Moore and Ashton Kutcher? Hugh Jackman and his wife? Cher, Madonna . . . the list just goes on and on. Don't you remember that movie with Diane Keaton and Jack Nicholson—the one where cutie Keanu Reeves has the hots for post-menopausal Diane? You know she even got an Oscar nomination for that role."

"Hollywood, Tucker. All of your examples are Hollywood. I'm sure if I were a millionaire movie star with houses in the Hamptons and Malibu, tadpoling would be a lovely option to consider, but this is the real world."

"My point exactly! The real world does nothing but obsess over Hollywood—trends trickle down, Clare, remember that. Trends trickle."

"Everyone! It's time to get started!" called Nan Tulley, our Cappuccino Connection hostess.

Although these sessions were nondenominational, even advertised in *New York* magazine's Personals, these evenings were actually part of the fundraising and outreach committee work for Grace Church over on Tenth and Broadway (one of the most magnificent examples of Gothic Revival architecture in the country, with lacelike stonework and gorgeous stained glass. New Yorkers always gape when they pass it, but few realize it was built in 1845 by the same architect who would later erect the monumental uptown landmark St. Patrick's Cathedral.).

"Come, everyone! Gather 'round . . ." Nan called again, clapping her hands.

Nan's regular job was managing the Wee Ones daycare center on Twelfth, which might have explained why I couldn't shake the impression I'd just entered an elaborate playgroup.

"Shoo, Tucker," I whispered. "I'm not really here to meet anyone anyway. You know that."

"If you say so, sweetie."

With an annoying roll of his eyes, Tucker was off to serve more caps to the crowd.

I moseyed over toward Nan, trying to keep my distance from my daughter, Joy, as I'd promised.

Right after my date with Brooks Newman two days ago, I'd phoned Joy and made her promise to quit the Singles-NYC on-line dating site. She agreed to try the tamer (a.k.a. "dud") sites that Brooks had scrawled on the back of his business card for me, but Joy also informed me that she'd decided to sign up for the Blend's Cappuccino Connection night.

I let it go for about twenty-four hours. Then I signed up, too.

Joy was furious.

"Mom, I can't believe you're doing this!" she'd said when I told her.

"It's got nothing to do with you," I lied. "They've been meeting in my coffeehouse two times a month for how long now—and all I've ever done is send my part-timers upstairs with trays of cappuccinos. It's about time I saw for myself how the whole thing works, don't you think?"

Joy really didn't buy it, but I promised her I wouldn't interfere with her participation—and she finally said that maybe it would be good for me after all.

My daughter was still under the delusion that I needed to discover that no man out there could hold a candle to her dad, an admittedly larger-than-life type, who, despite his inability to remain monogamous, had loved Joy unconditionally and with all his heart—and therefore could do no wrong in Joy's eyes. As exasperating as it was for me, I saw no reason to rob the girl of her love for the man, even though there were still times Matteo could make me angry enough to fantasize about pouring a few steaming hot Speed Balls down his pants.

Nan clapped a final time in a way that made me feel like I'd have to raise my hand before using the little girls' room.

"Quiet now, quiet! Okay, good! Now, I want you all to put your Listening Caps on. The first rule of connection night is that everyone must make at least three connections. Even if you think you've only met *one* person with whom you have chemistry, you *must* make dates with three people. This rule ensures that many of you will have more than one chance to connect! Isn't that great!"

Nan had the sort of enthusiastic voice I imagined worked very well on a dozen sugared-up four year olds. This crowd, however, seemed less than receptive. They murmured warily.

"Now, now, I know what you're all thinking!" Nan continued. "Why? Why do I need to ask people out with whom I don't necessarily feel a strong connection? Well, I'll tell you why: many happily married couples have had bad first meetings—and many fantastic first meetings have ended in bitter splits. You can never tell what may happen if you just give a person a chance to grow on you!"

"Like fungus?" some joker called.

"Hostility will get you nowhere," snapped Nan. "Remember, a bad first impression can still lead you to the right person . . . maybe not the *perfect* one, but the *right* one . . ."

I was dying to look around a little more, check out the people who'd gathered, but I didn't want Joy to think I was spying on her. The room was packed, too, which made it hard to see the entire field very clearly, anyway. So I just sipped my cappuccino and kept my eyes on Nan.

"Now, let's get started!"

The second floor of the Blend was quite roomy, with marble-topped tables and chairs as well as an eclectic mix of mismatched furniture. Overstuffed chairs and French flea market sofas, along with floor and table lamps, gave customers the feeling of relaxing in a bohemian living room. (With so many Village apartments being nothing more than tiny cramped studios and one bedrooms, it literally was that for many.) And tonight it was romantically lit with a roaring fire in the brick hearth at the front of the room.

To start what was termed the "Power Meet" session, our

chipper hostess told us she was going to position all the women around the room at different tables and seating areas. She would then select men at random and pair them with the various women.

But before Nan began seating us, I noticed her having a little side discussion with Tucker. It looked rather tense. I motioned him over.

"Everything all right?" I asked while Nan got busy seating the women around the room.

"Nan's upset," he whispered. "You're not going to believe this, but your group is actually short a woman—someone cancelled without calling."

"She just figured this out?"

"Yes, and she asked me to find someone downstairs who'd be interested in trying the Power Meet for free tonight."

The usual fee was forty dollars per participant, which included your three cappuccinos. It worked well for the Blend—since the cappuccinos were pre-purchased by the church group, we were guaranteed to move one hundred and twenty drinks right off the bat, and often couples would descend the stairs and hang out for another hour on the first floor, talking and purchasing even more coffees. All in all, the singles sessions were a boon for the Blend.

"Got any ideas?" I asked him.

Tucker shook his head. "I'll make the rounds. Latitia's down there, but she's already on a date with a guy from the symphony. Kira Kirk's doing a crossword, but that woman acts like she hates all men. Martha Buck is at a table editing a manuscript, but I think she's meeting someone. And Winnie Winslet stopped in, but she's already said this isn't her style."

I thought a minute. "What about Inga?"

Tucker paled a little. "You mean Inga Berg?"

"I do indeed. Maybe shop and drop Inga will actually meet someone here worth holding onto."

"Clare, Inga's dead."

"Dead!"

I'd said it a little too loudly. A few heads turned.

"Dead?" I whispered. "How? When?"

"Suicide. She jumped from the top of her building last Thursday night. I just heard about it from a *Voice* journalist doing a piece on it. The police kept the lid pretty tight on what happened at first, and she was so new to her building that the tenants weren't even sure of her name—"

"Which is why we didn't hear any rumors until now," I guessed.

"It's a terrible shame," said Tucker. "But I better get going. Nan's coming our way."

My head was still spinning after Tucker left and Nan guided me to an armchair by the brick fireplace.

Inga Berg and Valerie Lathem. Both Blend customers. Both attractive young women. Both seemingly had everything to live for—yet both had committed suicide within weeks of each other.

Coincidence?

I'd once heard Mike Quinn say, "In my business, there are no coincidences." And thinking of Quinn made me remember he'd been called to a crime scene the night of our dinner—and the night of our dinner was the night Inga had killed herself.

As Nan passed out small Hello Kitty notepads and pencils to everyone, I wondered if that was the reason I hadn't seen Mike. Had he been assigned to investigate Inga's suicide?

By the time Nan was done, Tucker had reappeared with the twentieth woman, Kira Kirk. She seemed a bit apprehensive, still clutching her crossword puzzle book. As usual, her hair was in its long gray braid, but she'd probably stopped in after a consulting appointment because she was dressed much nicer than usual—in a tailored black pantsuit rather than her usual oversized sweaters and jeans. And she was wearing makeup, too. She looked quite pretty, actually, and I was glad to see her up here.

My eyebrows rose at Tucker and he just shrugged. As Nan took Kira to a seat across the room, I motioned him over again.

"How did you manage to persuade her?" I whispered.

"Free, unlimited cappuccinos for two weeks, that's how."

"You'll have five minutes to get to know each other," announced Nan. With the women already seated, she quickly paired the men and women randomly. "When you hear the timer, shake hands and the gentlemen must then move one seat to the right. You then have a new five minutes to get to know the next person. There are twenty men and twenty women in this room, which means this session will last two hours. You'll have fresh cappuccinos delivered to you during the course of the night; and don't worry, we'll take a few breaks so you can visit the little girls' and little boys' rooms!"

I just knew I wouldn't get through this night without hearing Nan's rules for the little girls' and boys' rooms.

"Okay, remember, five minutes!" cried Nan excitedly, setting the dial on an old-fashioned kitchen timer. "On your marks, get set, go!"

Seven

~~~~~~~~~~~~~~~~~~~~~~~~~~~~~~~~~~~~~~

Mr. Slick.

Mr. Jock.

Mr. Type A.

Mr. Freeloader.

Mr. Superficial Artsy.

Mr. Far Too Old.

Mr. FunnyBook Boy.

Mr. Cabby/Musician.

Mr. Mama's Boy.

Mr. Moviefone.

Mr. Wall Street.

Mr. Borderline Clinically Depressed.

Okay. I know it's demeaning to reduce people to single-phrase descriptions, but what can I say? I'd been reduced to twenty separate five-minute "McMeetings" with twenty different men—and our hostess had given me a Hello Kitty notepad and pencil. So how else could I keep track?

Besides, label-writing was in my blood. I'd done it for years growing up in Pennsylvania, helping my immigrant Italian grandmother jar her tomatoes and peaches every August.

Consequently, given a uniform process, I couldn't see why selecting potential dates had to be any more complicated a recipe than preserving fruit. I simply pictured each man's face on a canning jar with a succinctly written summation of his chief identifying traits.

In any event, I was still reeling from the news that two of my customers, attractive and intelligent young women, had killed themselves within weeks of each other. And my only child was sitting on the other side of the room, ready to offer herself to one of these potential heartbreakers.

I looked at each with a mother's critical eye and the underlying question, "Okay, which of you jokers actually thinks in your wildest dreams that you're good enough to play with my daughter's affections?"

Scorecard at the ready, I showed no mercy.

Currently at bat was an attractive, well-groomed, well-dressed blond in his early twenties with the nametag "Percy." Graphic designer. Well educated. Good potential for my Joy.

"Okay, Percy, are you on any drugs or medication?" I asked him.

His gray green eyes widened. "No . . . well, just an antihistamine for my allergies."

"Have you ever been arrested?"

"Uh." He blinked. "No."

"Are you sure? I saw that blink."

"Well," he admitted, "when I was seventeen, I was swept up in a police raid of a club that allowed underage drinking. But that was it. Really."

I nodded. It sounded innocent enough. Next question: "What made you come here tonight?"

The young man crossed and uncrossed his legs, then nervously tapped one foot. "Well, I've been dating around on-line, you know? LoungeLife.com and SinglesNYC mostly, but nothing serious came out of those encounters, so I decided to try this. My last long-term relationship lasted for a little over two years though."

"What was the reason for the breakup?"

"Oh, we just weren't communicating. But mostly, he was insanely jealous, and I couldn't take it anymore. One of those high I.Q., high-strung types. Know what I mean?"

"Where do you see yourself in five years—" I stopped and looked up from the pink notepad. "Wait. You mean *she,* don't you? She was insanely jealous?"

"No."

"You're telling me you were dating a man?"

"Yes."

I frowned. "But tonight you're looking for a woman?"

"Yes."

Mr. Switch-hitter, I wrote.

"Aren't you familiar with the term *bisexual?*" he asked.

"Aren't you familiar with the movie *Far From Heaven*?" I responded.

"Okay, now your sounding like my ex, forever telling me to pick a team."

"Well, maybe you should."

"It's my life."

"Not exactly," I said. "Not if you involve another person in it and then change your mind."

"That's harsh."

"No, honey, that's a mother's point of view—the truth is, I'm screening you guys for my daughter, not myself."

"Oh," said the young man. His gaze shifted, first to my ringless left hand and then to my outfit.

I'd wanted to fit in tonight, so I dressed in what I felt

was appropriate—high-heeled black boots, black stock-ings, and a form-fitting dark green burnt-velvet dress with a sweetheart neckline. Nothing too upscale or down.

"But you're not married, right?" Percy said, gesturing to my left hand. "And you're pretty much a hottie, if you don't mind my saying so. Why not look for yourself while you're at it?" He gave me a flirty little smile.

"Thanks. Really. But I'm too old for this. And for you," I added gently.

"Nonsense. Haven't you heard of 'tadpoling'?"

Bing! went the kitchen timer. "TIME!" cried Nan. "Wrap up your meetings and shake, everyone!"

I stuck out my hand. "You should introduce yourself to my assistant manager, Tucker. He's right downstairs. Something tells me you two would hit it off."

Mr. Switch-hitter shook my hand and shrugged. "What-ever."

"All right, gentlemen," Nan called, clapping her hands. "Let's move to your next potential Ms. Right!"

I flipped the Hello Kitty notepad to a fresh pink page.

Next at bat: a muscular guy in his mid-twenties with a strong chin, short black hair, and a trimmed black goatee. He wore trendy, black-framed glasses, black jeans, and a distressed leather jacket. His nametag read "Mars."

He sat opposite me and stared.

"Mars is an interesting name," I said, trying to break the black ice.

"It's a nickname," he said without changing his expres-sion. Or blinking.

Mr. Intense, I wrote while waiting for him to say more. He didn't.

"We don't have to talk," I said. "I mean, if you've al-ready made your connections for the night."

"Connec*tion*," he said. "Singular. One. You've guessed correctly. I've already made it." He looked across the room—in the general direction of my Joy, which made me extremely nervous.

"Why don't you tell me about yourself anyway," I suggested, trying to remain calm. *Just in case my daughter completely ignores my pleas to shred your phone number and goes out with you anyway.*

"Whatever," he said, shrugging again.

I waited. Nothing. He just kept staring across the room.

"Are you on any drugs?" I asked pointedly.

That got his attention. He swung his dark, intense gaze back toward me. "Are *you?*" he asked.

"Yes. Caffeine," I said flatly.

His eyebrows rose, and there was the slightest lifting at the corner of his lips. The minimalist's version of a smile, I presumed.

"Okay," he said. "I'll play. I'm not on any drugs. At present."

"Have you ever been arrested?"

"Yes, actually."

Why was I not surprised? "What did you do ?"

The smile was slightly more pronounced. He interlaced his fingers across his chest. "Nothing you want to hear about, believe me."

Great.

"Try me anyway," I suggested.

But there was no answer. He just looked away, across the room again—toward my Joy.

"What do you do for a living?" I asked.

"Paint. I'm a painter. And a genius."

Bing!

"TIME!" called Nan.

Mars stood up, put his hands in his leather jacket pockets, and stared down at me intensely. "Charmed," he said, then walked away.

I shivered. Crossing my legs, I propped the notepad on

my thigh, scratched out *Mr. Intensity* and replaced it with *Mr. Weirdly Intense Painter.*

There was just no way I could let Joy near that guy. No way. If there was any prospective "connection" more potentially dangerous than Mars, I had yet to meet him.

"Well, well, well," said a familiar voice. "Together again."

I looked up to find the refined features and curly black hair of Brooks Newman. He wore a cream-colored crewneck sweater over tailored charcoal-colored slacks. Brooks seemed to be on the prowl because his hazel eyes appeared much sharper tonight as he looked me over.

"What are you doing here?" I asked. "I thought SinglesNYC.com was your stomping ground?"

Brooks shrugged. He moved to the armchair opposite me, sat down, and crossed his legs. "I told you I liked your cappuccinos."

"Decaf."

"Not tonight." A small smile lifted his thin lips. "Tonight I feel like I might enjoy some . . . stimulation. How about you?"

"I've had mine," I said flatly, holding up my empty French café cup.

"Yes," he said, leaning forward and lowering his voice, "but on a cold, cold night like this . . . wouldn't you like *more* to warm you up?"

"No."

"You look very nice tonight," he said, leaning back and surveying my green velvet dress. I instantly regretted the low cut of the sweetheart neckline, which is where his gaze remained fixed. "That color brings out your eyes."

Oh, really? That must be why you're staring at my cleavage. I glanced toward Nan, trying to estimate how many more minutes I had to endure this.

"I can't imagine you're enjoying yourself," I told him. "This sort of thing really doesn't seem your cup of java."

"Yours, either, Clare. I thought you weren't interested in hooking up with men. Just screening them for your daughter."

"As a matter of fact, that's exactly what I'm doing." I took the pencil and scribbled on the notepad. *Brooks Newman: Mr. No Way.*

His eyebrows rose. "I've met your daughter already—around the little circle here. Joy Allegro. I didn't consider your having different last names, but then, you're divorced, so I assume Cosi's your maiden name? Anyway, she's quite attractive. Very bubbly. Energetic. I can see the resemblance."

I frowned and changed the subject. "And how are you coming with the lingerie model fundraiser for vegans?"

My caustic tone didn't seem to phase him. His smile just broadened. "Younger women threaten you, do they?"

Not for the first time, I pictured pointing the espresso machine's steam nozzle at his face—with the valve opened full throttle.

"Listen, buddy, I'm not the one visiting Renu Spa every weekend to ward off the wrinkles."

"Clare, I know what women like you need," he said lowly. "And it's not a shot of caffeine."

"No?"

"No. It's a good, potent shot of sex." He leaned forward, toward my crossed legs, and with the tip of his finger, drew a little circle on my stocking-covered knee. "How about it? You and me . . . let's hook up tonight."

A shudder of revulsion ran through me, and I pushed his hand away.

"I'm not your type, Brooks."

He laughed. "To tell you the truth, the young ones aren't always as energetic as your daughter. Out of bed, and a lot of times in, too. And I'm betting a mature woman like you makes things interesting . . . between the sheets."

The man was dancing around his intentions, but I'd swear he was actually contemplating getting me and my daughter into bed with him at the same time.

If looks could kill, I gave him one that would at least send him to St. Vincent's ER. "Brooks, in case you haven't noticed, I'm being less than receptive."

"Where there's sparks, there's fire." He moved farther forward, and before I could stop him, his fingers were on my knee again and moving up my thigh.

Bing! Saved by the kitchen timer.

"Hands to yourself," I hissed, shoving him away a second time. "Move along. I mean it."

Man, what a creep, I thought with a shudder. Only Brooks Newman could turn Nan's innocent little playgroup into a play*grope*.

"All right, gentlemen," Nan called. "Let's move to your next potential Ms. Right!"

Still agitated, I flipped the Hello Kitty notepad to a fresh pink page. "More like Ms. Right Now," I muttered.

"Pleased to meet you, Ms. Now."

I looked up to find the next Power Meet participant, a fortyish man with chiseled features and a thick head of brown hair. His caramel-colored eyes looked curious and slightly amused by my comment. He held out his hand and smiled.

I shook it. A warm, firm shake.

"I'm Bruce," he said. "In case you can't read the 'Hello, My Name is' tag covering half my chest here."

My turn to smile. "I'm Clare."

I politely looked him over. A gorgeous suede jacket hung handsomely off broad shoulders. Beneath the jacket was a white, open-collared button-down that tapered into worn jeans.

"I've seen you here before," he said. "But downstairs."

He sat down and leaned back, crossing a workbooted foot

over a jean-clad knee. He seemed totally relaxed. "Comfortable in his own skin," was how Madame would put it in one of her favorite French phrases. In her view, too many urban Americans—"over-educated, over-stressed, over-anxious urban Americans" as she put it—too often weren't.

I looked at Bruce again. He did seem slightly familiar. "You're one of our customers?"

"I come in when I can. You have the best cappuccinos in the city."

Oh, I like this guy, I thought. *But not for Joy. Too old for Joy.* I relaxed with that thought, knowing I wouldn't have to grill him with my "Screening for Psychos" list of questions.

"Thanks," I said. "Are you from New York?"

"Originally, I'm from San Francisco."

"That's a real coffee town."

He nodded, his caramel-colored eyes brightening. "Absolutely. You know, your espressos are like nothing I've tasted before. They're like the perfect cross between the North Beach espressos I used to drink back home and the espressos I've tasted in Milan."

My jaw dropped. "You can't know that. Like ten people in the world know that."

He shrugged. "I can't pull an espresso worth a damn. And I can't tell you *why* it tastes like that. I just know it does."

I nodded. "It's the beans and roasting process. The Milanese Italians like a subtler, sweeter espresso. The North Beach Italians like the more pungent, rougher espresso. Madame likes to say we're geographically and gastronomically between the two."

"Fascinating . . ." He smiled, his gaze ever so subtly moving over me. "So how exactly do you get the different tastes?"

"A lot of ways. To get that more pungent, rougher version, you'd roast your beans darker—and you'd start with beans that have rich, acidy elements like a Kenyan AA or a

Sidamo. For the Milan taste you'd want softer profile Arabica beans—something like a Brazilian Santos. And you'd be careful not to add any beans to the blend with acidy elements. You might even add an Indian grown washed Robusta for sweetness—though typically Robustas are an inferior, foul little low growing bean, the sort you'd find in pre-ground tinned coffee, and you'd want to steer clear of them. The best beans are Arabicas, and they're grown at high altitudes—a good rule of thumb is the higher the altitude, the higher the acidity, and the better the coffee."

Bruce's eyebrows rose. "Wait. You *want* an acidy taste in your coffee?"

Give the man points for actually listening. "Acidity is an industry term. In coffee-speak it doesn't mean bitter or sour. It means a brightness, a pleasant sharpness. Basically, when you create a blend you want to pay attention to three major elements: acidity, aroma, and body. The beans that provide acidity are the high notes, the ones that provide body are the low notes. In the middle, you want beans that provide aroma, which can range from fruity to herby."

"Just like a musical chord. That's a nice way of explaining it, Clare."

His smile was genuine and I liked the way he said my name. "Thanks. That's nice of you to say."

"So give me an example of one of your blends."

"I'll give you a basic one: Kenya AA for acidity, Sulwese for aroma, and Colombian for body. But it's not just the coffee types that are important. For the perfect cup, what's also key is getting the highest quality beans possible, roasting and brewing them expertly, and enjoying them while they're still fresh."

"I'm getting it . . . and I can see there's a lot that goes into your business."

I shrugged. "We roast green beans right here in the basement. It's a century-old family business and every year it can change, depending on the worldwide coffee crops—not to mention the tastes of our customers. So you'd better love it and stay on top of it, or leave it, you know? And I do love it."

"Yeah, I love my business for the same reason—the constant challenge and the creativity."

I glanced at his workboots. "So what do you do?"

"I started out in construction, then became an architect to specialize in historical restoration—and I've done nothing but expand my business since I moved East. I've been in the tri-state region about ten years now, and I just moved down here from Westchester about two months ago. I'm divorced. No kids."

"What are you working on?"

Bruce laughed a little at my question. "I've got crews all over the city. Dozens of projects—interiors and exteriors. For myself personally, I'm jazzed about restoring the interior of a Federal townhouse over on Leroy. The exterior is more archetypal than your building here, even has a horse walk. Yours is a beauty, and its got a high level of integrity, but I can see there've been some liberties taken with alternations—I assume to make it workable for your business. The first floor's line of French doors and front windows for starters."

"Those were put in decades ago, sometime between 1910 and 1920, when the Blend shifted from being purely a wholesale roaster to a roaster and a café. I take it you're renovating the Leroy property for a residential owner then?"

"For myself. I bought it outright the second I saw it."

My eyes widened. This guy was a multi-millionaire. No question.

"How about you? What's Clare's story—in five minutes or less."

He smiled warmly again, and I tried to ignore the ridiculous pulsing of blood through my stupid veins. So this guy was drop-dead gorgeous, a self-made millionaire, charming as hell, and genuinely turned on by the perfect cup of coffee. So what? Underneath, he was probably as smarmy as Brooks Newman, looking to dangle a pretty package long enough to bait as many women as possible. Shop-and-drop. Grind 'em up. Spit em out . . .

Still . . . there was no reason *not* to be civil.

"Let's see," I began. "Well, I'd originally managed the Blend between the ages of twenty and twenty-nine. Then I got divorced, left this life for the hinterlands of New Jersey, and spent the next decade raising my daughter, fighting crabgrass, and launching a part-time career writing for trade magazines."

"Which?"

"*Cupping, In Stock,* and other magazines published specifically for the coffee and restaurant trade. Once in a blue moon, I come across a topic I pitch to a bigger publication. I had a Sunday *New York Times Magazine* piece run not too long ago about coffee-drinking trends."

"Impressive."

"That's nice of you to say, but my priority now is this place. Just a few months ago, my daughter moved to Manhattan to attend culinary school, so when Madame, the owner of the Blend, made me an offer I couldn't refuse, I came back to managing again."

"An offer you couldn't refuse? Let me guess . . . equity?"

"I'm impressed. Equity *and* the rent-free use of the duplex upstairs. You read tea leaves, too?"

"Not tea leaves—coffee grounds."

"You're kidding."

He shrugged his broad shoulders. "My grandmother taught me tasseography when I was just a little kid."

"Mine, too."

"No way," he said, skeptical.

"Way."

We both smiled that disbelieving smile two people smile when they share something special—something so few people share that it seems to bond you together, at least for the moment.

Bing!

Nan's kitchen timer.

Damn, I thought. *Damn. Damn. Damn.*

It was the first time in this entire evening I hadn't wanted the thing to bing.

"Wrap it up, everyone!" called Nan. "Say your goodbyes."

I shrugged. "Our playgroup leader has spoken."

"Playgroup," he repeated with a laugh. I liked his laugh. It was deep and genuine and reflected its bright energy in his eyes. "Yeah, you know, you're right. This whole thing is sort of one big sandbox, isn't it?"

"That or a Hopper painting," I quipped.

He glanced around. "Yeah, I can see it. The crowded yet lonely scene of couples *not* connecting in the stark light and shadows of the hearth's dying fireplace."

"An urban study in oil on canvas," I added. "Very *Room in New York.*"

"Or *Excursion into Philosophy,*" he said with a raised eyebrow.

Excursion was an odd choice, I thought, remembering Hopper's desolate couple: the man sitting fully clothed on a narrow bed, indifferent to the beautiful, half-clothed woman stretched out behind him, facing the wall, her red hair on the white pillow, her naked round bottom sunwashed, looking like ripe fruit ready to be enjoyed. Beside her, the man's face remains in shadow, full of angst. He ignores the fruit within his reach, staring instead at the floor, lost inside himself, possibly contemplating the book laying open next to him.

Did it represent the isolation of modern life? The depressive folly of the intellectual, brooding instead of living? Was Hopper laughing as he painted it? I used to wonder.

"I always saw that painting as the *end* of the road," I said. "No longer being able to connect. You know, years after the marriage vows. When disillusion sets in."

"Not for me," said Bruce. "I see it as the morning after the one-night stand, waking up with the wrong woman. He's tasted the fruit, and he's suddenly dejected, maybe even feeling a little fleeced, because she's not what she seemed. And he's no longer interested."

"You've seen the Whitney collection, I take it?"

"Maybe twenty times."

"You won't believe this, but my duplex includes two framed original charcoal Hopper sketches. They were done right here, too. It's amazing—one of the perks of living upstairs."

"I can't imagine a better one."

We smiled that disbelieving smile again—like we'd both found a three carat diamond in a Cracker Jack box.

"All right, gentlemen, and that means all of you!" Nan called in our general direction. "*Please* move along to your next Ms. Right. The clock will soon be ticking down!"

"Run, runner," I murmured.

Bruce laughed. "I hope I'm not ready for 'Carousel' yet."

My god, I thought. *He actually got my* Logan's Run *joke.*

As a Goth twenty-something with black lipstick and a tattoo approached us, Bruce rose from the chair. I held my breath as he extended his hand.

"Would you like to go to dinner with me tomorrow, Clare?" he asked.

OH, YES.

"Uh . . . tomorrow . . . yeah, sure. That would be nice."

I placed my small hand in his large one. To my unending delight, he didn't just shake and release—he held on.

"Bowman. That's my last name."

"And mine's Cosi. Clare Cosi."

"You have a nice smile, Clare Cosi," he said quietly.

"Thanks. So do you."

"Tomorrow then."

EIGHT

~~~~~~

"MOM! I cannot believe these notes of yours. They are, like, so out there."

As Joy flipped through my notepad's pages, I hung a blue Village Blend apron around my neck, brought the long strings to the front of my waist, and jerked them into a tight bow.

After the Cappuccino Connection had officially ended and most of the customers had departed, I had tried to "casually" discuss the evening's McMeetings with my daughter, but truthfully all I could think about was Bruce Bowman.

Bruce Bowman. Bruce Bowman. Bruce Bowman.

After shaking his warm, strong, slightly callused hand, I'd been on what felt like a super caffeine high, reciting his name like a New Age chant—until it hit me that every woman sitting on the Blend's second floor tonight was tracking Bruce's movements around the Cappuccino Connection circle.

Obviously, Bruce was the big Kahuna, the catch of the night, and Nan Tulley, the evil witch, had insisted all of us make three connections, at least. So it shouldn't have been a surprise to me when Bruce left the Blend with another "connection" on his arm. A tall, beautifully dressed red-headed woman.

I could have strangled her.

And him.

Of course, the fleeting flare of emotion quickly passed, and I coolly regained my composure, maturely resolving to forget about him forever.

Easy, right?

Wrong.

It was an hour later, and I still couldn't stop thinking about him.

Stupid, silly me just could not shake the feeling that we'd connected on some significant level, and I began to obsess about whether he'd actually keep his date with me tomorrow—and where exactly I ranked on his list of dates. Was it just under the redheaded amazon? Or was I farther down? Who else in the room had made "Cappuccino Connections" with him?

This was the state I'd been in when Joy rushed over to me to begin discussing the evening's men (and I couldn't remember any of them clearly but Bruce). Anxious to make sure my girl didn't end up with a loon, I'd resorted to reading over my notes.

Joy put up with my flipping back and forth through the pages for about two minutes before she'd snatched the Hello Kitty pad right out of my hand. "Let me see that," she'd cried.

Now she was leaning on the Blend's blue marble front counter, flipping through the pink pages, her eyes incredulous saucers.

"Tucker, you are not going to believe this. My mother

asked these guys about their personal drug use, their arrest record, and the reason for their last breakup. Then she *labeled* every guy she met. Like they were coffee blends or something!"

"Joy, not so loud," I cautioned from behind the counter. It was almost midnight and most of the customers had drifted out, but a few couples still lingered quietly at the far end of the main floor, near the first floor fireplace. Reluctant to throw them out, I decided to give them one last hour of romantic firelight—while Tucker and I cleaned and re-stocked.

"Coffee is not exactly a bad analogy," Tucker told Joy. "I mean, if you think about it, men can be like coffee blends. A very subtle blending of elements can form the most interesting tastes. Some are bolder, some rougher, some sweeter . . ."

"Some have whiney overtones," I quipped.

My assistant manager frowned at my caustic remark. Pausing in his cup-stacking duties, he wiped his hands on his apron and said, "Let me see that notepad."

Joy handed it over and he flipped through its pages.

With a concerned sigh, he began to read aloud, "Mr. Slick, Mr. Jock, Mr. Type A, Mr. Freeloader, Mr. Superficial Artsy, Mr. Far Too Old, Mr. FunnyBook Boy, Mr. Cabby/Musician, Mr. Mama's Boy, Mr. Moviefone . . ." Tucker looked up and wrinkled his nose. "Mr. Moviefone?"

I shrugged. "He had that voice."

"You mean the guy *sounded* like Mr. Moviefone?" asked Tucker.

"Yes, and I found it very distracting."

"I remember him!" said Joy. "He had a mustache and his cologne smelled like Gummy Bears. Did you know Kira left with him?"

"Really?"

"Yeah, they looked pretty chummy, too."

I nodded, remembering the man. "He did mention crosswords were his passion. Maybe I should have labeled him Mr. Crossword Puzzle Man."

"Clare, you know, I'm really surprised at you," said Tucker, shaking a finger. "Such catty, cynical evaluations are usually beneath you."

"It's not catty. It's practical."

"Practical? All right, this I gotta hear," said Tucker.

"If you've only got a first impression to go on, the most practical thing you can do is reduce the guy down to his basics. It's no different than my grandmother's method of putting up preserves. Very sensible. Boil the substance down and label it."

"I see," said Tucker. "So for you the only discernable difference between canning and courting is straining the guy in question and coating him with a thin layer of wax?"

"Technically yes," I said. "Even though I got the impression that some of these guys were just weird enough to consider being strained and waxed a vaguely kinky form of foreplay."

"Mom!"

"Sorry, honey. Forget you heard your Mommy say *foreplay*. But don't forget what I'm about to tell you. There are a few guys in my little notepad that under no circumstances you are to go out with should they call you, starting with a man named Brooks Newman."

Joy rolled her eyes. "Brooks Newman, what a character. I think he took the number of almost every woman he sat down with. Isn't he the guy who gave you those other online dating sites for me to try? The ones you said are more 'appropriate' for me than SinglesNYC?"

"Yes, but—" (Okay, so Brooks actually called them "duds," and it was me who told Joy they were more "appropriate" for a girl her age. But what else could I do? I couldn't very well tell my daughter she'd be better off on-line dating through two "dud" sites, could I?)

"Mom, I'm not in high school anymore. I can make my own decisions about my personal life. Don't you trust me?"

I didn't see any way to answer honestly without causing World War Three, so I didn't answer. Not directly. "Okay, then, why don't you just tell me and Tucker who you liked?"

"No. You'll just shoot them down."

"I won't," I said.

"Promise?" asked Joy.

My reassuring smile felt as though it were wilting into an anxious grimace. "I'll do my best."

"Okay, Mom, I'll tell you who I connected with. But only if you tell me who *you* connected with."

"I didn't make any connections. Your turn."

Joy narrowed her eyes. "I don't believe you."

"Believe me."

"But Nan said we were supposed to make three. Those were the rules."

"I know, honey. I just chose not to play by them."

Joy flipped though the notepad. "What about Mr. Wall Street?"

I closed my eyes, trying to picture that meeting. "Nice kid. Strong head on his shoulders, handsome, pleasant, good sense of humor. Late twenties. I liked him—for *you*."

"I liked him, too," said Joy. "And he asked me to lunch."

I smiled. "See. I was right, wasn't I?"

"Okay, so we agree on one guy."

Joy flipped through more notes. "I can't tell what you thought of this one." She pointed. "Mr. Weirdly Intense Painter."

"Mars?" *Oh, god, no.* "Did you know he admitted to be-ing arrested?"

"He *was* sort of intense wasn't he?"

"Sort of intense? That man would win a stare-off with Charles Manson."

"Who?"

"Never mind, honey. You didn't like Mars, did you?" My teeth clenched.

"It wouldn't matter if I did. He said he'd already made his connection."

I exhaled with extreme relief. "He told me the same thing."

"Yeah, but you know the weirdest thing about the guy wasn't his intensity—I found that sort of a turn-on actually. The weirdest thing was he said he'd *already* made his connection before he even started talking to me."

"Like I said, Joy, he did that with me, too. Don't feel bad."

"No, Mom, you don't get what I mean. It's not that I feel bad. It's that it doesn't make sense. I mean we all paid forty dollars each to supposedly meet as many people as we could in two hours, right? But I was only the second girl he sat down with."

"That is odd," said Tucker. "Who was the first? She really must have been something."

"The first woman he sat down with was this tall redhead named Sahara McNeil," said Joy. "She was sitting at the table to the left of mine and Mars just kept staring at her. It was kinda creepy, actually."

There was only one tall redhead in that room. The one Bruce had left with—and I had wanted to strangle.

"How did you find out her full name?" I asked. "Did you talk to her?"

"No, one of the guys mentioned her name," said Joy.

"Which one?"

"Let's just see," said Joy, smiling mischievously. She snatched my notepad back from Tucker and thumbed through it. "It wasn't Mr. Slick . . . or Mr. Cabby/Musician." Joy paused on that page. "I kinda liked Cabby/Musician. He invited me to see his band at CBGB Wednesday night."

Tucker snorted.

"What?" asked Joy.

"Sweetie, when you've lived in Manhattan a little longer you'll learn that every third or fourth straight little boy under thirty with a rock star complex gets his sucky band a call-in gig at CBGB. But look on the bright side—you're sure to meet his colleagues, friends, and family, because that's pretty much the only way these bands fill those Bowery seats."

"Now you're the one being catty," Joy said.

"Bring earplugs," Tucker advised.

With a sigh of annoyance, Joy went back to my notepad and kept flipping. "Here's the guy—the one who told me the redhead's name? It was this really cool dude named Bruce."

My heart sank. Completely sank.

"I need an espresso," I said.

I turned to put the coffee through the grinder. Funny how the hardest beans were no match for these sharp, little blades. When they whirred and spun, every whole little bean was aloofly chopped into unrecognizable bits—which is exactly what I felt was happening to me.

"Mom? What's wrong?"

"Nothing."

"Ohmygod. Look what you wrote here about Bruce."

"Give me that," I said reaching. Joy stepped backward.

"Mom . . . what does this mean?"

"Honey, it's just a few scribbles. Give it here!" I lunged but the counter stopped me.

"What does it say, Joy?" asked Tucker. "What did she label Bruce?"

"Mr. Right."

ΝΙΝΕ

~~~~~~~~~~~~~~~~~~~~~~~~~~~~~~~~~~~~~

"**H**ε just made a good impression on me, that's all," I tried to tell Joy.

"Mr. *Right?*" said Tucker. "I'd say that's a little more significant than just 'a good impression.'"

"Did he make a date with you?" asked Joy.

I studied my daughter's pretty, pensive face, dreading her reaction. I knew very well that a part of Joy had never given up hope that I would one day get back together with her father.

Her grandmother (my ex-mother-in-law) felt the same way. Madame's offer to me of equity over time—in the Blend and the duplex—was not a sole offer. She'd made the same deal with her son, Matteo, arranging our future so that we'd both one day co-own this building and its business, which, if fortune smiled, I assumed we would both eventually leave to Joy.

With her strategic little deal, my ex-mother-in-law was

clearly harboring the same hopes as my daughter—that I'd one day remarry Matt.

But I couldn't live my life by other people's hopes.

Not anymore.

Getting back together with my ex-husband was off the charts. Out of the question. I'd remain civil to Matt, of course—sometimes even more than civil. There were times when I actually enjoyed Matt's company, but as a friend. Nothing more.

I was through loving Matt too much. Through being infatuated with his larger-than-life presence. Through letting him hurt me. And if part of that meant becoming romantically involved with another man—or men—then so be it. It was time I moved on.

Still, I hated the idea of hurting Joy. This whole night was supposed to have been about my trying to prevent her from getting hurt.

I met my daughter's green eyes. "I'll tell you the truth, okay? Bruce Bowman and I had a very nice little meeting, but that's all it was. He asked me out, but I really don't think he'll call. He left with that Sahara McNeil person, and it's obvious he's much more interested in her than me."

"No, he's not."

I blinked. That was the last thing I'd expected Joy to say. "Of course, he is, honey. So just forget about it." I turned to my assistant manager. "Tucker, we need more cardboard heat sleeves. Can you bring some out from the pantry?"

"Sure, Clare."

I abandoned my espresso beans and turned to continue checking inventory, but Joy wasn't taking the hint that I'd closed this discussion. She came around the counter and began following me as I surveyed the shelves and cabinets.

"Listen, Mom, Bruce told me Sahara McNeil is just an old college friend. He was glad to see her only because he was hoping to reconnect with some other classmates they both knew."

"Honey, it sounds like this McNeil woman is an old flame, and he wants to date her again."

"No. Listen. When Bruce sat down, he told me right off the bat that I was too young for him—he was really nice about it, too, but he said he'd tried dating someone a year ago in her early twenties, someone who worked in his office, and it was a disaster, so I was definitely not even in the ballpark. So we just chatted in general and he mentioned being surprised at seeing his old classmate sitting at the table next to mine. I quietly asked him if he was interested in her, and he shook his head no. He told me she was always too far out for him. Too edgy. Said her real name was Sally but in college she'd changed it to Sahara because it sounded more artsy. I could tell by the way he said it that he thought that was sort of silly and phony. He said he liked more down-to-earth women. So, of course, I told him about you."

"You *what?*" I stopped checking inventory and faced my daughter in shock.

"I told him he should keep an eye out for someone special around the circle, a woman in a green velvet dress named Clare, because she would be the best connection he'd have a chance at making. Ever."

"You said that?"

"Yeah, Mom. I want you to be happy, you know. And I liked Bruce. So I'm glad you and he connected."

"I'm not sure we did, honey. But I'm . . . I'm very glad you're glad."

"Why do you look so surprised?"

"Because I thought . . ." I shook my head and took a break from checking inventory. I went back over to the grinder and processed more beans, enough for three espresso shots.

"What did you think?" asked Joy. "C'mon, tell me."

"I thought you were hoping I'd get back together with your dad."

Joy shrugged. "I do . . . but . . ."

"But what?"

"But I want you to be happy. And . . . to tell you the truth . . . well . . . you remember Mario?"

"Sure."

"You remember how I told Esther I hadn't really been into him or anything?"

"Yes."

"I lied. I really liked him, Mom, and I was really hurt when he broke it off with me . . ."

"Oh, honey, I'm sorry. Why didn't you tell me?"

"It was personal, and I was . . . I don't know . . . embarrassed, I guess. I thought it would be easier to pretend he didn't matter to me. And, you know, after the hurt, I was so angry with him, Mom, I could have killed him."

I sighed. "Honey, believe me, I know what you went through."

"Exactly . . . Look, remember when you said you wanted to try dating again? I wasn't thrilled at first, and I did want you to get back together with Dad, but then I thought how I would feel if you wanted me to get back together with Mario, even after he broke my heart and made me so angry and everything . . . and well, I wouldn't be very happy with you if you dumped that on me, you know?"

"That's different, Joy. Mario and I don't have a relationship. You and your father do. So it's natural you'd want me to get back together with him. But no matter what happens with me and your dad, your dad will always love you. And so will I. That's not going to change."

"Sure, Mom. You've told me that, like, a million times. And for a long time I still couldn't help feeling like the whole world would be right again if only you and Dad remarried . . . but I'm starting to think that maybe it's not realistic. And so . . . I figure if you and Dad aren't going to get back together . . . then there's no reason you shouldn't be happy. I mean, if any Mom deserves to be happy, it's you."

I reached under the counter—way under, behind the unopened coffee syrups and boxes of wooden stirrers.

"You know what this calls for?" I announced, motioning for Tucker to come over and join us.

"What?"

"Frangelico lattes."

Into each of the three cups, I splashed the translucent gold, added a freshly pulled espresso shot, poured in a tsunami of steamed milk, and topped it with a fluffy cloud of foam.

"She's underage, you know," teased Tucker as I handed out the drinks.

"She's old enough to vote, drive a car, have a baby, and fall in love. I say she's old enough for two ounces of hazelnut liqueur. Joy, just pretend we're in Milan."

"Okay, Mom," said Joy. She lifted her cup. *"C'ent anni, mama mia."*

"C'ent anni, mia fia."

"One hundred years," said Tucker.

And we all drank.

I sighed, tasting the sweet hazelnut flavor of the Frangelico, the glowing heat of its alcohol, the earthiness of the espresso, and the soft, milky froth of the steamed milk.

I hated myself for speculating, but I couldn't help wondering if Bruce Bowman could possibly taste this satisfying.

"Uh-oh," said Tucker.

Looking up from my pathetic, unattainable reverie, I saw why Tucker had complained. We hadn't locked the door yet, and a new customer had walked in, a young man in a long gray overcoat.

"Shall I tell him we're closed?" asked Tucker.

"No, I'll take care of his drink order and tell him it has to be to go. You grab the keys and lock up after him."

"What about the lovebirds?" asked Tucker.

The last three couples, spillovers from the Cappuccino Connection "Power Meet" session, were still nursing coffee drinks near the fireplace, heads together, talking with that intimate tell-me-everything-about-yourself intensity that always comes during the first fiery flush of an infatuation. I still didn't have the heart to pull the plug.

"We'll let them out one at a time as they approach the door," I said. "I have another thirty minutes' work here at least, then we'll kick their butts into the street."

"Sounds good," said Tucker.

He turned and strode toward the back pantry, where we kept our thick ring of shop keys on a hook. I took another satisfying sip of my Frangelico latte, waiting for the new customer to approach our coffee bar counter and place his order.

But he didn't.

Like a ghost, the young man drifted hesitantly over to those last three remaining couples. He approached one of the tables, hands in the pocket of his long gray overcoat. He stood there, waiting for them to look up. When they did, he mumbled to them. They shook their heads and looked away, then he moved to the next couple.

"Joy, something's up with this guy," I whispered. "Go get Tucker."

In less than thirty seconds, both Joy and Tucker were back.

By this time the lone customer had drifted to the second couple, with the same result. The man at the table, a slight guy in a navy sport coat and glasses, and the young dark-haired woman shook their heads; then the stranger moved along.

"Tucker, watch this guy," I whispered. "Something's not right."

The stranger moved to the third couple, spoke to them, and again was turned away. Finally, the man in the overcoat moved toward the coffee bar. He wasn't that old, maybe twenty-six or twenty-seven. He had pale skin, short brush-cut brown hair, and a very unhappy expression on his face.

"May we help you?" called Tucker, stepping in front of the counter to confront the man.

"Yes," said the stranger. The collar of his long gray overcoat was still turned up. He removed his hands from his coat pockets, took off his black leather gloves, and turned down the collar. "I'm looking for someone."

If the young man had sounded relaxed, I wouldn't have worried. But his tone was venomous, full of naked hostility.

"Tucker . . ." I said, trying to call him back.

"It's okay, Clare," he said over his shoulder.

"*Your* name is Tucker?" asked the young man.

"Yes," said Tucker.

The young man looked Tucker up and down. "And earlier this evening you talked to Percy?"

Percy? I thought to myself. Who the heck was Percy? A second later it hit me. Percy was Mr. Switch-hitter. The nice-looking graphic designer who'd advised me to consider "tadpoling"—the one I'd suggested get together with Tucker after the Cappuccino Connection night ended. The one with the "insanely jealous" ex-boyfriend. *Ohmygod.*

Before I could warn Tucker, he was already telling the young man, "Yes, Percy and I hit it off. Not that it's any of your business."

"Oh, but it is," said the young man.

The punch came so fast and so hard I stood completely stunned for a second.

"Call the police!" I told Joy and rushed forward to help.

But one of the men from the couples' tables, the slight guy with glasses in the navy sports coat, had gotten to Tucker faster. As the attacker was about to swing again, the slight guy body-slammed him, sending him soaring. Chairs clattered to the floor as the attacker's body flew into them. With an ear-shattering screech, a heavy marble table was dragged across the wood planks as the attacker used it to quickly pull himself back up.

By then, I was coming at him with a raised baseball bat—the one I'd kept behind the counter ever since my own frightening encounter with a bad guy a few months back. The attacker didn't tarry—he raced to the door and out into the black, cold night.

I dropped the bat and rushed to Tucker.

"Ah, shit, shit, shit!" he cried, blood pouring from his face, "I have an audition in three days! Do you think it's broken, Clare?"

"Take it easy, Tuck. Sit down."

I led him to a chair and had Joy bring out an ice pack. We had a first aid kit in back, of course, and I always kept ice packs in our freezer for staff burns or injuries.

"Honey, hold this against your nose," I told him.

After a minute, I had him remove the pack and took a look. "It's not twisted or misshapen. Do you feel a tingling or numbness?"

"No, but it hurts like hell."

"That's good, Tuck. It's probably not broken—just badly bruised."

"Well, thank God! And thank God Percy wasn't dating Mike freakin' Tyson or my career would be completely over!"

Within minutes a siren was screaming down Hudson. The red lights painted our front windows as the police car pulled up to the curb.

Officer Langley, a lanky young Irish cop, rushed toward our front door, nightstick in hand. His partner, a shorter, more muscular Greek cop named Demetrios was right behind him, one hand on the butt of his holstered gun.

I met them as they entered, and told them the attacker had fled. Then Langley put away his nightstick and pulled out his notebook, and Demetrios called in my description of the attacker over his radio.

"The cars in the area will look out for him, Ms. Cosi," said Demetrios. He and Langley had been regular Blend customers for a few months now—ever since they'd both helped Madame and me out of a few jams.

"Do you want an ambulance?" Langley asked Tucker.

"God, no. I'm a drama queen, but only on the stage."

I put a hand on Tuck's shoulder. "You need to see a doctor. I insist you at least get checked out at St. Vincent's ER."

"Fine," he said. "But I'm not going in a paramedic mobile, thank you very much. Flag a cab or something."

"We'll give him a ride," Demetrios offered.

"Thanks," I said.

Joy tugged my sleeve. "Mom, you go with Tucker if you want. I can lock up and take care of things here."

Was there any more rewarding feeling for a mother than a daughter rising to the occasion? "Are you sure, honey?" I asked.

"Yeah. No problem," she said. "Go. Take as long as you want. I can sleep over, if it's okay with you."

"Of course, Joy, you can sleep over anytime. You know that."

Joy fetched our coats, then shooed the rest of the customers away. I took Tucker's arm and led him forward, making sure he stayed steady on his way out the door and toward the back of the police car.

"God, it's freezing out here," he complained in a nasally voice. "And this damned ice pack isn't helping."

"Keep it on there," I insisted. "You'll thank me in a few days when your nose *isn't* swelled up like a balloon."

Demetrios held the back door of the car open. I climbed in and slid across the cold, black vinyl seat. Then Demetrios helped Tucker settle in next to me.

After the car door slammed shut, Tucker sighed. "You know, Clare, I was going to thank you for sending Percy my way. But now I have to tell you, I've got mixed feelings."

"I'm so sorry Tucker."

"Not as sorry as I am . . . you know, this *really* smarts."

Between the back seat and front was a metal grill. Through its wiry squares I watched Demetrios climb into the driver's seat and Langley settle in next to him.

The air was so cold in the dark car, our breath was condensing into little clouds. In the front seat, the radio was flickering with lights and a voice was chattering through static to another unit about the address of a tripped burglar alarm.

"Thank God for that Good Samaritan who body-slammed that jerk," I said quietly to Tucker as we pulled away from the curb.

"Who was he? Did you get his name?"

"Langley did. I saw him taking a statement. I only remember him by his Cappuccino Connection label."

"Which was?"

"Mr. Mama's Boy."

"You're kidding me?"

"Nope."

"Well, dear, sounds to me like you were way wrong about that one."

"No I wasn't, Tucker. He lives with his mother."

"Clare, living with one's mother means nothing these days, especially in this city, rents being what they are. Repeat after me: a guy who body slams a violent attacker is *not* a mama's boy."

I hated being wrong about people. But Tucker was right. That was one mild mannered bank teller I'd definitely misjudged and mislabeled.

"We better tell these guys to talk to Percy," I said, tipping my chin toward the front seat. "If they don't catch up to that jerk who hit you on the streets tonight, then they can catch up with him at his home tomorrow. Percy should at least have the man's name, if not his current address."

Tucker sighed. "I guess."

I shook my head. "I just can't believe this happened."

"Crime of passion, Clare. Crime of passion."

We arrived at the hospital in something like six minutes. While the Emergency Room doctor was checking over Tucker, I chatted with Langley and Demetrios in the too-bright fluorescence of the ER's waiting area.

"Your assistant manager's lucky that dude didn't have access to a gun," said Langley, propping his hip.

I shuddered. "Don't say that."

"Sorry, Ms. Cosi," said Demetrios, folding his arms across his chest, "but its true. You said this jerk was ready to take a few more swings at Tucker, and, quite frankly, head injuries can be fatal. He was obviously ready to go the distance."

"No . . . it wasn't that serious an attack," I insisted. "The jerk was just jealous."

Langley and Demetrios exchanged a look.

"What?" I asked, lowering myself into one of the chilly plastic seats. Suddenly, I felt totally exhausted. They obviously didn't. *Ah, youth.*

Looking down at me, Demetrios shrugged. "Jealousy's a deadly motivator, Ms. Cosi."

"Yeah," said Langley, "You never heard of O.J. Simpson?"

"He was acquitted," I pointed out, looking up at them.

The two officers exchanged another look.

I changed the subject. "So, have you two seen Detective Quinn around lately? I haven't."

"The guy's been buried under his caseload as far as I know," said Demetrios.

"Yeah, and the hottest one is that suicide over by the river. Lady took a dive off the roof of her new condo's building. Only Quinn doesn't think she jumped all by herself."

Demetrios nodded.

"What's he think?" I asked.

"Homicide," said Langley with a shrug.

"A pusher," clarified Demetrios. "And worse. He thinks the killer's struck before—and might just strike again."

TEN

Oh, my, my . . .

The Genius was impressed. Sahara McNeil was quite the chameleon. Marc Jacobs last night, and Frederick's of Hollywood this morning.

Given the transformation, the Genius almost didn't recognize her. Almost.

The flaming red hair had been the signal flag—so scarlet she didn't even have to color it to meet the fashion demands of her flamboyant colleagues. It was, the Genius recalled, the first thing he'd noticed about her.

Moving casually across the street, the Genius watched as Sahara pushed through the glass doors where she'd said goodnight to him just the other night.

It had seemed friendly. Catching up on old times, talking about friends and acquaintances, they'd left the coffeehouse, then went to a bar, and finally walked together to *this apartment building on West Tenth Street. And there they'd said goodnight.*

But the Genius knew that Sahara would not leave it at that. She'd taken his card. She'd be contacting him again—and soon.

That's why the Genius had waited for over an hour the next morning, across the street from Sahara's apartment building, scanning the faces of the professionals heading uptown and the stay-at-homes walking their dogs.

Any less vigilant and the Genius would have missed her.

If not for the flaming hair, the woman in the tailored slacks and tasteful makeup of last night could never have been matched with the cheap thing who'd just pushed through the glass doors of the West Tenth apartment building.

The too-short, too-jejune skirt. The mesh stockings. The shiny black dominatrix boots and animal print jacket made her look more like an exotic dancer than a legitimate art dealer.

Yet Sahara McNeil was a legitimate art dealer, as the Genius well knew. And was listed as an agent on a major six figure sale through Sotheby's just last month.

Pretty. Successful. Yet oh so sad and alone.

The Genius knew her type well. New York City was full of Sahara McNeils.

The Genius followed—from a discrete distance—as the redhead started her long walk to the SoHo art gallery where she worked. Most likely she made this walk daily, weather permitting. Rain or snow might drive her into a cab. But today she was on foot—likely ready to appreciate any male attention she might attract in that trampy outfit.

Yes, the weather was perfect at the moment. Still clear. Unfortunately, precipitation was predicted sometime in the next week, a chance of icy rain or even snow. If it

drove Sahara into a cab, that could be a problem. An um-
brella, too, might become a weapon, and the Genius
couldn't risk that.

On her walk to work, Sahara crossed busy boulevards
like the Avenue of the Americas and Houston. And she
strolled along twisting, narrow Village streets lined with
parked cars—a perfect place to await the coming of a dis-
tracted, fast-moving driver.

Why, there were so many opportunities for an accident.

It would be a challenge, but the Genius was up for it.
One simply had to think creatively. Murder was an art, like
any other.

No one knew that better than Sahara McNeil . . .

"You're not fanatical about your cholesterol level, are
you?" I asked as I approached Bruce Bowman with two
glasses of Campari and soda.

Better to discover his position on butter now, I thought,
than be forced to switch gravy recipes midway.

"Cholesterol and I are old friends," Bruce replied,
crouched in front of my living room's hearth. He'd offered
to start a fire and had done an admirable job. The flames
were just starting to crackle, the heat filling the chilly
room. "There are far worse ways to go than eating yourself
to death."

Great, I thought, ready to press on with my original
cholesterol-friendly, butter-happy menu.

It was early Sunday evening, the day after Cappuccino
Connection night, and, true to his word, Bruce had called
me around noon, telling me he'd made us dinner reservations at Babbo—a truly marvelous Washington Square
gourmet restaurant, co-owned by celebrated chef Mario
Batali, for which getting last-minute reservations was a
trick of David Copperfield–level magic.

Unfortunately, Tucker was off for the next few days,

tending to his nose (bruised but not broken, thank goodness), and I was worried about leaving the Blend solely in
the hands of my part-timers for long. I had yet to promote
or hire a second assistant manager, so I suggested instead
that Bruce come to my place—that way, I'd literally be two
floors away should any crisis come up downstairs. And
with Joy agreeing to surreptitiously baby-sit the staff, I
knew if they didn't call me, she would.

"Really, Clare," Bruce said, rising back up to his full
six-foot height. "It's very nice of you to go to all this
trouble."

"What trouble?" I said, handing him the Campari and
soda. "This is strictly a meat and potatoes meal."

Bruce shook his head. "Women don't cook for me. Not
New York women. Not ever. Especially not after I've asked
them out to an outrageously expensive restaurant."

I shrugged. "I like to cook."

It was also a delight to show off Madame's duplex to
someone who actually appreciated it as much as I did—the
antiques, the paintings, the furnishings were all of the
finest quality, as was the restoration of the hearth and windows, and Bruce Bowman noticed immediately.

My ex-husband had always been blasé about such things,
partly I think it was because he'd grown up with them, and
partly because he saw it all as part of his "mother's thing."

"I've seen this somewhere before," Bruce said, gently
pulling a lyre-backed chair away from the wall and giving
it the once over with a sophisticated eye. "I have a book on
church restoration with a picture of this very chair."

"Not *that* chair," I replied. "Probably one of its cousins.
That's one of only thirty or so still in existence. It was fashioned for—"

"Saint Luke in the Field! I know," said Bruce. "A col-
league of mine is working on a restoration project for
them. He'd love to see this."

The living room was comfortable—especially with the hearth's rising flames dispelling the brunt of the autumn chill—but we were never going to have dinner unless I got started.

"Follow me to the kitchen," I said as I led him through the swinging door.

"Oh, very nice," said Bruce.

I wondered what caught his eye: the brass fixtures, the granite sink, the woodwork, the restaurant quality appliances.

"You actually have three Griswold skillets?"

I smiled at the three cast-iron pans hanging over the counter.

"Actually we have five Griswolds. The other two we use for cooking, not decorations."

"Tiffany lamps, Persian prayer rugs, a Chippendale dining room, that lyre-backed chair . . . I can see why you love this place. It's a real treasure."

"A cozy treasure," I said as I hung a white apron around my neck to protect my cream-colored cashmere blend sweater, and tied the strings around the waist of my pressed black slacks. I lifted my arm, straining to bring down a hanging copper-bottomed pot.

"Here, let me reach that," said Bruce. He smiled at me as he easily stretched his long arm high and pulled down the cooking pot.

"Thanks. That's one of the drawbacks of being five-two."

"No problem. It does my ego good to come in handy."

I laughed. It actually felt a little strange to have a man in my kitchen. Well, strange to have a man other than my ex-husband.

Matteo and I were occasionally forced to share this kitchen during his mercifully infrequent layovers in New York, but the relationship wasn't one I'd call cordial. Even when we were married and generally getting along, the kitchen was never a place where we felt comfortable together—it was more like a cramped ship with two captains constantly arguing over navigation.

"What can I do next, Clare?" Bruce asked. He draped his camel hair blazer over a chair and rolled up his sleeves.

"Well . . ." I blinked, trying not to openly admire the nicely muscled forearms. "Um . . . how about uncorking that amazing wine you brought?"

"Sure, but it's nothing."

Nothing to a millionaire, maybe, but a 1995 La Romanée-Conti wasn't something I saw everyday. "You're kidding, right?" I told him. "The last time I saw a Grand Cru Burgundy, it was at a function of Madame's and royalty was present."

Bruce laughed as he turned the corkscrew at the small kitchen table, the muscles of his forearm flexing very nicely indeed. "I have a case at home."

"Oh, well," I said, working at the sink, "if you have a *case,* then one bottle of a wildly extravagant wine is nothing . . . sure!"

He laughed again. "Give me a wine glass."

I did, and he poured out a small amount.

"Taste," he commanded, holding the glass out to me.

I did and nearly swooned. "Whoa, that's good wine."

"It's an Echezeaux. There's layer after layer of complexity. Close your eyes and take another sip."

I did.

"Tell me what you taste."

"Blackberries?"

"Yes," he said. "What else?"

"Violets . . . and there's an oakiness . . . and something else . . . ohmygod . . . coffee!"

"Yes."

"It's really amazing, Bruce."

"I'm glad you like it." He came up behind me at the sink. "Okay, the wine's uncorked—and tasted. Now what?"

He stood so close the heat from his body was truly distracting. I felt my hands becoming moist, the paring knife in my fingers slipping.

"I think its safe to give you a knife," I said, clearing my suddenly dry throat. "What do you say, sailor? Peel these potatoes?"

"Aye, aye, sir."

I handed him five plump Yukon golds. He peeled while I knocked five cloves of garlic from a large head and stripped the dry white skin. Then I helped Bruce cut up his peeled potatoes into manageable cubes.

"I talked to your daughter downstairs before I came up," he mentioned in passing. "She's a good kid."

"Very. She's actually watching over the part-timers for me while we have dinner."

"Oh, so she gets a reprieve as soon as I leave?"

"Something like that."

"And what if I don't leave . . . right away?"

"That's a loaded question, Mr. Bowman. Keep your mind on the cooking, please."

He laughed. "She's a lot like you."

"She's stubborn like her father."

"She's got your features—the chestnut hair, the green eyes. You two look a lot alike."

I stopped cutting and looked up at him. "Don't say like sisters. I'm not that gullible."

Holding my gaze, he smiled. "No, I can see you're not."

When we finished cutting the potatoes, we both tossed them into boiling water, adding one smashed clove of garlic per spud. Then I pulled a pan from the stainless steel Sub Zero and removed the foil from the marinating meat. A powerful aroma filled the kitchen.

"What's that smell? Coffee?" Bruce asked, surprised. "You marinated the meat in *coffee?*"

I nodded. "One bite and all doubts will be dispelled."

"Okay, I'm game. I think."

"You better be—your wine has coffee overtones."

"True." He looked closer. "So what exactly have you got there?"

"Four thick, gorgeously marbled T-bones, courtesy of Ron, our local butcher. They've been marinating overnight in enough brewed and cooled coffee to cover them completely."

"Nothing else?" Bruce raised his eyebrow.

"Oh, ye of little faith."

He laughed. "It's just that I've never seen it done before."

"Actually, a chef who specializes in Southwestern cuisine told me he believed coffee was a fairly common ingredient in frontier cooking. There was a limited amount of spices available on the plains, and some of the gamier meats like horse and boar needed both flavoring and tenderizing."

"I've heard of using *beer* as a tenderizer."

"You're thinking of Kobe beef. In Japan they ply live cattle with malt liquor daily. It results in fatty, well-marbled meat. This is different."

"Okay, but I'm sure I remember hearing the Japanese do *something* odd with coffee."

"There's a Japanese beauty treatment that uses coffee grounds fermented with pineapple pulp. The citric acid from the pineapple cleanses, and the caffeine firms and tightens the skin—smoothes out wrinkles."

"Oh, I see . . ." His brown eyes fixed on me. With the backs of his slightly callused fingers he gently touched my cheek. "Is that your secret?"

I blushed. "What am I supposed to say to that?"

"You're beautiful."

"I'm cooking," I said, determined to keep my head.

We barely knew each other, and even though the man's proximity was having an embarrassingly unnerving effect on my state of mind, I resolved to maintain control of this situation. A public restaurant may have been a better bet for that reason—but it was too late now.

Disregarding his irresistible smile, I pressed on.

Using a cool, professional, pre-trial Martha Stewart tone, I explained that a carefully chosen coffee brewed strong not only imparts a nutty, earthy flavor to the meat, but tenderizes it as well. "You want an acidic bean, because it's the acidity that does the tenderizing. Most Latin American beans will give you enough acidity for this recipe, but I usually go with a Kenya AA."

Bruce raised an eyebrow. "I'm not yet convinced," he teased.

"The only way these steaks could be better is if I grilled them over mesquite—though I do love them with eggs in the morning. Nothing like a coffee-marinated steak to really jolt you awake. You'll see."

A slow smile spread across his face. "Is that an invitation for tomorrow morning?"

Oh, god. What did he think I was implying?

Bruce took in my expression and laughed. "I'm kidding."

"Right."

I hastily refocused my attention on browning the T-bones in the cast-iron skillet, trying like hell to forget about the incredibly charming man leaning casually against the sink a few feet away—and watching my every move.

"Smell that?" I asked. The aroma of roasted coffee and sizzling beef filled the apartment.

"Mmmmm. I see what you mean. Nice combination . . ."

After both sides of the thick steaks were properly seared, I placed them on a rack in the broiler and deglazed the pan with a splash of beef consomme.

"There's actually another way of getting the coffee flavor into the meat. I wrote a piece on it last year. Restaurants in Seattle, San Francisco, and Colorado rub the steak with coarsely ground coffee. But I'm not a fan of the crunch, you know? So I prefer to get the flavor through the marinating process—it's more intense this way anyway."

"Intense? Mmmmm. I'm up for intense."

"You mash the potatoes while I make the gravy," I commanded, handing him a potato masher.

"Do you have enough butter in there?" Bruce asked, peeking into my copper-bottomed sauce pan.

"I seem to recall you were friendly toward the subject of cholesterol."

After the butter melted, I whisked in the flour, then added the deglazed drippings from my steak skillet, more beef consommé, and coffee.

"More coffee? You're kidding," Bruce said, still mashing up the garlic potatoes.

"I never kid about coffee, or gravy."

The dining room table was already set, the candles lit, the homemade butter biscuits in the lacquered basket, Madame's Spode Imperialware at the ready, the tomato and avocado salad in the crisper. My marinated steaks were sizzling on the rack—quite rare now, but darkening more with each passing minute.

"How do you like your steak?" I asked, turning—right into Bruce Bowman's arms. How did *that* happen?

"Hot," Bruce replied softly.

And then he was leaning in, closing his arms around the small of my back, pulling me close. Ladle in hand, I closed my eyes and let his mouth cover mine. All feeble attempts at keeping my head were now completely and utterly lost.

He was rough and sweet at the same time, like that peculiar taste we'd achieved downstairs, between the espressos of North Beach and Milan. Warm and rich and tender . . .

"Nice," he said softly against my lips.

"Very." My eyelids felt heavy, my limbs heavier. "But we hardly know each other."

"I know. I just had to see how you tasted."

Oh, god.

He smiled. "You know, I have yet to see those alleged Hopper sketches you claim are in this place."

I laughed. "It was all a lie to lure you into my apartment."

"I've got news for you, Clare. I would have come anyway."

"They're upstairs, in the master bedroom."

"I thought so."

He lifted one hand from around my waist, reaching up to massage the back of my neck. "Maybe after dinner? You can show them to me?"

"I don't think that would be a good idea," I said, fairly breathless. "Like I said, we hardly know each other."

He laughed. "You need to know me better to show me your . . . Hoppers? Is that what you're telling me?"

"Yes. Exactly."

I felt his hand move even farther north, tangling in my hair and prompting a tiny voice in my head to argue, *It's been too long, Clare . . . just let him touch you a little . . . there's no harm . . . just a little . . .* Cradling the back of my head, he kissed me again.

Warm and rich and tender . . . oh, yes . . . and, lord help me, I wanted more. Unfortunately, a booming voice wasn't about to let me get it.

"Nothing says welcome home like coffee steak and gravy!"

Oh, God, no.

It was Matteo. My oh so unwelcome ex-husband, back from his East African expedition (without fair warning!). He'd used his key to barge right into the duplex—and back into my life.

ЛEEÐLESS to say, the evening pretty much deteriorated from there. There was an awkward moment or two or three, of course. Accusatory looks exchanged, uncomfortable silences, and understandable tension made all the more intense by the presence of sharp steak knives and the fact that pretty much everything at this meal—including dessert—was laced with caffeine.

With trepidation I recalled the ominous words of an unnamed Hindu philosopher who warned against the pernicious influence of "that black bean from Africa" and compared peace-loving Asian tea drinkers with the warlike European coffee-consuming nations.

But then I remembered *Mon Journal,* by French social critic and historian Jules Michelet, which essentially attributed Western Civilization's Age of Reason to the transformation of Europe into a coffee-drinking society.

So, against all reason, I remained civil when Bruce actually invited Matteo to sit down and have dinner with us. It wasn't all that insane, really, given Matteo's exhausting hours of travel. It was the decent thing to do, actually, and I didn't object, figuring that if coffee could enlighten Europeans it could pretty much accomplish miracles—and boy did I need a miracle now.

After hastily cooking another T-bone, adding a place setting, and pouring the magnificent two hundred dollar bottle of Burgundy Bruce had brought, I sat down to dinner between my ex-husband and my date for the evening. As Madame would say, we were all acting so civilized we were almost French!

"I'm surprised you didn't leave a message, *to let me know you needed the apartment,*" I said to Matteo, not really surprised in the least.

"I called from the Rome airport," my ex replied. "Maybe you should check your machine once in a while."

"That's quite a tan you've got, Matt. Especially for autumn in New York," said Bruce, attempting to interrupt our thinly veiled bickering.

Matteo grinned. His teeth shone white against his now darker than dark skin. His sleeves were pointedly rolled up six inches higher than Bruce's, displaying his biceps in addition to his muscular forearms, both browner than a hazelnut and just about as hard.

"The African sun will do that to you." He stabbed a chunk of T-bone with his fork and chewed it with relish. The coffee-soaked meat was obviously the jolt he'd needed to melt away the jet-lagged miles. "And nice to have fresh meat again," Matteo said around the mouthful. "You can get real tired of *doro wat.*"

"Doro . . . ?"

"An Ethiopian dish," said Matt. "Stringy old chicken cooked in a stew with rancid butter. Kind of like Hungarian *paprikas csirke,* but much, much hotter."

"Sounds delicious," I said dubiously.

"The heavy spices cover a multitude of sins," said Matt.

"Including ptomaine poisoning?" I asked.

Matteo gave me one of those pitying looks he often used during our marriage. A look that said so many things, like: "What do you mean you won't go bungee jumping with me?" or "Why can't we buy twin Harleys and cycle across Mexico?" or even "Are you really too uptight to try a night with Tiffany and me?"

"So Clare tells me you're a coffee buyer," said Bruce. "Is that why you were in Ethiopia?"

"Who said I was in Ethiopia?" said Matteo with barely

disguised hostility—so much, if fact, that I suddenly wished I'd marinated the steaks in Prozac instead of coffee.

Bruce paused, his fork halfway to his mouth. "Well . . . I . . . thought you just did . . ."

Matteo set his fork down and sat back, smirking. "Yeah, I was in Ethiopia looking for coffee. May have found some, too. Nice enough cherries this season, but they'll be better next year. I'm looking at the C market—futures."

"Why Ethiopia?" asked Bruce. "There are safer places to buy coffee, aren't there?"

"Ethiopia's the motherland. Folks were drinking coffee in Ethiopia while Europeans were waking up to beer and mead." With that, Matt lifted his glass of Bruce's La Romanée-Conti Echezeaux and took a long, deep draft. Most of the glass had instantly vanished, and he reached for the bottle to refill. "Damn, that's good wine."

I met Bruce's eyes and tried not to burst out laughing. He smiled, then tried again to make polite conversation.

"I heard things were bad there. In Ethiopia."

Matt shrugged and resumed attacking his coffee-marinated steak like an East African predator. "They're getting better. The coffee market in Harrar is coming back to life and the bull market in Jimma never stopped. The new farms near the Somali border are not producing yet, but I managed to take a Jeep trip to Jiga-Jiga without getting killed."

"Sounds dangerous," said Bruce.

I gave Matteo a look that told him I knew he was exaggerating the hazards of his trip—even though I also knew it was entirely possible he was not.

Matt winked at me as he told Bruce, "Remember *that* the next time you gulp down your morning blend."

"Speaking of coffee, I'll get the French press," I said, rising from the table.

Matteo and Bruce both jumped to their feet so fast to help me that they nearly collided.

"I can handle it," I said, waving them back down.

"So," I heard Matteo purr as I hurried to prepare coffee. "What is it that you do, Bruce?"

When I entered the kitchen, I smelled gas and wondered if a pilot light had gone out. I checked the stove and found nothing.

For desert I'd prepared my new recipe for Three Chocolate Mocha Pudding—a second attempt. Detective Quinn had left before having it when I'd cooked dinner for him, so I gave it another shot for Bruce's dinner.

I pulled out my favorite French press and three of the Spode Imperialware cups and saucers. Before Bruce had arrived, I'd brought up Jamaica Blue Mountain beans from the Blend's special reserve (thirty-five dollars a pound), and they sat sealed in a dark, airtight container on my shelf, waiting to be ground and brewed.

When I noticed some dust on the coffee cups, I went over to the kitchen's carved granite sink to wash them off. The brass faucet refused to turn on my first try. It had been giving me trouble for a couple of weeks and I'd vowed to get it fixed. Using both hands, I tried again.

This time the faucet came off in my hand—followed by a powerful blast of cold water that doused me from head to foot.

I screamed as water gushed everywhere.

The door burst open and Bruce and Matteo rushed in.

Matt took one look at me and burst out laughing while Bruce hurried to my side.

"Are you okay?"

I nodded more worried about the water that was gushing everywhere.

"Where's the cutoff valve?" Bruce cried over the noise of the water.

I looked at him blankly. In the months that I'd lived here, I never needed to know about the plumbing. I shrugged. Bruce turned to Matteo, who stopped laughing and came up blank, too.

"Never mind," said Bruce, scanning the kitchen. "It's probably behind this plate." He pointed to the embossed tin plate under the sink.

I'd seen it before but figured it was ornamental. Bruce knew differently. He immediately sat down in the growing flood of water, drew out his keys, and opened a tiny screwdriver attached to the chain.

In a flash he unscrewed the plate. When he yanked it off, the powerful smell of natural gas flooded the kitchen.

"Open the window!" Bruce called. Matteo complied and cold autumn air dissipated the odor.

Behind the plate, I saw a hole filled with pipes. Bruce reached in and twisted a valve. The flow of water slowed, then stopped.

After the noise and chaos came a moment of eerie calm. Finally, Matteo spoke.

"So, Bruce. I take it you're a plumber."

CLAD now in dry clothes—I had hastily thrown on jeans and an oversized T-shirt—I escorted Bruce Bowman to the door. Matteo casually followed us, hovering in the foyer.

"I can't believe what happened," I said for about the tenth time.

"I'm just glad I was here," Bruce replied. "Those gaslight pipes should never have been left behind the wall. They were filling with gas for half a century or more. Luckily the leak behind the faucet rusted the gas pipe enough to let out the pressure. Otherwise, there could have been an explosion."

"I don't know what I would have done if I'd been here alone," I said.

"You weren't alone," Matt snapped from behind me. "I was here."

"Matt, you didn't even know where the cutoff valve was," I reminded him.

"I'll get the pipes taken care of first thing in the morning," I told Bruce.

"Good-night, Matt," said Bruce, extending his hand.

Matt hesitated but shook. "Yeah. 'Night."

"Some privacy?" I whispered over my shoulder to my ex-husband.

Matt frowned but didn't argue. He drifted off, back into the dining room.

"Bruce, I—"

"Don't say 'I'm sorry.' Not again. It's not your fault."

"I should have listened to those phone messages. We could have gone to a restaurant."

"It's okay. Now the ice is broken, right?"

I couldn't believe it. Our romantic first date was completely ruined, and Bruce was trying to see the bright side.

"Hey, look at it this way," he added. "Joy gets to go home early. I'll even offer to walk her, okay with you?"

I nodded, grateful. "Can I make it up to you?" I asked.

"Oh . . . let me count the ways." He smiled and touched my cheek. Then he leaned in for a long, sweet, good-night kiss.

"I'll call you," he promised, then turned to descend the back service staircase, the one that would lead him out by way of the Village Blend.

When I closed the door, I turned to find Matt leaning against the dining room door frame, nut-brown forearms folded across his chest.

He shook his head. "When did you start dating plumbers?"

Eleven

~~~~~~

LIKE a desert wind, Sahara McNeil burst out of her apartment building and moved quickly toward the SoHo gallery where she plied her trade. Her flaming red hair caught an icy gust as she ate up the sidewalk on red leather boots with four-inch heels.

Best of all, the woman was fiddling with her portable CD player, totally oblivious to her all too familiar surroundings. She was so oblivious, in fact, that the Genius matched her quick steps directly behind without the woman even noticing.

This morning's mission was supposed to have been a dry run for the real event, which would occur when every aspect of the planning had been thought out. But the weather was getting unpredictable, and this moment felt too perfect.

All the planning in the world added up to nothing without the boldness required to carry it out, and the Genius believed any set goals could never be achieved without a *certain amount of risk. Even Napoleon said he would rather have a lucky general than a smart one.*

As if on cue, a dirty white New York City Sanitation Department truck came rumbling down West Tenth Street. Two men sat in the cab, talking, not looking at the road even as the vehicle rolled forward toward the empty intersection.

No one else was walking on this part of the block, which was predominantly residential—the only place of business was a retro bar called the Blue Lounge, and it was dark at this early hour.

No witnesses, *thought the Genius.*

Absent mindedly, Sahara halted at the end of the block to wait for the truck to pass before she crossed. She did not look up. Instead she popped open the CD player and fumbled in her bag for a new disk.

The truck continued forward. The workers continued chatting distractedly.

A push. Timed just right. One simple push.

Then Sahara would never again bother him.

"God, what is it about this place and death?!"

Esther Best had made her typical existential outburst earlier than usual, and loud enough for everyone in the Blend to hear. It was just after noon on Friday, a busy time for us. Customers' noses lifted out of books, their eyes peered over laptops and newspapers. Esther stood in the Blend's open doorway, her gloved hand on the old brass handle, a blast of icy November drizzle sweeping in behind her black overcoat.

"Close the door, Esther," I said. "You're letting in the cold."

She did. Then she trudged over to the coffee bar.

Most of the customers returned to their business. All except Kira Kirk, who was sitting close to the counter, still looking up from her crossword puzzle.

"And where exactly is 'this place'?" she asked Esther, peering over the tops of her horn-rimmed reading glasses. "I mean as it pertains to death? This coffeehouse? The West Village? New York City? Or are we talking the universe itself? You must be more specific."

Esther gave Kira a sidelong glance through her own black-rimmed glasses. Then she pulled off her gloves. I was working behind the pastry case, refilling the empty muffin baskets with blueberry, apple spice, pumpkin carrot, and banana walnut. She sidled over to speak to me.

"Sorry I'm late," she snapped, her tone not exactly apologetic. "A woman got killed across the street from my new apartment. Hit by a garbage truck. Police everywhere."

Tucker made a face, not unlike the one my superstitious grandmother used to make after she'd heard someone speak ill of the dead and before a hasty sign of the cross.

At a table near Kira's, Winnie, the tall, raven-haired Shearling Lady lawyer, who'd arrived an hour before, looked back up from her book, interested. Martha, a young editor from nearby Berk and Lee publishers, glanced up from a manuscript, too.

Esther carted her coat to the back pantry, then came out again, looped a blue apron over her neck, and tied it.

"I'll work late to make up the time," she said, still averting her eyes. Then Esther tied back her wild dark hair, grabbed a cloth, and began dusting the shelf of our one-pound House Blend bags until the labels threatened to peel away.

Obviously, the accident had upset her. Not that I blamed her. Expiring under the wheels of a New York City Sanitation truck was just a wrong way to die. Not that there was a right way.

"Did the victim live in your building?" Tucker asked.

In New York City, a question like that was akin to "did the victim live in your neighborhood," because in New

York, most apartment buildings had the population equivalent of a small town street, if not an entire block, which often made your co-op board (if you had one) the equivalent of your neighborhood block association, the repository for rules about such things as the proper disposal of garbage, leashing of pets, and hours to have a party.

Esther stopped dusting.

"I didn't see her face. Just her legs. They were sticking out from under the truck, you know?" She shuddered. "A couple of cops went over to the big co-op building on the corner. One of them was carrying her bag. Expensive one, too. Coach."

"How do you fall in front of a garbage truck?" Tucker asked.

"When your number's up, it's up," said Winnie.

"Probably she slipped," said Kira. "People slip and fall all the time. Some even die in their own homes."

Myself, I was thinking "pushed," but maybe that's because the last slip and fall I encountered (my late assistant manager Anabelle) turned out to be premeditated murder. Or maybe it was Quinn's influence. That man's dark vision of the universe sometimes rivaled Schopenhauer's.

"She probably just killed herself," stated Esther.

Or Esther Best's, I amended.

Esther was facing us now, her eyes brightening at the reaction her words elicited.

Now *that* was the Esther I knew. I was fond of the girl, don't get me wrong—and I felt bad for what she'd had to witness this morning—but most of the time, Esther wasn't exactly Sister Mary Sunshine. As Tucker put it, while some folks saw the silver lining in a dark cloud, Esther would search compulsively for the lightening strike. And then endlessly wallow in the painful disappointment of this discovery via free-form verse at a St. Mark's Street poetry reading.

"Now, Esther, why would you think it was suicide?" Kira asked.

"I guess I was thinking of that Valerie girl in the subway, and Inga Berg, too. It's like there's some epidemic of suicides in the New York air or something. It's like these girls got up one morning and went out and just killed themselves for no reason—on a whim, even though they had everything to live for."

"Suicide is not an act of whim. Nor is it contagious," said Tucker.

"It can be a fad, though, Tucker," Kira noted brightly as she drained the last of her cappuccino.

Kira had been in exceptionally good moods since the last Cappuccino Connection night. I'd noticed she'd started to wear makeup regularly again, and I assumed Mr. Moviefone/Crossword Puzzle Man was the reason. Still, I couldn't let a morbid remark like that go unchallenged.

"What do you mean suicide can be a fad?" I blurted. "Like the hulahoop or skinny neckties?"

"Or maybe mass Macarena-style masochism?" quipped Winnie, sharing a glance with me.

I shook my head.

"A *literary* fad," Kira clarified. "The Werther epidemic is a case in point."

"Don't know that one," said Esther.

"Rings a bell," said Winnie.

"When the German poet Goethe published his novel *The Sorrows of Young Werther*, it became an overnight sensation. Napoleon told Goethe he'd read it seven times. But Goethe's biggest influence was on middle- and upper-class youths. Some were so influenced by the tragic love story of Werther and Lotte that a number of them actually emulated the hero and committed suicide. It became the fashion in Germany, France, Holland, and Scandinavia for unrequited lovers to kill themselves dressed like Werther, with a copy of the novel lying open nearby, marking a favorite page or passage. It got so bad that clergymen denounced the novel from their pulpits."

"You've got to be kidding." I gave Kira a doubtful look.

"Where did you learn that?" asked Tucker. "And for heaven's sake, *why?*"

Kira laughed. "I told you before, I'm a genius."

Tucker and I exchanged a look that said, *join the club.* In our experience, a formidable fraction of people sitting in New York City coffeehouses thought they were prodigies—primarily because their mothers told them so.

"Actually, I read the Penguin edition of Goethe's novel," admitted Kira. "As for why . . . A few years ago a *Times* crossword question was 'before Faust was damned, this protagonist committed suicide.' The right answer was 'Werther' but I didn't get it. When that happens, I learn all I can about the subject so it never happens again."

"See what I mean?" said Esther. "Tragedy and death are under the surface of everything. It's part of our entertainment, our popular culture. I mean, violent movies, violent music, suicide in a crossword puzzle? And look at us! Everyone here is obsessed with suicide. Somebody mentions the subject and that's all anyone can talk about."

Tucker's face pruned up. "But, Esther, you're the one who mentioned—"

I laid my hand on Tucker's arm, silencing him. "Nobody who really has it all commits suicide," I told Esther. "And I doubt—the Werther epidemic notwithstanding—that one human being can influence others enough to drive them to suicide."

"You forget Jim Jones and his Kool-Aid-drinking followers," pointed out Winnie.

"And suicide bombers," Tucker added. "Someone's putting the idea in their heads to strap on explosives and visit the Middle Eastern version of mini-malls."

"Okay, those are exceptions. But most people have deeply personal reasons for ending their lives. Reasons that have nothing to do with fanaticism, religious or otherwise."

"There has to be a screw loose," said Winnie. "Healthy, self-actualized people turn their aggressions outward, not inward."

"You'd think a healthy person wouldn't have any aggressions," said Kira.

Winnie gave her a look that said, *don't be so naive.*

"It's just really hard for me to believe that Inga Berg actually committed suicide," said Esther. "Life was her oyster. Especially in this town. At least, she gave us all the impression it was."

"It was all those damned decafs," said Tucker. "A couple of weeks ago Inga Berg started ordering decaffeinated coffee in the evenings. Said she was having trouble sleeping. I think she should have stuck to regular. Might have saved her life."

"Maybe that was it—lack of sleep. Maybe she wasn't in her right mind because she was so tired," said Esther.

"No. You're not getting my point. People who drink caffeinated coffee are actually less likely to kill themselves. I saw a news story on it a few years ago."

Esther rolled her eyes with skepticism, but I spoke up.

"Tucker's right. I wrote a piece on it for a trade magazine. A Harvard study concluded that women who drank more than three cups of coffee a day were at one-third the risk of suicide compared to those who didn't imbibe."

"What about us men?" said Tucker.

"The study wasn't done on men. It was done over a ten-year period with female nurses. I think because they roughly paralleled the general population in rates of depression, smoking, obesity, drug abuse, and other bad habits. Sorry."

"Good for the goose, good for the gander," said Tucker, refilling his empty cup with our freshly made Breakfast Blend.

"Whip me up another one, Mr. Barista," said Kira, waving her own empty cup. "Nice to know my addiction will keep me from slashing my wrists."

Esther wasn't convinced yet. "Valerie and Inga were both coffee drinkers, and they both killed themselves."

"The study said one-third less likely to commit suicide, not one hundred percent," noted Winnie. "Nothing is one hundred percent in life. Except that more than half the women who come to this town looking for fulfillment through a man or a career will end up disappointed."

Winnie was starting to sound like Esther now—whose philosophy could probably be summed up in one phrase: Expect the worst and you won't be disappointed.

As the tide of conversation in the Blend was getting more and more grim, I actually welcomed the fresh blast of cold air that heralded the arrival of a new customer.

I looked up to see Mike Quinn standing at my counter. It was good to see him there. It had been so long, I was starting to give up hope of ever seeing him again.

The police detective had obviously been on hard duty for quite a while. He looked haggard, his iron jaw displaying the stubble of a dark blonde beard that was substantially more than a five o'clock shadow. His lean cheeks looked wind burned and his overcoat appeared in need of a good cleaning.

"Can I speak to you?" Quinn asked in a voice of dry ice.

"Sure," I said, turning to fix his usual latte. I figured we could chat while I whipped it up.

When he said, "NOW," I froze.

Quinn wasn't the most charming guy I'd ever met, but he was usually polite—at the very least, civil. Obviously, the man's nerves were raw.

I turned back to face him. "Go ahead. I'm listening," I said.

He glanced from me to Esther and Tucker, whose gazes were now glued to him.

"We need to speak somewhere more private," he said, his voice suddenly calmer.

I nodded. "My office. Just give me a minute."

I crossed to the coffee urn and filled two grande-size paper cups with piping hot Breakfast Blend.

I felt Esther's and Tucker's eyes on my back, and Kira's and Winnie's, too. Mercifully, the other customers were either seated too far away to have heard Quinn's remark or simply had no interest.

"Follow me," I told the detective, and made a beeline for the back service staircase and my second floor office. Quinn's heavy shoes fell right behind.

TWELVE

~~~~~~~~~~~~~~~~~~~~~~~~~~~~~~~~

As we entered my small, utilitarian office, I thrust a cup into Quinn's hand.

"Have a seat and drink this," I said.

The store's safe was here, along with a somewhat battered wooden desk, a computer, and files of our employee and general business paperwork.

He slumped into the easy chair next to my desk and held the cup under his nose. The aroma slightly eased his grim expression, and after he sipped I could see the full-bodied brew wash some of the tension out of his wind-burned face.

"This is good," he said.

"It's a medium brown roast in the West Coast style, but we use a nice blend of Indonesian and Costa Rican." I set my own cup on the desk, untied my blue apron, and hung it on a hook on the back of the door. "You get a fruit-toned complexity from the Indonesian, and a nice resonance from the less subtle Latin American bean, with just the right amount of dry acidity. In my opinion, most breakfast blends are bitter and dry. But not ours."

"Right."

I closed the door, then smoothed my khaki slacks, adjusted my pink long-sleeved jersey, and sat down in the desk chair. "Too much information?"

He raised an eyebrow. "In my opinion, you can never give a detective too much information."

I raised my own eyebrow. "Then you should also know we change the blend every year—mainly because the Indonesian beans tend to be inconsistent from season to season due to the old fashioned way they're processed."

Quinn took another sip and sat back. "Ah, the vagaries of international agriculture."

I sampled my own cup and we sat quietly for a moment.

"I didn't mean to be short with you downstairs," he said.

"It's okay. You look like hell. I gather you were over near the West Tenth accident this morning?"

Quinn's face froze in mid-yawn. "And you know that *how?*"

"Esther Best, one of my part-timers, lives on that street. She got here a little while ago and told us what happened."

"I'd like to talk to her," Quinn said. "Find out if she saw or heard anything."

"She didn't," I replied. "Just the gory aftermath. Has her pretty rattled, though."

"Yeah. Me too." Quinn sighed as he rubbed the back of his neck.

"I didn't know you investigated traffic accidents."

"I don't. This morning's 'accident' was a homicide."

I stiffened. The idea of someone being crushed accidentally under the wheels of a ten ton sanitation truck was bad enough—hearing Quinn confirm it was no accident gave me an unnatural chill.

"You're sure?" I asked.

Quinn nodded. "We have two witnesses. The assistant manager at a nearby bar came in early to clean up. Heard a woman scream the word 'no' and glanced out the window just in time to see Ms. McNeil fall under the truck's wheels."

"Wait a minute," I said. "Did you say *McNeil?*"

Quinn reached into his pocket and drew out a dog-eared leather-covered rectangular note pad.

"Sally McNeil, a.k.a. 'Sahara' McNeil. West Tenth Street, apartment number—"

"I know the name," I said.

Quinn closed his pad. "You want to tell me how you know her? Regular customer?"

"Yes, I've seen her here before, but it was more than that. She came here last Saturday night for our Cappuccino Connection."

"Alone?"

"Yes."

"You see her leave alone."

"No. She left with a . . . mutual friend."

Quinn sat up. "Male or female?"

"A man," I replied. "An old college friend of hers . . . I understand."

"His name?"

"Bruce Bowman. But I don't think—"

It was Quinn's turn to blink. "You know Bruce Bowman?" His tone was even but his eyes were hard. I suddenly felt like one of his collars sitting under an interrogation room spotlight.

"I just met him . . . during this last Cappuccino Connection," I stammered, smoothing my khaki slacks compulsively now.

"Did you meet Bowman professionally, as the manager of this place?"

"Well, actually, I participated in the Cappuccino thing,

too . . . just because, you know, Joy wanted to do it and I wanted to screen the men who'd signed up . . . screen them for my daughter, but then—"

"But then you made a date with Bowman yourself?"

Though Quinn was wearing his detective hat, his questions were getting far too personal.

"The Cappuccino Connection is just a neighborhood social introduction group," I told him defensively. "It's run by a local church. Bruce Bowman was there, Joy was there, too. And everybody meets everybody for a couple of minutes. It's all innocent fun . . ."

Quinn gave me a look he probably gave pickpockets who claimed they had "absolutely no idea" how that woman's wallet and credit cards got inside their coat. "The reason I ask," he finally said, "is because Bowman's name has turned up during my background checks of two women: the late Valerie Lathem and the late Inga Berg."

"How is Bruce connected?"

"Bruce . . ." repeated Quinn, leaning slightly forward.

I shrank back in my seat, suddenly feeling like Alice after she'd eaten the mushroom.

Quinn continued. "*Mr. Bowman* dated Valerie Lathem for about three weeks in October. They met through her job at an executive travel agency."

"And Inga Berg?"

Quinn paused and took another sip of coffee, a lengthy one. He set the cup down and observed me long enough to make my palms sweat.

"What I'm about to tell you is strictly confidential. But if you or your daughter is considering a date with Mr. Bowman, consider this first: Bowman was involved with Inga Berg for a short time. Starting in late October and ending at the beginning of November, just before Ms. Berg's death. This relationship with Ms. Berg was sexual. And Ms. Berg was not always discrete in her encounters."

"I'm not sure what you mean by 'not always discrete.'" I said, not sure I wanted to know either.

"One of the tenants in Ms. Berg's buildings saw Ms. Berg having sex in her brand new sports utility vehicle on the rooftop parking lot a few days before she died. Now, why the hell she chose to mess around in her car when she had a nice cozy bed in her apartment five floors below is a mystery to me—unless you want to factor in Ms. Berg having a particularly interesting kink."

I didn't believe it. "You're not saying it was Bruce in the car with her?"

"We don't know that," Quinn replied. "The tenant didn't see the man's face. I'm just saying it's possible, if she was into this sort of behavior, and he was involved with her sexually, that it could have happened. I have Ms. Berg's phone records, and she called his number the day before this incident occurred. Unfortunately our witness can't remember much beyond naked bodies flailing around."

"Well, then, you don't know it was Bruce," I said.

"We also found a ripped-up note addressed to Inga in the rooftop garbage can," said Quinn. "We know it was put there on the night of Ms. Berg's death because all older garbage had been emptied a few hours prior. The note was an invitation to come up to the rooftop lot and meet someone by her car for a "special surprise" of some sort. Given what we've uncovered, it's not hard to guess what Ms. Berg thought she was getting—quite different from what she actually got. Or maybe the same, depending on your use of vernacular."

I frowned. Why was it that Quinn's gallows humor always reared its ugly head when I least felt like laughing?

"Have you analyzed the handwriting?" I asked.

"It wasn't handwritten—and, of course, you'd expect it of a note like that, a supposedly casual and personal note. The person who wrote that note to Inga used a Hewlett Packard DeskJet, a small computer printer, model . . ." Quinn checked his notebook. "Model 840C. The lab is still working on identifying factors in the stationery's composition."

"And you're sure Inga's death wasn't a suicide—and Valerie Lathem's, too, for that matter?"

"I was never convinced Ms. Lathem's death was a suicide. Unfortunately, I haven't been able to produce enough evidence to convince my captain otherwise, but in the case of Inga Berg there is enough physical and circumstantial evidence to warrant further investigation."

"But wasn't Inga dating a lot of men? She told me herself that she was. With her it was almost a point of pride. Why pin it on Bruce?"

"Just how well do you know *Bruce?*"

"I've spent a lot of time with him since we met last week, and I feel I know him well enough to say I think you're barking up the wrong suspect's tree."

Quinn just gave me that infuriating cop stare of his.

Thank goodness I wasn't guilty of anything—I mean, here I sat, innocent as an Easter lamb and still I was quaking as if Quinn were accusing me of these alleged murders. Suddenly, I felt as though I were closeted in a confessional with the toughest priest in the diocese.

"Clare, the note was signed."

"How?"

"With a B."

I shook my head. "That still doesn't tie it to Bruce beyond a shadow of a doubt and you know it. What about your second witness to the death of Sahara McNeil? What did that person see?"

"Nothing, like the bartender. A dental hygienist in a first floor apartment was getting ready to go to work. She heard the scream. She also heard someone running on the sidewalk. But by the time she got her window open enough to stick her head out and look down the street, the person doing the running had vanished around the corner."

Quinn gulped more coffee, then drained his entire cup.

"There's a third witness, but less convincing. The driver of the sanitation truck heard the victim scream, too, and claimed she flew in front of the truck like she was pushed. But any judge would say he's just covering his ass."

Quinn stood up. So did I.

"I'll still speak with your employee . . . Best was it?"

"Esther."

"Esther Best. But I thank you. You've given me more to go on than I expected."

I crossed the office and stood in front of him.

"Just why *did* you come by today, Mike?" I asked. "You haven't been here in two weeks. Why today?"

"Been busy," said Quinn. "And I actually came by to follow up on some notations in Ms. McNeil's date book. She'd written down the address of the Village Blend along with last Saturday's date and a time. It was a long shot, but you came through with the explanation—your Singles group—and an even bigger lead."

"Bruce."

Quinn nodded. "With your help, I've now linked Mr. Bowman to three suspicious deaths. One death could be happenstance. Two might be construed as a coincidence—although you know what I always say about coincidence."

"I know, in your business you don't think there are any. But, Mike, you're reaching and you know it."

"Three deaths, Clare? In my book, that's not a reach. And if I'm right, the violence is only going to escalate."

"How?"

"Look, the killer's working out what looks to me like a lot of rage. These women may have been killed as a result of a disappointment or perceived betrayal. Or it could be the killer just snaps based on a trigger. With Inga, there was a note left behind that confounds the issue."

"How does the note confound the issue of rage?"

"Because it points to premeditation. Yes, the killer may have used the note to lure Inga to the roof for sex only, then disposed of the note in the rooftop garbage after the encounter went bad—"

"Went bad? You're saying the killer snapped, went into a rage, and pushed her? Then picked up the note, threw it away, and fled?"

"Maybe. Or the killer may have planned to murder Inga from the start, luring her to the roof with the promise of sex, then all of a sudden she's airborne. Either way, the killer obviously fled the scene and got rid of any connection to the crime as soon as possible—specifically that note. Better to throw it away than be caught holding it, which was a distinct possibility if the killer had been seen coming down from the roof by a tenant and then was stopped, questioned, and searched by the police. It's also probable the murderer assumed Inga's death would be instantly ruled a suicide—just like Valerie Latham's—and never expected us to search every inch of that rooftop and find that evidence. But we found it, which was a break for us. And a few hours ago it's likely that same killer committed a murder in broad daylight in front of witnesses, which was another break for us. Now those witnesses didn't give us much to go on, but it's enough for us to treat Sahara McNeil's death as a homicide instead of an accident, and I'm sure the murderer never thought that would happen either . . . It's sloppy, it's reckless, and I think this killer is unraveling. The next time, the killer may not worry about witnesses or evidence or trying to make it look like anything in particular. The next time, the killer may just compulsively want to kill first and worry about consequences later. And that's when I'll nail the son of a bitch."

"But another woman has to die first."

Quinn's eyes met mine.

"Stay away from him, Clare. Though I'll grant you I can't prove a thing yet, certainly nothing that would hold up in court, there is one fact that is indisputable: the women who get close to Bruce Bowman end up dead."

"But, Mike, it makes no sense. Bruce is an accomplished, successful, seemingly well-adjusted architect. What in the world would motivate him to murder these women?"

"If I had to guess? I'd say the man's looking for Ms. Right. And when she turns into Ms. Wrong in some way, he takes the disappointment very badly."

Quinn turned and reached for the doorknob. "Thanks for the coffee," he said over his shoulder.

And then he was gone.

D**AMN** *you, Quinn,* I thought. *Damn you and your messed-up marriage.*

I didn't go back downstairs right away. I spent the next half hour pacing my office, trying to process everything Quinn had just told me—and my feelings about it . . . and my feelings about Bruce . . . and Quinn.

I liked and respected Mike Quinn, but I couldn't for a second believe what he was saying about Bruce. What I *could* believe, however, was that Quinn had become a bundle of raw nerves, operating on the edge. Obviously, the breakdown of his marriage was getting to him as much as his inability to find evidence to support his theory linking all of these supposed "push" murders of women.

For a fleeting second I even considered maybe, on some remote level, this whole "stay away from Bruce" thing of Quinn's was the twisted result of his feelings for me.

He and I never dated, but we'd certainly flirted enough— and with his marriage going down the tubes, he might have been conflicted about the fact that I was out looking for a date instead of waiting around for him to make a decision about whether to break things off with his wife or work things out.

Okay, so Quinn had been eyeing Bruce as a suspect even before he knew I'd met him—and before he found out about the Sahara McNeil connection. He'd said Bruce's name had turned up on background checks for both Valerie Lathem and Inga Berg. But it sure seemed to me he'd upgraded Bruce's suspect status the second he realized I was seeing him.

I didn't believe Quinn was a dishonest cop. In fact, in my opinion, Mike Quinn had the morals of a freaking Arthurian knight. (Notwithstanding my ex-husband's assertions that no police officer could be trusted—an unfortunate result of Matt's frequent experiences with corrupt officials in banana republics.)

In any event, I certainly wanted to think Quinn would be the last cop in the world to frame a man, if for no other reason than the fact that he knew the real criminal was still out there.

But if Bruce Bowman *was* a murderer, that sure didn't say much for the process I'd used to screen my daughter's dates.

Could I be misjudging men that badly? First mislabeling Mr. Mama's Boy, now finding out "Mr. Right" is on Quinn's list as "Mr. Dial M for—"

No.

No, no, no, no, no!

Since Sunday evening, I'd laughed with the man. I'd kissed the man. And I'd spent long hours getting to know him. In my heart I knew Bruce Bowman was not a murderer. He *wasn't*.

My thoughts were interrupted by a knock at the door.

"Clare," Tucker called. "Your pride named Joy is here. And she's brought a gentleman caller."

"Thanks, Tuck. I'll be right down."

I smoothed my slacks again, tied my apron over my pink long-sleeved jersey, ran my fingers through my hair, and opened the office door.

Downstairs, I spied my daughter near the counter. Curiously, I looked around, trying to find Joy's mystery escort. Then I noticed a man was crouched down, examining the selection in the pastry display. Finally, he straightened up. He was tall, and his face was turned away from me.

He said something to my daughter and Joy laughed.

Then the man turned, and I saw his face.

It was Bruce Bowman.

THIRTEEN

∿∿∿∿∿∿∿∿∿∿∿∿∿∿∿∿∿∿∿∿∿∿∿

"Hey, Mom," my daughter waved. "Guess who I ran into on the street after class?"

"It was hard to miss her," said Bruce, his smile dazzling. "Especially with that coat."

I nodded. Barely an hour ago I had unwittingly implicated this man in a series of murders to an exhausted New York detective. I was feeling a dozen different emotions—none of them remotely resembling delight. Nevertheless, I lifted the corners of my mouth in what I thought was a pretty game smile.

"I hate this thing," said Joy, unzipping the big bulky parka.

"It keeps you warm, doesn't it?" I reminded her tightly—and not for the first time.

She frowned. "But, Mom, just look at it! The thing's bright yellow with black stripes."

"Yellow's the traditional color of rain slickers, isn't it?" I pointed out.

"This isn't a rain slicker. It's a way heinous too-puffy parka," complained Joy.

Bruce laughed. "It's not that bad."

"You've got to be kidding," said Joy, rolling her eyes. "I look like a pregnant bee."

My daughter hadn't stopped complaining about the coat since I'd bought it for her three weeks ago on the clearance rack at Filene's. I knew Joy didn't have the money for another coat—and I had yet to find the time to shop for anything else. So, for now, she was stuck with it.

"Hang in there till Christmas, honey," I said. "I'll get you another."

"You know what my classmates do when I pass them on the street?"

"No."

"They buzz."

"There's a solution for that, you know," said Bruce.

"What?" asked Joy.

"Well, doesn't that thing come with a stinger?"

"Just shut up," she told him, punching his arm. "You're not helping."

Bruce laughed.

And my heart broke. How could a man who laughed so genuinely, who kissed so sweetly, and who acted so considerately be a murderer? How?

Forget the fact that he also looked good enough to put in my pastry case. His own fleece-lined leather coat emphasized broad shoulders and tapered down to lean, jean-clad hips. Beneath it he wore a caramel cashmere sweater that matched his eyes. His face was rosy from the cold air and he exuded an air of confident high spirits.

Since our Sunday night dinner, he'd been intensely busy with his various restoration jobs, checking on crews and projects during the day, and tied up with business dinners or official meetings at night. Yet every day this week he'd found ways to steal time away from his work schedule and stop in to see me—sometimes three times in one day.

I'd take breaks when he stopped by, of course, and lead him up to the second floor, which we kept closed until evenings. He'd light a fire and we'd just relax and have coffee and talk for an hour or two before we'd both part for work again. We'd gotten to know each other better, and I was looking forward to our next official dinner date.

I never imagined that when the moment finally arrived it would be under such bizarre and ambiguous circumstances.

"So, what have the two of you been up to?" I asked Joy, trying to sound casual.

"I told Bruce about that restaurant my friends want to open, and he drove me over to Brooklyn to see a great retail space that's available."

Drove her. In his SUV, no doubt. A very sick part of me remembered that SUV of Inga's. The one Quinn told me she'd used in lieu of a hot-sheets motel. The one I was certain Bruce had *not* been in. (God, why was it murder victims had to have their most embarrassing peccadilloes exposed to the general public? Wasn't being murdered enough?)

"Joy's colleagues had their hearts set on a location in Carroll Gardens or Brooklyn Heights," Bruce explained. "But rents are so high along Court, Henry, and Hicks Streets these days that they'll pay twice as much for half the space, and Columbia Street is just too downscale for the kind of eatery they have in mind."

Joy stepped forward and nodded enthusiastically. "Bruce showed me a wonderful vacancy on the other side of Montague Street—a location near the Brooklyn Promenade, the Brooklyn Academy of Music, and downtown."

The Promenade was on the very edge of Brooklyn

Heights. It was a long, narrow, tree-lined walkway on the edge of the East River that looked out across the water toward the spectacular towering skyline of lower Manhattan's financial district—a view that was once dominated by the twin towers of the World Trade Center.

Bruce nodded. "The restaurantrification of South Brooklyn hasn't penetrated that far yet, but with the new Nets stadium project in the planning stages and upscale apartments being constructed in the vicinity, that part of Brooklyn is earmarked for major improvement. Best to be a pioneer, get in on the ground floor."

"That's great," I said, the tense smile still plastered across my face.

Joy looked up at Bruce. I could see in her face that she trusted and admired this man—just like me.

"We stopped at a great little place in Carroll Gardens for lunch," said Joy. "A real Italian neighborhood place. I haven't had veal that tender since you made it, Mom."

"I did the design work for a restoration project on Clinton Street," Bruce explained. "The workers told me about a local place called Nino's. What a find! Veal Marsala that melts on your tongue, and the best garlic broccoli I've ever tasted. Fridays are my favorite, though. They serve up an array of seafood, including the best conch, squid, and octopus salad this side of Sicily. I can't wait to take you, too, Clare."

Joy glanced at her watch.

"Well, I've got to go," she said. "I've got this cool 'special menus' class in a half hour. We're covering Kosher, vegetarian, and lactose-intolerant. And the instructor's already picked me to be part of a student team helping her cater this big vegetarian benefit thing at the Puck Building tomorrow night, so I don't want to screw up and end up late for class. She'll assume I'll be late for the catering job, too, and that would be totally bogus because I'm never late."

"Can I drive you to class?" Bruce asked.

"That's okay," said Joy. "It's like a fifteen minute walk tops. No big. I still have time to grab an espresso to go."

"Coming up," said Tucker, who'd been working quietly behind the counter.

"Can I get you anything?" I asked Bruce, my voice not quite there.

"Actually I have to go, too," he replied. "But I wanted to ask you something."

Bruce motioned me to follow him through the coffee-house to a far corner of the Blend's first floor. The lunch crowd had pretty much dispersed, even Kira and Winnie had left.

We sat down at one of the marble-topped tables.

"I wanted to ask you to dinner, tonight," Bruce said. "I know it's short notice, but the Manhattan Borough President's Office just cancelled a meeting on me and I figured I'd take advantage of the unexpected free time. You know I've been trying to find an evening for us to spend some time together, and tonight's the first night I could manage it."

I mentally checked my social calendar and came up empty as usual. Still, I didn't want to seem too eager. And then, of course, there was that pesky little issue of my personal friendship with a detective getting Bruce Bowman's name bumped up a suspect list in a number of recent homicides.

I wanted to tell Bruce everything, but I didn't dare. Our relationship was still new and fragile. Trust was important. I could think of no way to bring up the subject that wouldn't sound sordid and accusatory and possibly send him running.

As for being in any way worried about my own safety, that was ludicrous. I didn't believe Quinn's theory about Bruce. Neither could I let it ruin my chances of deepening a relationship with this man.

Bruce was one of the very few men that I'd been attracted to since my divorce, and I wasn't about to let Mike Quinn do my thinking for me.

Here Bruce was, the suspect himself, sitting across from me in the flesh, for me to judge. I looked into his face, his eyes. I didn't see a murderer. I just saw Bruce . . .

"When and where?" I said, smiling, finally, with conviction.

"My place, say seven thirty?"

"Your place? But I thought you said it was a mess inside, still under reconstruction . . ."

"I figured something out. Something cozy. You'll see— and with your ex-husband back, you know we'll have a better chance at privacy over on Leroy."

Why not? I asked myself. Couldn't a woman get to know a man better by seeing the place where he lives? And, who knows, maybe I could actually uncover something that would take him *off* that suspect list. That thought alone boosted my convictions tenfold.

After all, I'd solved the murder of my assistant manager, Anabelle Hart, hadn't I? Whether Quinn liked it or not, maybe it was time to put more than one detective on this case.

"Can't wait," I told Bruce, and meant it.

Fourteen

⟨∿∿∿∿∿∿∿∿∿∿∿∿∿∿∿⟩

An hour after sunset, autumn abruptly changed to winter in the Village, giving me my first New York snowfall in ten years. Icy flakes were falling, coating cobblestones, blanketing rooftops, and clinging to stately bare trees.

As eager as I was to see Bruce, I didn't hurry as I made my way down Hudson. The next morning or afternoon, the temperature would undoubtedly rise again, and all of this would melt. Tonight, while I had the chance, I wanted to take my time and enjoy the radiant charm of streetlights glowing through gauzy lace.

They say time slows for people in this part of the city. The pace is more leisurely, the objectives more mannered than midtown's lean, reaching towers of commercial sport. On a twilight evening like this, however, with a thick white blanket muting sounds of car traffic, ambulance sirens, and cell phones, time didn't just slow, it stopped altogether. I was no longer in twenty-first century Manhattan. With the ghostly low clouds erasing even the tops of skyscrapers, I'd entered the pages of Henry James or Edith Wharton.

My boots crunched with every step as I walked, breathing in air that smelled fresh and crisp, enjoying the intimate stillness of the streets, the hush of all things around me.

The row houses of the eighteenth and nineteenth century looked more like dollhouses waiting under a Christmas tree, sweet as gingerbread; the snow, a final dusting of powdered sugar on delicate confections.

I turned onto St. Luke's Place, one of the most desirable streets to live on in the Village. No more than three-quarters of a block in length, it carried an open and airy feeling, with dozens of tall ginkos lining a row of fifteen beautifully preserved Italianate townhouses. Facing a small park, these homes sat back from the wide sidewalk, their brownstone steps railed with ornate wrought iron, their arched doorways crowned with triangular moldings.

November was far too early for carolers, but given the preservation of historic detail on this stretch, I could almost hear a group of girls singing at the corner, see their buttoned up boots, long, layered skirts, thick velvet coats, and matching fur muffs.

As St. Luke's curved, turning into Bruce's street, Leroy, it crossed the line—and so did I. With a few steps, I was no longer in the officially designated historic district. This particular area of the West Village was not considered protected.

Inappropriate demolitions, alterations, or new construction could legally occur at the whim of the property owner. The Greenwich Village Society for Historic Preservation, founded in 1980 to safeguard the architectural heritage and cultural history of the Village, had been working to change this, and extend the historic district protections.

My steps slowed as I neared the address Bruce had given me. The house was a charming Federal-style with two full stories above ground, topped by dormer windows, indicating a usable attic. Basement windows were also visible below the short flight of railed steps leading to the high stoop and shiny green front door. To the left of that entrance, at street level, was a rustic little door of rough wood. Directly above that small door was a small window.

"The horse walk," I murmured aloud, watching my warm breath create a pearl gray cloud in the frosty air. I didn't see this feature too often, but this home was archetypal Federal just as Bruce had said. The horse walk was simply a secondary entrance that provided access to a rear yard—during the 1800s, there would have been a stable in the back or even a second, rear lot house.

Clearly, this property was a choice one, and even though it was beyond the historic boundary, it certainly appeared to deserve landmark status.

I stood for I don't know how long, watching the snow fall on the place, enjoying the refined simplicity of its lines, the straightforward elegance of its faded bricks and newly painted white-framed windows, and I could almost see it becoming a home—each wide ledge displaying a flower box in summer, a single candle in winter, a wreath on the door every year at Christmas.

Suddenly, the brass lamp fixtures flanking the house's entrance came brightly to life and the green front door opened.

The light from inside created a silhouette of the man standing in the doorway. The dark shape moved forward, peering onto the sidewalk from the stoop above me.

"Joy?" called Bruce sharply. "Is that you?"

"It's me," I called back. His mistake was understandable, given my attire—the same bulky bright yellow and black parka he'd seen Joy wearing earlier today. I even had the hood up.

"Oh, thank God," said Bruce after hearing my voice. He stepped forward and descended the snow-covered steps. I could see him more clearly now. He wore faded jeans, a black cableknit fisherman's sweater with a crew neck, and steel-toed workboots. God, he looked good.

He stopped in front of me. "For a second there, I was worried something was wrong and you sent Joy to tell me," he said softly. "What's with the pregnant bee parka?"

I shrugged. "I just couldn't take the whining anymore—hell hath no complaint like a daughter forced to look uncool—so I simply swapped her winter coat for mine."

He smiled. "And you don't care how you look, I take it?"

"It's a very warm coat, thank you very much. And it's really not that silly, is it?"

"Not if you like honey."

"In that case, you give me no choice." I bent down, scooped up a handful of wet snow, and made a big, icy ball.

Bruce folded his arms across his black sweater and raised an eyebrow. "You're not actually thinking of throwing that at me."

"Try me."

"A snowball fight is a serious step, Ms. Cosi."

"Just make one more crack about this coat. I dare you."

"Only if you give me a peek at your stinger."

I cocked my arm. "You've got three seconds."

Bruce turned and beat it up the stairs. I let fly, nailing him right in the back of the neck.

"Ow! Damn, that's cold!"

I laughed, walking up the steps to join him. "Never underestimate a former softball player's ability to hit her target."

He was laughing by now, too—and a little bit darkly, but I didn't suspect why.

"Come on in, then . . . and get that arctic gear off," he said.

I unzipped and unhooded as he closed the door—and then, from behind, he struck.

I never saw it coming.

He rubbed the icy ball against my cheek first, then dropped it right down the back of my sweater.

"Bastard! Ahhhh! That's cold!"

"Yes, it is, and I should know," he said with a laugh as I jumped around his foyer.

"How the hell did you manage that?" I demanded.

"I scooped snow off the outside handrail as I was coming in. Never underestimate a man who knows how to improvise."

I managed to tear off my coat and lift my sweater enough to get the half-melted lump out. Bruce was still laughing—until he noticed what I was wearing beneath the puffy yellow parka.

Suddenly, he stopped laughing.

I hadn't worn the outfit in years. The little red plaid woolen skirt had been hemmed to fall about mid-thigh. (Longer than the dancers in a Britney Spears video, hopefully, but short enough to show some leg.) Black ribbed, winter-weight tights, knee-high black leather boots, and a form-fitting sweater with pearl buttons and a daring décolleté completed the (admittedly) cheeky ensemble.

Being petite sometimes felt like a disadvantage in a town laced with Amazonian fashion models and long, lean dancers. On the other hand, Matt once told me that most men weren't into height necessarily. What they were after was a shapely form, and my petite size and small waist did seem to call attention to the size of my breasts, which, despite my height, were not by any measure small. When I wanted to, my shape was easy to hide under large blouses and oversized T-shirts. But tonight, with Bruce, I didn't want to hide. More than ever now, I needed to know how he really felt about me.

With one brief, burning look of naked attraction, Bruce wiped out any guesswork on my part. I no longer had to wonder whether the man would notice my figure and like it, whether he was truly physically attracted to me. One searing look said it all.

"*Killer* outfit," he rasped.

Damn. Why did he have to use that word? On the slow walk down, I had tried to forget my anxieties, that oppressive feeling of guilt for talking too much in front of Quinn. Now all I could think about was Quinn's suspect list—and how to get Bruce off it.

"Clare? What's wrong? Are you feeling all right?"

"Sure. I . . . uh . . ." I put my hands to my cheeks, which I didn't doubt had gone pale. "I'm probably a little chilled from the walk, that's all."

"Let me get you warmed up then." He smiled, put his hand around my waist, and led me down the hall.

The place was clearly still under interior renovation. Drop cloths, ladders, and construction materials cluttered the scuffed hall floor. In the back, beyond the stairs to the second floor, I glimpsed part of the kitchen and saw it was a complete mess with peeling, old wallpaper and dirty tile. He guided me through a doorway to the right and I found myself entering a long, rectangular space. This room was devoid of any furniture—but it was obviously finished. The vast wood floor was highly polished, the walls and moldings carefully restored, and the crowning achievement had to be the fireplace.

"I've got furniture in the master bedroom upstairs, but nowhere else," he explained. "So I thought we'd have a little winter picnic."

"It's charming," I said, and meant it. He'd laid a thick futon flat on the floor, in front of the fire. Big velvet and embroidered pillows were piled in a crescent shape on top. He sat me down in the arch of the crescent, wrapped a soft, chenille throw around my shoulders, and began to rub.

"Warm yet?"

Staring into the fire, I put a hand on his, stilling it. "Yes."

In that instant I knew that if I looked up, into his eyes, he'd kiss me. And if he kissed me, more would happen.

It wasn't that I didn't want to be physically closer to Bruce. I did. But for my own peace of mind, I had to push him away right now and find a way to question him about the women he'd known.

This wasn't going to be easy to do without admitting the reason, but I had to try. Coming out with "By the way, did you know you're a suspect in a murder investigation?" wouldn't exactly inspire him to keep trusting me. Sure, I could try to explain it all away. But "I really didn't mean to finger you in a conversation with my detective friend" wouldn't inspire much confidence, either.

"I'm fine," I told him stiffly. "You can stop now."

I could feel the awkwardness of the moment, but Bruce did his best to respect my signals. Reluctantly, he removed his hands and moved to a covered basket warming beside the fireplace.

"I bet you're hungry," he said, smoothing over what I'm sure he felt was a gentle rejection. "And have I got a special surprise for you."

A special surprise? Like Inga Berg's special surprise on that rooftop? I suddenly thought.

I closed my eyes. God, I wanted to strangle Quinn. Because of him, I knew too much—and not enough. And it was killing me.

"Actually, maybe the dinner can wait?" I said. "I'm really dying to get a tour of this place."

"Really? It's a huge mess."

"I don't care. I love these old places. I was admiring your exterior, you know, that's why I was standing out there in the snow so long."

"Thanks." He cocked an eyebrow. "For admiring my exterior."

I laughed. "You're terrible."

"I know."

"Well, anyway, you weren't kidding about this place being archetypal Federal."

"Yeah. It's hard to believe, but there are about three hundred of these Federal row houses still standing in lower Manhattan."

"Three hundred?"

"Not all are in pristine condition, some have been altered almost beyond recognition. But many have maintained their integrity."

"You've been working with the preservation society, I take it?"

"Yes. And they do good work. For this place, they've already finished the researching, documenting, and petitioning of officials. The New York City Landmarks Preservation Commission will most likely agree and grant this place its deserved landmark status. What most concerns me—and the Village Society for Historic Preservation—is that more than half of the three hundred Federal row houses have no protection at all. The other half either lie within the boundaries of an official historic district, or else they have individual landmark designation."

"More than half are in jeopardy? You're kidding!"

"They could be lost at any time." Bruce looked away, disgusted. "What a waste."

"Do you know what year this one was built?"

"1830. You know the history, right?"

I nodded. Back then, people residing in the crowded colonial enclaves near lower Manhattan's ports were looking to escape the regular outbreaks of disease, including cholera and yellow fever, so they came up here. The Village was only two miles north, but it was a vastly different world for them, bucolic, with fresh air and space, and they began building in earnest.

"These small row houses were an escape, weren't they?" I said.

Bruce looked around the room a little cryptically. "It's been one for me."

The remark seemed to my ears loaded with meaning. "How so?"

He held my gaze a moment, as if deciding whether to talk about what was on his mind. Instead, he shrugged. "So . . . what do you think of this room?"

I kept hold of his gaze. He was changing the subject. We both knew it. For the moment, I let it go. For the moment.

"The work's fantastic," I said. "The fireplace mantel especially. Is that marble?"

"No. It's wood, made to look like marble."

I rose and moved to the hearth, ran my hand along the smooth finish, which was an unusual color—a sort of orange-tinted gold with deep yellow blended in a way to give the impression of carved marble.

"Remarkable. And you're telling me this is authentic Federal?"

"Damn straight. Federal period designers liked to bring light and bright colors into their living spaces—that coloring is authentic and so is the technique. Strangely enough, they liked to play with the look of wood like that, making it look either like stone, marble, or even wood of another species."

"It's beautiful."

"Thanks, Clare."

"So . . . how about that tour?"

He started by explaining that this large parlor room had been two rooms when he'd originally bought the place. He'd knocked down the wall because the house's original Federal scheme, although calling for a front and rear parlor, provided a sliding door between the two that could be open, as it was now, to turn the two rooms into one larger space.

We glanced in the kitchen, which was a total mess, and I laughed when I saw the only two new and possibly working appliances were a small, office-size refrigerator and an espresso/cappuccino machine.

"I like your priorities," I said, walking over to the large machine. "And it's a Pavoni. Good taste."

"I'll be honest with you, it was a gift from a client. I haven't figured out how to use it yet. No time to read the instructions, you know? But I did buy a bag of your espresso blend and I have whole milk in that little fridge."

I smiled. "I'll whip us up some after dinner—and give you a tutorial. Good?"

"You don't have to do that."

"It's my business, buddy. Let me show off."

"Then let me show off mine a little more for you. Okay?"

I nodded and he took my hand. On the stairs, he told me the third floor was the attic, which had once been used for servant's quarters.

"At the moment, those rooms are pretty stark and filled with nothing but paint cans and building materials, so we'll skip them for now. But I think you'll like the second floor."

The second floor had two bedrooms. The smaller one was obviously the "before" picture, with peeling wallpaper, a stained ceiling, broken moldings, and a hideous pink shag carpet, possibly circa 1970, over the wood floor.

"Oh, yuck."

"I take that to mean you think I have my work cut out for me?"

"Yes. That's the technical definition of yuck."

The master bedroom, however, was nowhere near yuck. In fact, it had been as beautifully restored as the downstairs parlors. He'd uncovered the old fireplace, refinished and polished the wood floor, restored the ceiling and its moldings, and even started furnishing the bedroom with a four-poster bed and matching bureaus. In the corner, I noticed a workspace with a drawing board and shelves beside it, full of books and blueprints. Propped on one shelf was a map of the Village and SoHo covered with arrows of different colors and little colorful circles.

I wandered over, curious. "What are these arrows?"

"The green ones show the direction of the traffic flow. The red, blue, and yellow circles refer to sanitation pick-up schedules—its three times a week in Manhattan and twice in the boroughs."

"Sanitation pick up?" I repeated, trying not to picture Sahara McNeil's legs sticking out from under a ten-ton garbage truck. "Why would you need to know that?"

"Those big trucks can stop traffic dead. If my crew has exterior work or needs to move equipment in and out of a particular block, it's better to do it on a day where we won't have to worry about the city's pick-up times—it's been known to fluctuate from early morning to after dark."

It sounded like a reasonable answer. Quinn couldn't fault him for that. I wanted to ask him about Sahara, but since it had happened just this morning, I thought it might be better to wait.

Wandering over to his bookshelf, I skimmed the spines. "Oh, I see you have a big book on the New York subway stations here."

He nodded. "I'm a fan of that restoration project. It was massive. All that gorgeous mosaic tile work."

"Have you been in the Union Square station?" I asked as casually as possible.

"Sure."

"Isn't that the one where that poor woman jumped to her death at the beginning of the month?"

I watched him carefully. He looked away without expression. "Yeah. I'm sorry to say I knew Valerie. That was her name. Valerie Lathem."

"I'm sorry, too. Were you good friends?"

"We dated a couple of weeks. She and I kind of mutually agreed we weren't right for each other, and we said we'd remain friends. She booked my travel. Worked at an agency."

"I'm sorry, Bruce."

"I hated reading about what happened in the papers. Felt bad for her family."

"Was she . . . depressed . . . or anything . . . when you two broke up?"

"Not at all. In fact, she even suggested I try her on-line dating service, SinglesNYC."

I blinked in surprise. Valerie Lathem had sent Bruce to SinglesNYC? That's how he must have hooked up with Inga. I filed that little piece of information away.

"She had everything to live for," Bruce continued. "I don't know why she . . . did what she did."

I nodded. "Do you think it's possible it wasn't a suicide then?"

"What do you mean? Like an accident?"

"Or . . . something else. Could someone have wanted to hurt her?"

Bruce's brow wrinkled. "What makes you say a thing like that?"

"Uh . . . just . . . I don't know. . . . I guess I thought maybe it didn't add up. Young woman, just promoted, beautiful . . ."

"Those things are true about Valerie . . . but, to be honest, she didn't strike me as having the kind of personality that would make someone want to push her onto subway tracks. She wasn't a party girl per se, either . . . although she was a little naive. I'm sorry to say anything negative about her, but if you're fishing as to why we decided to part ways, it had to do with the fact that her job ended at five o'clock, and my job never ended. You know how it is to run a business, right?"

"Sure."

"Well, she didn't. She wanted the kind of guy who'd be at the happy hour down the street at five fifteen every night. A guy who could jet off to the islands on a spur of the moment low-fare deal. I wasn't that guy."

I observed Bruce carefully as he spoke. He didn't seem angry or guilty or disturbed as much as melancholy about the whole thing. He didn't seem very evasive, either.

Okay, I thought, one down, two to go.

(And I still intended to follow up with him on the one time he *had* sounded evasive—when he talked about this place being "an escape.")

I noticed there was an oak desk beside the drawing board. It was a roll-top, and it had been rolled completely down.

"Thanks for telling me about Valerie," I said. "I'd really like to know more about you."

Bruce nodded. "Likewise."

I moved toward the roll-top desk. "This is a nice piece."

"Thanks, unfortunately, the rolling cover sticks sometimes. But I like the look of it. I keep my laptop under there."

"A computer?"

Detective Mike Quinn's voice suddenly boomed in my head: *The person who wrote that note to Inga used a Hewlett Packard DeskJet 840C. A small computer printer. Model 840C . . .*

I cleared my throat. "Do you have a printer?"

"A computer printer? Yeah, sure. But the printer under that roll-top won't impress you, its just a dinky thing I use for personal correspondence. I know what you want to see—the way I design digitally, right?"

"Uh . . . right."

"Well, I can show off some of my fantastic software in a few weeks. But at the moment all my work equipment is in storage while my offices are moving from Westchester to Chelsea. Tonight, I'm afraid, it's not part of your Federal house tour."

Bruce took my hand and pulled me back out of the room. "Come on, our dinner's going to get cold. You must be hungry by now."

"Sure," I said, letting him take me back downstairs.

What else could I do? I couldn't force the issue of looking at his computer printer.

I would just have to figure out some other way of getting myself back into Bruce Bowman's bedroom.

Fifteen

~m~m~m~m~m~m~m~m~m~m~m~m~m~m~m~

" ... But for me, the divorce wasn't as ugly as the last few years of the marriage itself, know what I mean?" asked Bruce.

I nodded, swallowing a succulent forkful of pork loin. "I can relate."

We were finishing an amazing dinner of braised fennel salad, pumpkin lune (little ravioli "moons" with butter), and pork loin alla porchetta with mirto (Italian for myrtle, which added a delightful and surprising herbal bite to the dish).

Bruce had picked up the basket from Babbo, the Washington Square restaurant where he'd made reservations the night I'd made dinner instead. As an expensive, celebrated gourmet restaurant, Babbo was not your average "take out" place, but Bruce had apparently consulted on some restoration work for the owners, and they always treated him well.

"Your ex give you any problems this week?" he asked.

"No. When Matt's in the city—and these days, it's rare—he stays out of my way and I stay out of his. The night you came to dinner, I'm sorry to say, was the exception."

"What a disaster." Bruce laughed. "I have to be honest, that's the only reason you're drinking the same wine. I'm usually not so boring that I'd drag out two bottles of the Echezeaux in the same week. But you'd seemed so excited about it before Matt showed—"

"—and rudely drank most of the bottle."

"I wasn't going to go there."

"Go there, be my guest. I've got a catalog of Matt's flaws filed away somewhere in storage."

Bruce smiled. "That's a loaded comment, you know? I mean, you must be starting the list on me by now."

"On you? Oh, sure. Let's see . . . you're too darned thoughtful and generous. I hate that about a guy. And you're too nice to my daughter, too. You're also too hard working, funny, intelligent, and talented . . . and let's not forget you have way too much good taste, not to mention that superior . . . exterior." It was my turn to cock an eyebrow. (And keep the whole murder suspect thing to myself, of course.

"You know, Clare, with me, flattery will get you everywhere."

He moved his hand to the back of my neck and gently pulled me close. I let him. The incredible wine had relaxed me and he just looked too good in that black fisherman's sweater not to taste. His mouth was warm and soft and I could smell the myrtle from the pork loin and the subtle, sophisticated mix of blackberry, violets, and coffee from the Grand Cru Burgundy.

"Mmmm . . ." he said as we parted. "Full-bodied, elegant, and complex . . ."

"The wine?"

He looked into my eyes. "You."

Oh, no . . . no, no, no. I couldn't let him do this to me, I hadn't finished my interrogation (as unorthodox as it was) . . . and I had to take care to keep my head . . .

"Are you telling me the arrangement with Matt doesn't upset you?" I asked, pulling farther away.

"No," he said leaning closer.

I leaned back.

"Why doesn't it?" I asked, curious.

A barely perceptible sigh came out of him—a subtle exhale of frustration over what would probably feel to him like my second rejection of the night.

He shrugged. "Because I see my ex around, too, just like you see Matt."

"She's in the city then? She's around?"

(*She's alive?* is what I was really asking—because if Quinn's theory about Bruce's having a trigger and snapping out violently were true, it would probably have first manifested on his wife.)

"Oh, yeah, she's around. And I hate to tell you, I've seen her in the Blend. You'll probably meet her soon enough, but I hope it'll be later rather than sooner. It's understandable she's come to the city. The Westchester place was this vast thing. Lots to care for—grounds, tennis courts, but at least I'm not sharing a space with her."

"Is that what you meant earlier when you said this house is an escape?"

Bruce shifted. "Yeah, it's an escape . . . from her . . . from the bad marriage . . . and just . . . from my past . . . yeah."

My past? What did he mean by that exactly?

Bruce poured more wine for us both. "So you're telling me that Matt's a really stubborn guy, then? Won't give up his rights to the duplex?"

"No . . . but then neither will I . . ."

"Joy just as stubborn?"

"I always say she gets it from her father. But I know I can be stubborn, too."

"Thanks for the warning."

"Oh, come on, and you aren't?"

"Yeah, I can be, I guess . . . I was in the divorce."

"Over what?"

"Ten years ago, when Maxi and I first moved East, Maxi had put up the money for the Westchester house, but I'd put in a decade of sweat equity. We split the proceeds from the sale after a really long, ugly fight in court. She was determined to keep it all, but I was stubborn about my position, too. My years of work had more than doubled the value of that property. The judge agreed, even though New York's not a community property state. She made every possible argument, but the judge split it down the middle. She still says I don't deserve a penny."

"She put up the money originally?"

"Yeah . . . to be completely honest with you, Clare, ten years ago, before I started my own company, I didn't have much. Remember I told you how I grew up in Napa?"

"Sure."

During his visits with me at the Blend this week, Bruce had told me some general things about his background. Surprisingly, we had a lot in common. Like me, he'd been brought up primarily by his grandparents. Also, like me, he'd grown up without much money, which made his appreciation of the finer things in life all the more poignant. Frankly, I felt the same. It always amazed me when I'd meet people in Madame's social circle. Some of Madame's friends were old money, some new, but to many (not all, but many), the finer things were just a function of entitlement or prestige. Appreciation for the history and artistry of a thing was far from a prerequisite to ownership. I didn't feel that way. And, obviously, neither did Bruce.

In any event, Bruce had told me it was his grandfather who had given him an early mastery of basic carpentry, plumbing, and the general set of "This Old House" skills. It led him to start working in construction, then restoration, and eventually architecture.

"Well . . ." said Bruce slowly, "what I didn't tell you was that my grandfather was a handyman on a Napa Valley estate. That's where I grew up, on the estate itself. It was Maxi's family's estate . . . and when she and I got involved, her family didn't like it. But Maxi was used to having her way. She's very bright, too, but she couldn't make a career work, didn't play nice with the other kids, you know, kept getting fired from jobs and kept losing well-heeled fiancés, too."

"Sounds like a real gem."

"In a lot of ways, she is. Maxi's beautiful. Brilliant. Rich. She can be a fantastic person when she wants to be. And there were a lot of reasons a lot of men gave her multiple chances, but she was a princess, too, and a lot of men wouldn't put up with her games. So, when the last fiancé broke it off, she ended up living back in her parents' home. She was thirty-two at the time and very worldly, and I was barely twenty-four and, in a lot of ways, just a stupid, gullible kid. We fell in love, eloped, and I was too young to see she was using me as a way to stick it to a family she saw as trying to rule her life."

"Were they?"

"No. Looking back on it, her family just wanted her to get a grip. But she saw them as controlling. Only, she was the one who was controlling . . . it took me a lot of years to see the picture clearly. It's hard to get perspective when you're a twenty-something ignoramus dude, you know?"

"I can't imagine you were any such thing, Bruce. You

were just young." I knew, all too well, that waking up to reality was the toughest thing of all in a bad marriage. His brutal honesty about it impressed me. "So . . . it was a hard thing for you to come to terms with?"

"It took a long time to understand how Maxi saw me, if that's what you mean . . . or, anyway, how she wanted to keep seeing me. It was her father who decided if he couldn't get Maxi to use her degrees for anything constructive, if he couldn't make anything of her, then he'd make something of me."

"They helped you?"

"Yeah, they paid for my education and helped hook me up with some prestigious projects. I was dutiful and grateful and I stuck it out with Maxi for a long time, even after she became very hard to live with . . . very damaging. I was changing and she didn't like it. I wanted to improve things, and I thought moving East would do it. I wanted to make my own mark anyway, start my own business, and I thought if I did that, and we got away from her family, I could prove something to myself as much as them . . . as much as her . . . and I did . . . I built my own company . . . doubled the value of the property Maxi bought, like I said—"

"But you still feel guilty?" I could hear it in his voice. "You still feel you owe something to your ex? To her family?"

"Yeah, part of me does, I guess . . . but part of me doesn't. Part of me feels used, Clare. I spent a lot of years with a woman who made me feel as though I were nothing—barely worthy of her. Maxi's beautiful, like I said. She's rich, she's cultivated. She taught me a lot. And I really did love her. But she also made me believe I was worthless for a long time. Then one day, I stopped believing it."

"That's the way it happens. One day, you stop believing the lie."

"So you can see, that's the very reason I'm not threatened by Matt. Maxi and I, we ran our course. I'm a different person than I was when we first met. In many ways, I think she still can't accept it, but there it is. And I know you must have your own reasons for divorcing, too. So that's why I'm not threatened by Matt. Do you understand now?"

"Yes, I do . . . I do . . ." I said slowly, but, my feelings weren't quite as resolved as Bruce's seemed to be.

Not that I would ever admit it out loud. But, in my heart, I hadn't lost all affection for my ex-husband. Matt was still a business partner . . . a father to my child . . . and a friend. The truth was, I didn't necessarily want my ex out of my life as completely as Bruce wanted his gone from it.

I found myself staring into the flames of the fire.

"Clare?"

"Sorry. I was . . . uh . . . thinking about—"

The investigation, I told myself. *Keep going, Clare, keep him talking.*

"—about the woman you left the Blend with last week. After the Cappuccino Connection . . . Joy mentioned that you knew her from school or something?"

"Yes," he said with a nod. "Her name is Sally McNeil. Crazy girl. Back in college, she changed it to 'Sahara' to sound more exotic." He laughed. "I know her from college, that's all. We hadn't spoken for years—not since Maxi and I moved East, anyway. So we just had drinks at a bar that night, and I walked her home. I'll probably stay in touch with her to be honest with you, but just as a friend."

Why was he speaking about her in the present tense? The woman had been killed this morning . . . unless . . . he didn't know she'd been killed yet . . . my god . . . he doesn't know. . . .

"Just last night, she e-mailed me the phone numbers of two old friends I hadn't seen in years. They'd dated her—

in succession. To be honest, I never saw why. She's such an artsy phony. Pretty superficially out for herself, too, you know? Not my type at all . . . you know why?"

"No."

He smiled. "*You're* my type."

Bruce leaned in. I leaned back.

"And what about other women? You mentioned Valerie Lathem already . . . and that didn't work out . . . but you said you tried on-line dating?"

Bruce laughed. "You're seriously going to give me the third degree?"

"Yes."

"Okay. All right. For me, dot-com dating was an unmitigated disaster. It just was the wrong thing for me to get involved with."

"How many women did you meet?"

"About six or seven, I guess. Maybe ten tops."

"Anyone in particular strike your fancy?"

"If that's a cute way of saying did I sleep with any of them, yes, I did. One of them."

Oh, god. I didn't know if I really wanted to hear this, but it wasn't just me wondering, it was Quinn . . .

"Tell me. I want to know. Who was she? Did you practice safe sex?"

"Of course, I practiced safe sex, and her name is Inga Berg. She lives in one of those new condos by the river, and I used to see her at the Blend, although not lately, and frankly, I'll be happy if I never see her again."

I noticed Bruce's verbs were present tense. He was talking about Inga as if she were still alive. Like Sally McNeil, he didn't seem to know about Inga's death. It wasn't all that hard to believe, actually, since the news of Inga's plunge hadn't hit the front page of the papers like Valerie's had. With all the crime and death in this city, Inga's was just one more. There'd been a small item in two of the tabloids, but that was it. If you weren't a daily reader of either paper, you could easily have missed it.

"You want my unvarnished word for her? You'll probably think I'm a pig, but I found her . . ." He sighed. "Disposable."

"Oh, that's not a good word to use, Bruce."

Especially when Quinn questions you tomorrow or the next day, or whenever he's got enough of a case to pressure you into a "confession."

"I'm sorry, but Inga Berg is such a psycho. She's attractive, sure, but she made me sorry I got involved with her in pretty much less than two weeks."

"So you went to bed with her?"

"No *bed* was involved."

Not the SUV. Please not the SUV.

"I want to know."

Bruce sighed. Not happily. "Your really want me to totally wreck the romantic ambiance of this evening of ours, don't you?"

"I just . . . I just need to know . . ."

"Fine, you want to know everything, I'm an open guy, I want you to trust me, so I'll let you know everything. Inga wanted to sleep together from the beginning. She wanted to do it in her new SUV on the roof of her building, but I said no. We ended up against the wall of her apartment's living room the first night. After that, she wanted to hook up in public places, which I dissuaded her from.

"Our last night together, she'd taken her panties off at dinner, put my hand under her skirt, which gave the waiter a thrill but not me, frankly. Then she went crazy in the back of the cab home. She was just all over me . . . I wasn't that turned on by her, but she was aggressive and I went with the momentum. But the event was more sordid than sexy, frankly."

"Really?"

"Really. The idea of this stuff may fly in a fantasy porno magazine, but in reality, when you're not young and drunk and you can't stop worrying about one of your crews showing up on time for an important job the next day, it's just . . . skeevy. The cab driver kept glancing in his mirror and . . ."

Bruce took a long swig of wine. "I'm just not an exhibitionist, I guess. When she got out of the cab, she was half naked, and didn't seem to care. So I made sure she got up to her apartment safely—then I left. For good."

"I see."

"I like sex. I like hot sex. But I'm a conventional guy, Clare. I actually like the finer things. I like romance. I like elegance. To be blunt, I don't want to worry about a woman I'm escorting embarrassing me. I've got too much on the line with my business, city officials, my work, everything I've built. I think at least one former president will agree that we may all be just one intern away from disaster. Anyway, the bottom line is, my work aside, I could never respect a woman that out of control. And if I can't respect a woman, I can't love her, can I?"

I swallowed uneasily. He sounded angry now. This really was turning into a wrecked evening. But . . . I had my answers.

Bruce had a plausible reason to leave the Cappuccino Connection with Sahara McNeil. And I'd always known Inga Berg liked to "shop and drop" men. Now I also knew she could be a reckless woman, one who could have gone out with any number of men who'd snapped and gone violent on her. And, clearly, Bruce was not the SUV guy. Unless he was lying to me, but with the wine and the emotion in his voice, I could tell he wasn't.

"Thanks for being honest, Bruce. I needed to hear what you had to say."

"Well, I'm sorry you had to hear it."

"I'm not."

He sighed and poured more wine. We'd come to the bottom of the bottle.

"You're entitled to ask me the same questions," I told him.

"I don't need to. I'm with you now, no matter who you saw in your past, and I'm interested in being with you—and making you happy enough to want to be with me . . . maybe even . . . eventually . . . exclusively."

Whoa. Did I just hear what I thought I heard?

"You haven't known me very long to say a thing like that," I said softly.

"Clare, I'm too old and too freaking busy to play games. These days, it doesn't take me long to know what I want. But . . . I can see you need time . . . and I can respect that."

"I think I know what I want, too, Bruce," I said softly. "You won't have to wait long."

He smiled. "Good."

I smiled, too. "Are you ready for some cappuccino, maybe?"

"Sure," he said.

I set up the Pavoni for him on the scratched counter of the old, unfinished kitchen, filling the water reservoir, plugging it into the electric socket, and quickly assembling the portafilter parts. This was an extravagant home machine model—probably worth around four hundred dollars—and it included its own grinder, doser, espresso maker, and steam wand for creating foamed milk.

I hated to tell him I still had the five dollar stovetop machine my grandmother had brought over from Italy with her—and it still made the best espresso in town as far as I was concerned.

"Remember the night I met you at the Blend?" asked Bruce. "I warned you I can drink espressos all day and night, but I can't for the life of me make them myself."

"It's not that hard. Remember, you're a man who can improvise, right?" I teased.

"Still steamed about that snowball, huh?"

"Now pay attention, Rookie. The requirements for making a good espresso can be summarized by the four M's."

"The four M's. Check. Will this be on the written portion of the exam?"

"*Macinazione*—the correct grinding of coffee blend, *Miscela*—coffee blend, *Macchina*—the espresso machine, and, of course, *Mano*—barista. That's you."

"Check."

I ran through the basics with him, then ground the espresso beans, dosed it into the portafilter, tamped it, clamped it, and asked, "You have whole milk in that fridge?"

"I'll get it."

I rinsed out the stainless steel pitcher and half filled it with cold milk. "You should really prepare your milk before you draw your espresso, so your shot doesn't deteriorate. At the Blend we dump anything that stands over fifteen seconds."

"Whoa, that's a tough window."

"Better to lose a twenty-five cent shot than a regular customer."

Bruce nodded. "I feel that way in my business, too. I'd say 'Quality Is Job One' but somebody in motor city stole my motto."

"Fancy that." I laughed. "I only wish I could clone your attitude for a few members of my part-time staff. Sometimes they can be hard to motivate."

"Tell me about it. Hey, I meant to tell you, I tried that trick you told me about on my downtown crew yesterday, and it worked like a charm."

"Late workers come on time when you tell them to be there a half hour earlier than you need them. I use that on Esther all the time."

He laughed. "Okay, so how about some more tips for me—I'm very receptive. *Very* receptive."

The tone was suggestive, but I stayed cool. "Let's do the milk," I said, redirecting my attention. "When you're just steaming milk—for a latte, for example—then you want to place the wand's nozzle close to the bottom of the pitcher."

"I see."

Bruce's eyes were on me so intensely, I felt a little flustered all of a sudden. "For a cappuccino, however, you want to do more than steam. You want to create an angelic cloud of froth, which means you need to add air, so you want to place the tip of the nozzle just beneath the surface of the milk and gradually lower the steaming pitcher as the foam grows."

"Go ahead and show me," said Bruce.

I did, filling the pitcher halfway with whole milk, clearing the steam valve, then placing the nozzle inside the container.

"Rookie baristas think it looks cool to move the container all over the place," I explained. "Up and down and round and round—but that's not the way to do it."

Bruce stepped up behind me. "Wait. I want to get this straight. Let's go over it again."

"Which part?" I swallowed, trying not to let the heat of his body affect me, which was about as easy as trying to keep an ice cube from melting on the surface of the sun.

He placed his hands on the hips of my little plaid skirt, gently but insistently pulling me against him. "Up and down? And round and round? *Not* the way to do it, you say?"

Slowly, he moved my hips with his.

"Uh, not when it comes to foaming milk. No. You just want to lower the pitcher slowly as the foam builds. That's why you only fill the pitcher halfway—to leave room for the foam to grow."

"Room for growth?" he said, his hands still moving my hips with his. "And round and round and up and down?"

"No," I said softly, "you don't want to do that. It gives you an inferior product. Overly aerated foam with big short-lived bubbles and lousy texture."

"I'm hearing you. What else do I need to know?" I felt his mouth on my hair, gently inhaling, then kissing and caressing my neck.

"Ah, let's see . . ." Still trying to stay in control, and barely managing, I licked my lips and cleared my throat. "The milk shouldn't spurt or sputter, either, but should sort of roll under the tip of the wand. A gentle sucking sound is what you should hear—"

"Say that again."

"What?"

"What you just said."

"A gentle sucking sound?"

I felt his mouth, warm against my ear. "Again."

"Bruce . . ."

"Say it."

I inhaled sharply when I felt his lips touch my earlobe.

"Gentle sucking sound," I whispered.

He turned me in his arms. The kiss wasn't gentle, it was full of heat and hunger and I wasn't stopping him.

When we came up for air, he reached behind me and hit a button on the machine. The little ON light faded out.

"Change your mind about that cappuccino?" I asked.

"Yes," he said. "I think I'm stimulated enough."

I smiled as he covered my mouth with his again, and the world went away.

This time when we finished, he took my hand and pulled me gently back into the parlor and onto the soft futon in front of the fireplace. He kissed me deeply, then stretched out beside me.

"Are you okay with this?" he asked.

His eyes were kind and warm and waiting for my answer. "Better than okay," I said, touching his cheek.

And then, for a long time, there were no more words.

Sixteen

∿∿∿∿∿∿∿∿∿∿∿∿∿∿∿∿∿∿∿∿

Twenty *years ago.*

The Mediterranean sun was a lemon in the sky. Brightness full of promise yet painful, too, like a squirt of citrus to the eye.

A young man played with a dog on the sand. He wore fraying combat fatigues cut into shorts and nothing else, the woven hemp choker appearing white as spun sugar against his deeply tanned chest.

The young woman was not a native of this Italian village. She was just visiting, staying with her father's relatives so she could study art history for the summer. One week before, she'd been ogling the works of Michaelangelo in Rome, and she looked at this romping man the same way—like a sculpted statue come to life.

She admired how his chiseled calf and thigh muscles contracted and relaxed as he ran along the sand. How his flexing bicep flung a Frisbee into the surf over and over again for a happy, excited dog to fetch. She found it mesmerizing, and, at the time, had no way of knowing this was simply a "rest day" for the young man—a brief break from his typically more strenuous pursuits of bicycle racing, wind surfing, rock climbing, and cliff diving.

She didn't know his name, had never been introduced to him or his family, and, despite her admiration of him, or maybe because of it, she kept walking.

It was the big black mixed Lab that for some reason came right for her. Probably the heavily perfumed shampoo she'd bought in the village, which gave off a strong lavender scent, most likely the same scent as someone the dog knew and loved. As if they were old friends, he bounded right up, jumping high, his big paws landed and she was slammed down into the sand.

"Mama mia! Scusi, signorina."

Long, damp black hair, loosed from its ponytail, hung into his face. It was a pleasant face. Open and joyful. It was the kind of face that took pleasure in everything it could. And the brown eyes were curious and kind.

"It's okay," she said, surprise reverting her to English. "I'm not hurt."

"You're American! You're from home!"

The pair chatted amiably. He told her he'd been backpacking across Europe and was passing through, visiting extended family and friends all over the Continent. He invited her to dine at his cousins' house that evening. But she declined his invitation and kept walking.

The young man would tell her, much later, after they were married, that he'd kept his eyes glued to her ass the entire time she'd walked away. Her chestnut hair had reached all the way down her back then, and he'd been mesmerized, first by her green eyes, then by the way she'd looked leaving him, her long, dark wavy hair swinging just above what he'd call her "sweet-looking blue-jeaned booty."

A few days later, she found him reading at a café. When she asked about the cast on his forearm, he explained that he'd broken his wrist spinning out on a motorcycle. He wasn't sexually aggressive in the least with her, just warm and genuine. And when he politely asked if he could accompany her on her next long trip to Rome, she found herself agreeing.

Maybe it was the cast and the helpless way he asked. He seemed almost touchingly pathetic—at total a loss for what to do with himself next. And she couldn't get over the fact that he'd been visiting Italy on and off for over a decade of summers and had never bothered to visit the Vatican museums. So she became his guide.

She'd already resolved not to sleep with him, to fend off any aggressive advances, but he wasn't the kind of young man who came at a girl head on. He was more like a cup of espresso, warm and inviting, yet still very potent. He knew how to relax and excite at the same time. And when her guard was finally down, he played her with his light fingertips and laughing mouth and she melted like morning chocolate, right into his hands.

In the end, she would often become melancholy thinking about the way they'd met—the prophetic nature of it. How the sun had been so bright with promise it proved painful, making her smile and squint at the same time, ultimately limiting her vision.

How he'd wanted her most when she was walking away.

I opened my eyes.

How odd, I thought, *to dream of Matteo.* To recall so vividly my first time making love with him—which had also been my first time, period. The dream didn't disturb me. For some reason, I found it strangely comforting.

On the futon, Bruce's arms were still around me, his body warm, but I was cold. It was hours later, and the flames in Bruce's hearth were dying. He was sleeping deeply beside me, and I knew it was now or never.

Easing away from him, I reached for his black fisherman's sweater and slipped it over my head. The garment was huge on me, reaching almost to my knees, the sleeves extending far past my hands. I shoved the sleeves up and rose on bare feet, tiptoeing toward the staircase.

Okay, so sleeping with Bruce may not have been the smartest thing I'd ever done, but it was the most satisfying thing I'd done in years. Like the snow on my walk earlier in the evening, I knew I wanted to enjoy this moment while I could . . . because I had no idea if any of what had happened between us tonight would actually last.

I wanted it, too, of course, but I couldn't control it any more than the early snow . . . and, in the end, I had to accept that it was all right.

Twenty years ago, when I'd first met Matteo, I'd needed things to last. Security was paramount, and I was desperate for permanence. Maybe it was because of my crazy, unpredictable, lawless father, or maybe it doesn't matter who your father is. Maybe every young person feels insecure to some degree because nothing is decided yet, and the future is such a long, untraveled road.

I felt less frightened of the future now than those years when I was Joy's age, more resigned to the notion that the one thing to be counted on was that nothing could. The only unchanging idea was that everything changes, everything is fluid, and nothing can be possessed.

Over time, the various occupants of this very house had flowed in and out, changing from rich to poor then rich again, and they would continue to change and flow through for decades to come.

Certainly nothing living and breathing could be possessed, either. Not friends, not spouses, not aging parents, not even children.

Sometimes I would look into my little girl's green eyes and see that wary child, clinging so tightly to my hand in front of her elementary school. Then instantly she'd be grown again, transformed like a magician's dove. And, laughing with relish, she'd fly away from me, a beautiful young thing with her brand new life.

Maybe it would be good for me to finally let go of the notion of permanence . . . or at least loosen my grip. Maybe in the end all I really needed to do was let go of holding on so tightly.

It certainly felt good earlier to let go of my inhibitions, to trust myself with someone new. I wondered what Matt would think if he could see his ex-wife now, with another man's sweater over her naked form, sneaking up to his bedroom to snoop for evidence that he was not in fact a serial murderer.

Yeah. Sure.

I certainly didn't believe it. Not for a minute. Not for a second.

No man who made love like that, so tenderly, so considerately . . . No man who opened himself so completely could be as cold blooded a killer as Quinn claimed. I just had to find the evidence to make that clear to my detective friend. Starting with that printer.

I crept up the old unfinished staircase, the wooden steps rough against my bare feet. An icy draft flowed down the long hallway from the front door, sweeping up the stairs and up through the bottom edge of Bruce's heavy cableknit, chilling my thighs, and making me shiver as I hit the fifth step. On the sixth came a noisy creak.

I froze and listened intensely, but the house remained completely still. With a quiet exhale, I resumed my climb.

At the top of the stairs, the darkness was thick. I felt my way along the wall and stepped through the master bedroom's doorway. The large room was in shadow, front windows giving enough light from the street to make my way around the great four-poster bed, which sat on one end of the room like a hulking giant. I reached for the small, bedside lamp and turned it on.

The antique roll-top sat by the window. I began to push back its cover. When it stuck midway, I cursed and pushed harder, but the damn thing was more intractable than my ex-husband.

Bending over and peering under, I could make out Bruce's sleek little laptop computer. It sat open, the screen black. I could see the edge of what looked like a small printer, sitting at the back of the desk's large surface.

For a few more minutes, I struggled with the cover. Finally, I smacked and shoved, and suddenly, with a loud rattle, the cover gave, rolling all the way up with a bang.

I closed my eyes, held my breath, and listened.

The desk had made a terrible racket, and I stood in dread, my mind racing to concoct some story. I was certain Bruce was already up, about to furiously bound up the stairs and demand I explain why I was snooping around his bedroom in the wee hours.

For a solid minute, I stood, hearing no sign of movement downstairs, so I swallowed, and resolutely turned back to the desk to quickly examine the printer at the back.

"Hewlett Packard DeskJet," I whispered. "Model 840C."

It was the same brand, the same model as the printer Quinn was trying to link to Inga Berg's murder. I closed my eyes. *Dammit*. Quinn would take this to the bank. But I knew it was just a coincidence. It had to be.

I wrestled for a moment with telling Bruce everything, suggesting he get rid of the printer. But I knew I couldn't. Not yet.

A part of me, a very thin slice of my being, couldn't help asking the question: Was there a chance Bruce Bowman could be a murderer? Was there a chance?

I knew I needed more to go on—one or more threads to follow, something more to pursue myself or give to Quinn.

On a little prayer, I smacked the laptop's spacebar. The screen jumped to life. *Bingo.* It had been in sleep mode. I searched the computer's desktop for anything that might look like a lead.

It appeared he was hooked into a DSL line for the Internet, and he'd set his password to automatic. I quickly logged on and checked the "New Mail" box. It was empty. He must have been answering e-mails just before I arrived. The box was completely cleaned out.

I flipped over to the "Old Mail" box, looking for correspondence from any of the victims. I was fishing blindly, not sure what, if anything, I'd find, but praying I'd know it when I saw it.

The "Old Mail" box screen was set up to scroll mail from oldest to newest. The first date was thirty days ago, and I assumed this box, like my own, expired mail at that time, dumping it into a back-up folder. I didn't have time to search for that folder, so I just began to scroll down.

There were a number of e-mails from people in his company—the URL address was tagged with "@Bowman-Restoration.com." I ignored those. There were also dozens of e-mails from someone named "Vintage86."

Bruce had grown up in California wine country, so it didn't seem out of the ordinary to have a correspondence with a person who also liked wine.

At random, I opened one, my eyes scanning the long, rambling text.

"Nobody thought you were very smart. They used to say I was slumming. I was. You were just a sex toy. Nothing of any consequence. . . ."

The words were ugly. Harsh. And they went on and on.

I shuddered. If this were his ex-wife, Maxine, then I could see why Bruce considered this new life, this new house, an escape.

I hated myself for doing this, but I clicked on the "Sent" box to see how he was answering. This was a terrible invasion of privacy. I knew that. But I had to know. Was he just as cruel? Was this a sick back-and-forth, a pattern he was maintaining? Was he really the man Quinn painted him to be—someone who could snap, give into rage and hate, someone who had the ability to kill, maybe at the moment one of these women started belittling him like his ex-wife?

The "Sent" box was set up like the "Old Mail" box. There were thirty days worth of correspondence here. Not one was addressed to "Vintage86."

The realization stunned me. Not even I could have read those attacks and not fired off a few choice words. But Bruce hadn't written one e-mail to Vintage86, at least not in the last thirty days. It appeared he was reading her e-mails, reading all that ugliness, all that terrible stuff, but giving none of it back.

Maybe he'd written some in the past and had simply gotten to the point where he chose to ignore her—just let her blow off steam. Either way, though, it was clear he was a man who could in fact hold his temper, even in the face of verbal abuse, not to mention in the face of my interrogation of him tonight. He'd been annoyed with me at times, even a little angry with my prying questions, but he'd always been reasonable, never lashed out, never lost his temper or turned on me, and he certainly never raised a hand.

I exhaled a breath I didn't realize I was holding.

He's innocent. I knew it then for sure, knew it with every fiber of my being.

Quickly, I went back to the "Old Mail" and continued scrolling. In the days just prior to her death, I saw a few from "IngaBabe34_24_32," the numbers sounding like her measurements, which was in character for Inga.

The last one read, "Where've you been? Are you traveling? I've been calling. Let's get together and . . ."

The e-mail degenerated into a profane description of sex acts.

I flipped over to the "Sent Mail" and found Bruce's answer.

". . . and I'm sorry. You're a beautiful woman, but I'm not the man for you. And you're definitely not the woman for me. Good-bye and good luck. B."

I shuddered, seeing that *B,* remembering that's how Quinn said the note to Inga was signed. But Bruce wouldn't have kissed her off like this in the e-mails if he'd intended to meet her again. It had to have been some other man she'd been involved with.

I flipped, one more time, back to the "Old Mail," scrolling all the way to the end of the long stack of e-mails. My eyes caught on one labeled Sahara@darknet.com. The date and time indicated it had come in the evening before.

"Okay . . . last one . . ."

I opened the mail, my eyes scanning. Sally "Sahara" McNeil had provided the names addresses and phone numbers of two men she called "my old flames and your old buds . . ."

These had to be the old friends from college that Bruce had wanted to get back in touch with. Sally came through for him. More text below these addresses talked about how she had enjoyed seeing him again and how she'd love him to come to a gallery show the following week. She also provided a hyperlink at the bottom of the e-mail, which she said would give him more info on Death Row.

"Death Row?" I whispered, shuddering. "What the heck is Death Row?"

"Clare?"

I heard the voice. Faint and distant. *Damn.* Bruce had woken up.

It would take him at least sixty seconds to get up here. I held my breath and clicked on the hyperlink. The DSL was fast and quickly connected me to a web site for an art gallery.

In the blink of an eye, I skimmed the home page. There were a number of links listed. They looked to be artist's names, and the tagline on the site read, "Journey into Violent Art and the Art of Violence."

It seemed Sally McNeil's gallery was dedicated to "art inspired by lust, morbidity, and obsession."

When I heard the creak of the sixth step, I began quickly closing all the active windows on the laptop.

"Clare?"

The voice was louder now, slightly tense.

"Bruce?" I called as innocently as I could manage. "I'm up here. In your bedroom."

I took hold of the open roll-top's cover. *Please god don't stick.*

It didn't. The cover smoothly and silently rolled down, giving me about five seconds to get to Bruce's bureau before he appeared in the bedroom's doorway.

When I looked up from an open drawer, he was standing there barefoot. He'd pulled his jeans back on, zipped them, but hadn't bothered buttoning them. In the soft bedroom light, the brown mat of hair on his naked chest appeared a shade darker than the coarse stubble now shadowing his jawline.

"I was cold . . . so I came up here . . . thought I could find some extra blankets or something to sleep in . . ."

Bruce smiled. "I like you in *that*."

I pinched a bit of the black cableknit. "This old thing? Oh, I just picked it up somewhere."

He yawned. "It's *way* too early in the morning for bad jokes."

"Agreed." I headed toward the doorway, still nervous. Still certain he'd heard the roll-top going down, would suspect what I'd been up to and hate me for it.

"Wait right there," he said, putting his hands on my shoulders. "I was kidding. I have something for you to wear."

He moved to the bureau, opened a drawer, and pulled out a pair of flannel pajamas. "You take the top, I'll take the bottom."

"Thanks."

"And I have something else to keep you warm . . ."

I thought for sure he was setting me up for another seduction, but instead, he reached for one of two Saks shopping bags leaning beside the bureau.

He reached in and pulled out a classic, floor-length shearling with exposed seams, turn-back cuffs, and a hood. "It's for you, Clare. Try it on."

"Bruce? What did you do?" The coat was easily over a thousand dollars.

He·shrugged. "You and Joy were going at each other just because of a stupid-looking parka. I thought it was silly. So I bought you both early Christmas gifts. You can give Joy's to her next time you see her."

"Bruce, it's too much—"

"No, it isn't." He cut me off. "It's a gift, Clare. Don't turn it down. I didn't turn down the dinner you made for me, did I? So don't tell me you can't accept this."

"It's too generous."

"It's just a coat. You'll make me happy if you wear it." He held it up, waiting for me to slip my arms in its sleeves. "Come on, try it on."

I did, slipping my arms into the fleece-lined garment and wrapping the buttersoft leather around me. For fun, I even flipped up the hood. "It's really warm. And it's really beautiful. To tell you the truth, I've been admiring the shearling on one of our customers, and I've always wanted one, just could never afford it. Is Joy's like this one?"

"Exactly."

I laughed. "She'll love the coat, but hate having one just like her mother's. We haven't had mother-daughter matching clothes since she was four."

"Well, you can always exchange it for another style—or she can. I just figured one of you might like this version enough to keep it."

"Thank you," I said, then turned and kissed him. He smiled, held the kiss longer than expected. My hood slipped off as he pulled me closer, just as I was pulling away.

"You know I have to get up in less than four hours to open the Blend," I warned him.

He nodded, went to the four-poster, and pulled down the bedcovers. "Okay . . . I'll set the alarm, and then drive you."

"You don't have to—"

"I'm driving you, Cosi, so drop it. Now let's go to bed while we can."

Seventeen

~~~~~~

It was twenty-five minutes to six in the A.M. when I unlocked the front door to the duplex above the Village
Blend. That meant I had twenty-five minutes to wash,
change clothes, and be back downstairs to unlock the door
for our morning pastry delivery.

I didn't even want to think about the snow removal on
the sidewalk—although I knew I'd have to think about it
soon, or else risk a very hefty fine from the Sanitation Department. The city gave property owners four hours to
clear their sidewalks after the snow stopped falling. I figured we were just about due for the massive ticket.

Matteo wasn't scheduled to fly out again for another
week, and I made a quiet entrance, trying not to wake him.
It wasn't that I was worried about his beauty sleep. In fact,
I'd probably be pounding on his door in fifteen minutes,
telling him to start shoveling the walk. I just didn't want

him to see me coming through the front door, at this hour, dressed like this.

Too late.

"Well, well," said Matt in an injured tone. "So you finally made it home."

"Good morning," I said, meeting his gaze. He stood there in tight, scuffed jeans and a crinkled gray turtleneck.

I took off the beautiful shearling coat and hung it in the closet. Put down the Saks shopping bag with Joy's and faced Matteo to find him staring at my outfit, his disapproving eyes moving from the low cleavage of my tight, pearl-buttoned sweater to the short hemline on my red plaid skirt.

"I know you were wearing Joy's yellow parka when you left here—and I won't even ask where the hell it is now—but you haven't actually been borrowing the girl's *clothes,* have you?"

"Certainly not," I replied. "I'd never let my barely adult daughter go out in public wearing an outfit like this one."

For a change, Matteo was speechless.

"Coffee?" I asked. "You're up so early you probably need it."

I headed for the kitchen and my drip coffee maker, Matt on my heels.

"Someone had to get up early," he said. "In case you didn't make it home. Someone would have to open the coffeehouse."

"Please," I said with a wave. "In all the time I managed this place for your mother—during our marriage and since I've returned—I've never once missed the opening. You, on the other hand—"

Matt put up his hand to stop me.

"Let's not go there. It's the here and now we're talking about."

Matteo sat down at the table while I scooped beans into the grinder.

"Anyway," he said, "I wonder how much longer you'll be able to keep that sterling employment record going? Especially with millionaire Bruce Bowman—a.k.a. *Mr. Right*—in hot pursuit. Or is the pursuit technically over now?" Matteo glanced at his watch and raised an eyebrow. "Gauging the hour—and your choice of attire—I'd say Bruce got pretty much what he was after. How about you, Clare? Happy?"

Matteo had learned the many ways to bait me early in our marriage. For the first few years, I refused to sink to his level, but soon we were fighting fairly regularly. It was possible my hostility gave him some kind of sick justification to seek comfort elsewhere—not that he'd ever really needed an excuse.

In the years since the divorce had become final, however, I'd had little to no patience with Matteo's games.

"Yes, as a matter of fact, I am happy," I tossed over my shoulder. "Bruce made me very happy. And correct me if I'm wrong, wasn't it you who always said I was too uptight and should lighten up? You're just mad because I didn't lighten up while I was married to you."

"That's a load of—"

I pushed the button on the electric grinder, drowning out his reply. Grinding beans too long would create a bitter brew, but frankly I preferred having the bitterness on my tongue than in my ear.

When the beans were pulverized I turned off the grinder and dumped them into the drip machine's cone filter to the sound of silence. I got the whole thing brewing, then grabbed two large mugs and set one in front of Matteo.

The nutty smell of freshly brewed Breakfast Blend gradually filled the kitchen. I yawned, leaned against the granite sink, and let the earthy aroma revive me.

It slowly dawned on me that through some bizarre circumstance of karmic justice, Matteo and I were both reliving an all too common scene from our past—only in reverse.

Back when we were married, Matt had been the one who invariably partied the night away, usually with some vivacious little bubblehead, as a result of a networking party, while I played the part of the responsible, long-suffering, faithful, injured spouse. I didn't like my role, but what Matt saw as my "uptight" morals allowed for no other choice of lifestyles. Just because Matteo strayed at the drop of a thong, didn't mean I would.

If I remembered correctly, it was Matteo who usually made coffee on those bleak mornings, still dressed in the clothes he went out wearing the night before—pumped full of adrenaline, or testosterone, or cocaine, or all three. He'd make coffee while I sat at the table or gazed out the window, sulking, and contemplating the end.

Now if I were a cruel person, I would take pleasure in this remarkable turning of the tide—and maybe I was a cruel person because a part of me knew Matt wanted me back, and I was honestly enjoying this moment. On the other hand, maybe I wasn't cruel. Maybe I was just human.

When the pot gurgled its last, I carried the hot carafe to the table.

Matt spoke again. "Your friend Detective Quinn stopped by last night, around closing time."

I froze in mid-pour, dribbling three dark drops. Matteo swept his hand across the table, wiping them away.

"Quinn put a tail on Bruce," he continued. "From the report he received late last night, it appeared a woman with a bright yellow parka entered Bowman's house. He thought it was Joy who had gone in. He came here, alarmed, looking for you. He found me instead, and I explained you'd borrowed Joy's yellow parka. What his plain clothes officer saw was *you* going in. That's when Quinn told me—"

I finished pouring and sat down at the table across from the father of my child. "I know what he told you. He told you Bruce Bowman is a suspect in a murder."

"*The* suspect, in *three* murders."

"Quinn exaggerates," I said evenly. I tasted my coffee and found it bitter. I added an extra dash of cream—and, uncharacteristically, a heaping teaspoon of sugar.

"So maybe Bruce only killed one woman instead of two or more," said Matt. "Yeah, I could see how Detective Quinn was exaggerating just a tad. Nothing to worry about."

I shook my head, disturbed. "Matt, listen to me. Bruce is not a murderer. Quinn's wrong. Misguided, over-wrought, and . . . wrong. And if he's telling you about it, then he's obviously trying to convince you to persuade me to stop seeing Bruce. But I'm not going to. Instead, I'm going to do something else."

"Like what?"

"Like prove Quinn wrong."

"Whoa, Clare—"

"Don't 'whoa Clare' me," I said a little too loudly. "You want to know what I think? I think both you and Quinn are jealous. You with your public parade of serial flirtations, and Quinn with his messed-up marriage and all the baggage that comes with it. Frankly I'm sick of the both of you."

"Aren't we being a little harsh?"

I gritted my teeth and glared at Matt. "I meet a man. A nice man. More than a nice man. A remarkable, talented, tender, and hard-working one. Someone sane, reasonable, adult, self-aware, and brutally honest about the mistakes of his past, and you and Quinn conspire together to ruin things for me."

"Clare, you're starting to sound paranoid. I can't speak

for Quinn, but I'm not out to frame your boyfriend, or hurt you, believe me."

"Not out to hurt me? That's rich. Just what did you think you were doing all those times you had a fling with some barmaid, stewardess, or mutual friend's wife?"

For a long minute, he had no reply.

"I didn't do it to hurt you, Clare," he finally said softly. "You know that."

Sadly, I did. It had taken me years to come to terms with the idea that Matteo and I had very different attitudes toward sex. For him, physical love was just another exhilarating activity—like mountain climbing, surfing, getting falling-down drunk, or bungee jumping. Sex was no big anxiety-producing ordeal—and there certainly didn't have to be any complicated meaning behind it. What meaning was there in a drunken binge or a bungee jump?

But for me there had to be more than the excitement of the chase, or the thrill of the seduction. Much more. I had to respect the man, and like him a lot, if not love him completely. Sex meant relationship. Sex for me could never be a one-night stand.

I know now that Matt never really understood what his little infidelities were doing to me back then. It was like he was missing some gene, or had an amazing psychological blind spot where the result of his own behavior on others was concerned. The cocaine didn't help either, frankly. But my cognitive comprehension of my ex-husband's shortcomings didn't go very far to ease the pain in my heart. Or stop the anger I still felt toward him at times.

Like right now.

I picked my coffee mug up. We drank in silence.

"I'm not out to hurt you and I never was, Clare," Matteo said after a long pause. "I just didn't get it, you know? I do now." He met my eyes. "I do . . . right now."

I was a little taken aback. Just when I was angry with him, he said something like that—which was about as close to an apology for his past indescretions as I would ever get.

"Maybe you can help me, then. Help me find out the truth about Bruce," I said slowly, hopefully. "These murders, if that's what they are, and Quinn's suspicions about Bruce . . . I can't sort it all out myself . . . Matt, they're like dark clouds hanging over what could be . . . well, what I think could be something very important for me."

Matteo shifted impatiently, then gulped his coffee. "I'm not a cop. You'd do better getting your buddy Quinn to help."

"You and I did pretty good the last time . . . with Anabelle Hart. We solved a real crime, didn't we? We put a real killer in jail. That was something."

Matt shook his head. "We got lucky, Clare. We could just as easily have ended up in jail for breaking and entering, or for impersonating federal officers—and need I remind you that you almost got yourself killed?"

I sat back in my chair and ran my finger along the edge of the warm coffee cup.

"You need Quinn," said Matteo.

"I can't go to Quinn. I can't trust him with this."

I paused, then decided it was time to come completely clean.

"His marriage isn't going well, Matt . . . and he was telling me about it one night, and I think he might have been interested in seeing me . . . or at least I think he was thinking about it . . . before I got involved with Bruce."

Matteo snorted. "I told you the man wanted you."

"Christ, I didn't say *that!*"

"You said he seemed interested. What about you? Were you?"

"I don't know."

"Honestly."

"Okay, I like Quinn. He laughs at my jokes, and I usually enjoy his morose sense of humor and I find him a little bit sexy—in a rumpled, hard-boiled, film noir sort of way. And, okay, we've been flirting pretty heavily with each other since we first met. And it's probably Quinn, now that I think about it, who helped me start to believe that I should give the opposite sex a chance again—"

"Clare."

"What?"

"This is way more information than I need to hear."

I threw up my hands. "Quinn has too much baggage. His marriage is falling apart, he loves his children and is clearly ripped up about his unresolved feelings for his wife. Anyway, I'd never get involved in a tangled mess like that and he knows it. But I also think he wasn't thrilled to hear I was dating anybody again, let alone Bruce, and I really think Quinn's grasping at straws where Bruce is concerned."

"I see," said Matt.

"I'd rather trust you with this . . . investigation . . . or whatever you want to call it. Helping Bruce is what I want to call it."

Matteo smiled. "I'm flattered."

"Why?"

"Because you feel you can trust me. That makes me want to help you, but the truth is you still need Quinn. He's been investigating these crimes for weeks, he's talked to people we don't even know about, and he has all the facts at his disposal."

I sat straighter and leaned across the table.

"Quinn doesn't know everything," I whispered. "I did a little investigating on my own. Last night, while Bruce was asleep, I logged onto his computer and read his e-mails."

"You logged onto the man's computer and read his e-mails? Without his knowing, I take it?"

"Of course."

"Jesus Christ, Clare, you've got nerve . . . no wonder you found out about Daphne and me. And I thought I was so careful."

"You were flaunting her, Matt. Even Madame knew . . ."

"Mother knew?"

"Yes, but she forgave you. I doubt she ever forgave Daphne, though."

It was sad, really. Madame and Daphne had been friends for years before Daphne made a play for her best friend's son.

The direction of the conversation was obviously making Matt uncomfortable, so he changed it.

"Clare, if you logged onto his computer, that means you had some suspicions of your own."

"No," I lied. (Okay so I'd had a moment of doubt after I saw the model number on his HP DeskJet, but the truth was I wanted to look for anything that might contradict the picture Quinn was trying to paint of Bruce, and I had.)

"So what did you find out from all of your investigating?"

"I think the key to this whole thing is Sahara McNeil. She was someone Bruce hadn't seen in years, not since he was first married. He didn't even know she was in New York until Cappuccino Connection night—"

"And then he found out Sahara was living in the city and he killed her," concluded Matt.

"That's not where I was going."

"That's where Quinn would go. And what about the subway victim? And Inga Berg? Wasn't Bruce connected to both of those women, too?"

I sat back and took a sip of my coffee.

"He was involved with both of those women, true," I said. "But *for a short time,* and I think that's just coincidence. New York is a big city, but the circles in some of these dating services are really quite small. Bruce admitted to me that he'd dated a lot of women since his divorce, including the dead women, but I'll bet a lot of other men dated them, too. Inga, certainly. Ask Tucker. She used to yammer on about her dates every weekend. And Bruce told me Valerie liked the happy hour scene—and she was the one who told him about SinglesNYC.com, the on-line service where he met Inga."

Matt folded his arms. He didn't seem convinced yet, but at least he was still listening.

"So why do you think this Sahara person is the key?"

"Sahara McNeil sent Bruce an e-mail link to a web page. It was a promotional site for the art gallery where she worked. It's in SoHo, a place called Death Row. Ever heard of it?"

Matt shook his head. "Never."

"They don't exactly specialize in our kind of thing," I told him. "The tagline on the site said something about dealing in 'violent art' and 'art inspired by lust, morbidity, and obsession.'"

Matt scratched his unshaven chin. "That's creepy, but I still don't exactly see where you're going."

"It seems possible to me that Sahara could have been done in by one of the artists her gallery represented. In fact—wait just a second, I'll be right back."

I rose and went to my bedroom, then returned with the Hello Kitty notepad I'd filled out on Cappuccino Connection night. I quickly leafed through the pink pages.

"One of the men I was screening for Joy called himself Mars. He had that intense kind of stalker look and said he was a painter. But the strangest thing was that he spent most of his time ogling Sahara McNeil. He kept repeating that he'd already made his 'connection' for the night, and Joy said he'd told her that, too, which was truly odd since she was only the second person he'd sat with. The first one was Sahara."

"So you think that this Mars may have killed Sahara? And since he's a painter he may have known her through this Death Row gallery thing?"

"It's a place to start," I replied, trying not to sound totally desperate.

Matt sat gazing in silence at the steam rising from his coffee cup.

"Look at the facts," I said after a pause. "Valerie Lathem hasn't been ruled a homicide. Inga Berg's killer could have been any number of men, and Sahara McNeil . . . I think she's the real key. If I can find other suspects, I'll bring them to Quinn's attention. I just need some ammunition to prove Bruce is being framed."

Matt nodded.

"Okay," he said, slapping his palms on the table. "What do you want me to do?"

Just then the downstairs door buzzer went off, a faraway sound from up here in the duplex.

"First, I want you to let the pastry man in while I change clothes," I said. "And then I want you to clear the sidewalk." I glanced at his tanned skin, the familiar bronzed coloring of the perpetual equatorial summer. "You remember how to shovel snow, don't you?"

Matt raised his dark eyebrow and gave me a look that seemed to say *I'd* been the one doing the shoveling for the last few minutes. Lucky for him, I had a coffeehouse to open.

Eighteen

∽∽∽∽∽∽∽∽∽∽∽∽∽∽∽∽∽∽∽∽∽

Until the 1840s, SoHo—the truncated term for the neighborhood in lower Manhattan south of Houston Street—was a sleepy residential section of Manhattan. Then the building boom of the 1850s transformed it into an area of expensive retail stores and lofts built to house light manufacturing.

During this commercial building spree, the use of then-inexpensive cast-iron materials instead of carved stone became the vogue, making opulent, Italianate architecture like the 1857 Haughwout Building on Broadway near Broome Street the norm. Iron columns, pedestals, pediments, brackets, and entranceways were mass-produced for so many SoHo buildings that the area became known as the Cast Iron District.

By the 1960s, however, the facades of these structures were looking pretty worn from a century or more of neglect, and the once pricey lofts had begun to house cheap sweatshops. At that time, an entire floor of an industrial building could be rented for next to nothing, and impoverished artists did exactly that. Within a decade SoHo became the East Coast mecca for art, and by the 1970s hundreds of art galleries, large and small, mingled with antique dealers along West Broadway, Broome, Greene, and Barrow.

Transformed into a bohemian colony, the exhilarating mix of art, design, and architecture attracted the uptown crowd to the area, and by the late 1970s a new brand of tenant was buying up lofts. It was the era of the art patron rather than the starving artist, the latter forced to search the west side's warehouse districts and the outer boroughs to find inexpensive industrial space. By 1980, the newly renovated lofts of SoHo were more likely to be written about in *Architectural Digest* than in Andy Warhol's *Interview*.

Fortunately, the "artsy" character of the neighborhood never truly faded, and within the irregular borders of SoHo—and in some areas around it, too—the largest concentration of galleries and museums in North America could still be found.

A promising artist or designer could work anywhere he or she liked, but a showcase in a SoHo gallery was *the* essential element in a truly successful artist's or designer's portfolio, which was why the ambitious still poured into New York City year after year upon art school graduation.

On this bright, blustery, and cold Saturday afternoon, the narrow streets of SoHo were crowded. Last night's snow appeared fluffy and white on rooftops and car hoods, but on the streets and sidewalks, foot and car traffic had turned the early snowfall into slushy black puddles.

Tucker was now baby-sitting the Blend, so Matt and I could be free to take off. By the time we reached the perimeters of SoHo, all clouds had vanished in the blue sky. In the streets, we mingled with tourists, day shoppers, and the lucky few who could afford to live in this trendy, too-swank neighborhood.

It was strange to be here again with Matteo at my side. I had been so busy managing the Blend that I had not been back to SoHo very often since I'd returned to New York City, and much had changed. Long-established art dealerships like the Perry Gallery, the Atlantic Gallery, and The Richard Anderson Gallery still resided side-by-side with edgier art showcases like the Revolution Gallery and Ferri Negtiva. But the area had become so upscale that Prada, Armani, and Chanel had established their presence here, too, rubbing shoulders with Pamela Auchincloss and the First Peoples Gallery.

Salons of designer jewelry and haute couture also seemed to be edging out the smaller galleries and antique shops. But the most noticeable difference was the absence of the World Trade Center, whose twin towers had once loomed over the neighborhood like giant silver sentinels, guarding New York Harbor.

Despite the many changes, my memories of this area were rich. Early in our marriage, Matt and I enjoyed shopping here, often accompanied by Madame, who was always pleased to dispense her wisdom and good taste in judging our selections. These days—post Matt's cocaine habit, our divorce, and the raising of Joy—there was no way in hell we could afford to shop in most of these pricey outfits.

Though gentrification had spread through much of SoHo, there were still tiny pockets of low rent stores, dive bars, and tarot card parlors. Death Row was located on such a block, an area north of the exclusive Mitchell Algus Gallery on Thompson.

Along a row of three- and four-story buildings as yet untouched by the latest spurt of renovation, Matteo and I found several storefronts for minor galleries, low-end antique dealers, and vintage clothing stores.

"According to the address it should be right around here," Matteo said, glancing at the handwritten note he'd scribbled down before we left the Blend.

I scanned the dingy storefronts and found the Belleau Gallery, Shaw's Antiques, Velma's Vintage Clothing, Waxman's Antique Stoves and Fireplaces, but no sign of Death Row Gallery.

Matt touched my shoulder. "There it is."

The exterior of the exclusive art gallery that had employed Sahara McNeil did not look anything like I had expected. Instead of a trendy storefront, Matteo directed my attention to an anonymous three-story building with a dingy antique shop on the first floor. Next to the antique shop entrance there was a flight of concrete steps leading down, below the level of the street to a basement door. Above that door, painted in five-inch stenciled letters were the words DEATH ROW.

Negotiating the irregularly constructed stairs, we stood before a barred steel door—not an aluminum security gate so familiar to New Yorkers but a real cast-iron door taken off a nineteenth century prison cell. The door was locked. A black iron doorbell fixture in the shape of a skull hung next to the entrance.

Matteo pressed the bell, and I heard a funereal gong sound deep inside the building. I almost expected Lurch from the Addams Family to appear—instead it was a clone of Uncle Fester who buzzed us in.

The man stood at the end of a long hallway lined with framed art. Inside, the air was warm and close, and the lighting had a subtle scarlet tinge I found unsettling.

"Welcome. The gallery is this way," the fat man said jovially, waving us toward him.

The walls of the nondescript hallway were insulated brick painted institutional green. The floor was covered with cheap green tile as well. Though dismal and ugly, the hall was hung with expensively framed art prints and original theater posters. I didn't recognize any of the artists and the plays were mostly unknown to me.

I spied a poster for an Off-Broadway musical called *The Jack the Ripper Revue: A Tale of Saucy Jack*. There was also a marquee for a Broadway version of Mary Shelly's *Frankenstein* which opened and closed sometime in the 1980s, and another Broadway poster for a musical version of Stephen King's *Carrie*. It was the King poster that jogged my memory.

"I understand the décor of this hallway," I whispered to my ex. "It's from the Stephen King story 'The Green Mile.' The long green hall of the prison the condemned walked to the place of execution."

"Well, this *is* supposed to be Death Row."

"And so it is," said the big man, standing in front of us. Though portly, he was clad from head to toe in black Armani—slacks, shirt, and jacket. He held his hands behind his back so his bald, pink, oversized head was the only splash of color in a shadowy silhouette. As was the fashion of late, the bald man's shirt was buttoned tightly around his neck, and he wore no tie.

When we reached him, the man thrust out a puffy hand for Matteo to shake. I noticed pink flesh bulging over the tight collar under the man's cherubic face, which was free of all facial hair, including eyebrows. As he motioned us through a narrow door, I noted that his shoes appeared to be Bruno Magli, his watch a Rolex.

"Welcome to Death Row. My name is Torquemada."

I glanced at Matteo. "Torquemada?" I murmured. For some reason, I associated the name with some heinous historical atrocity.

Matt lifted an eyebrow. "Nobody expects the Spanish Inquisition."

The suffocating hallway suddenly opened into a massive, bright art gallery that dominated the entire basement. Though this interior gallery had no windows, strategically placed mirrors, a high white ceiling packed with ductwork, and a polished hardwood floor increased the illusion of brightness and space. The lighting was subtle but intense enough to highlight the work displayed, and the whole space was well appointed and tastefully done—which was more than I could say about the art.

I noticed several other people in the gallery. A young, trendy-looking couple seemed to be browsing, and two middle-aged Japanese men were locked in conversation with a tall, well-proportioned young woman who looked like Prada's version of Elvira. Matteo's eyes were immediately drawn to her.

"An amazing space," Matteo told Torquemada. "I never would have imagined such a splendid gallery could be found at this address."

Torquemada lowered his eyes and his lips turned up slightly at the compliment.

"Are you looking for anyone's work in particular?"

At that moment, my eyes locked on a grisly painting depicting a scene of brutal murder and mayhem. The central figure was a woman, slashed and mutilated, hanging over the edge of a bed. Blood seeped from her wounds and pooled on the floor. The figure was crudely done yet very detailed. The colors were lurid and intense—so intense they almost seemed to glow. A window dominated the upper right corner of the canvas; through it, a bland street scene was depicted, totally lacking in detail, as if the artist had showered all of his obsessive attention on the doomed figure in the foreground.

"This work is called *Lustmord*, a German phrase that roughly translated, means 'sexual murder,'" said Torquemada as he stared up at the image. "The original was painted by Otto Dix in 1922. Sadly, this is only a print produced in Germany during the Weimar Republic in the 1920s, but quite rare nonetheless. This example is signed and numbered."

"Interesting," I said, averting my gaze.

"Is this what I think it is?" Matteo asked, resting his hand on an unfinished wooden chair with crude metal electrodes attached to it.

"That's the actual electric chair that serial killer Jonathan Fischer Freed died in, but don't ask me how I got it," Torquemada said conspiratorially. "I'm sorry to say that item is not for sale."

"Oh, that's too bad," said Matteo dejectedly.

Browsing, I came upon a section of the gallery dedicated to clown paintings. That's right. Clown paintings. Just like the ones you'd find in any flea market in America. Competently but not expertly rendered, each picture featured a different clown. Odd, but innocuous, I thought.

"These are a series of works painted in prison by serial murderer John Wayne Gacy," Torquemada explained. "He turned out hundreds of oils for avid fans before he was executed on May 10, 1994."

"Electric chair?" Matteo asked.

"Lethal injection," Torquemada replied. "I recently acquired these particular works from a collector who passed away . . ."

I looked at one of the paintings and thought I saw a cruel glint in the eye of the supposedly innocuous clown. The painting was called *Pogo the Clown* and was subtitled *A self-portrait*.

"Gacy tortured and murdered twenty-eight young men in a homoerotic frenzy," Torquemada continued. "He was struck with a swing as a child and the injury resulted in a blood clot that he insisted clouded his sense of right and wrong. Despite this real or imagined infirmity, Gacy was a talented painter and a prominent businessman who was active in his community. Dressed as Pogo the Clown, Gacy entertained sick children at the local hospital and helped with their fundraising activities. He was so influential in Chicago politics that he once had his photograph taken with First Lady Rosalynn Carter."

Slowly edging closer to Elvira, Matteo came upon a bookshelf made of old bones—human bones by the look of them. I might have found this shocking, except for the fact that I'd seen shrines in Italy made of human bones and they were often quite lovely in a macabre sort of way. And I have no doubt that Matteo had seen more unsettling things than this simple bookcase in the Third World. Indeed, Matteo's eyes quickly moved past the bizarre furniture to scan the books themselves.

On a rib-caged shelf, a glass case held a shopworn magazine face out to display the cover, which featured a photograph of a woman's torso and head completely encased in black leather.

"We have a complete set of John Willie's *Bizarre* magazine, all twenty-six issues," Torquemada said. "If you are not acquainted with the title, *Bizarre* was an underground fetish magazine published in the forties and fifties. We don't deal in much erotica at Death Row, but we have a bit here and there if the items are collectable enough."

"What type of art *do* you deal in, Mr. Torquemada?" I asked.

"Just Torquemada, Ms.—?"

"Cosi," I said.

Torquemada folded his hands.

"To answer your question, primarily Death Row Gallery provides an outlet for the violent outcasts of our society to exhibit and market their creative endeavors."

"You mean you sell art by murderers."

"You put it crudely, Ms. Cosi, but accurately."

He shifted his gaze to Matteo, then back to me.

"You're obviously searching for a particular item. I'm sure I can be of service."

"Actually, I was looking for the work of a particular artists," I said. "A young man who calls himself Mars . . ."

Torquemada stared at me doubtfully. "Mars?"

"Sahara McNeil told me about him. Recommended his work."

At the mention of Sahara's name, Elvira turned in our direction.

"Mars?" Torquemada said tersely. "You can't be serious."

The couple seemed oblivious to the change in the tone of our conversation, but the Japanese businessmen were now glancing in our direction, too.

Torquemada gripped my arm, none too gently.

"Will you both please follow me to my office," he said with forced politeness.

I shook my arm loose from his grasp as I followed the dealer through the gallery to a door marked PRIVATE. He quickly unlocked it and motioned us inside. Torquemada followed Matteo and I through the door and closed it quickly.

The office was small and stark, with off-white walls displaying framed posters announcing Death Row gallery shows. An Apple computer with a sleek, thin monitor sat on the desk and a slew of art books and catalogs packed a set of tall shelves. Stacks of black leather artist's portfolios leaned against the length of one wall, and the corner of the room, behind the desk, was dominated by a human skeleton posing with a silver tray in its hand, as if it were serving lunch. There were some items on the tray, but Torquemada spoke up before I got a good look, calling my attention away.

"Now what is this all about?" Torquemada demanded, his face florid. "I already spoke to a police detective. If you two are more of the same you should at least identify yourselves as such."

"We're private detectives investigating the death of Sahara McNeil," Matteo smoothly stated without a second's hesitation.

"What's to investigate?" Torquemada said, his arms wide in an open shrug. "She was flattened by the Sanitation Department, end of story."

"You don't seem broken up about it," I noted.

"No, I don't, Ms. Cosi. And neither would you. Little Sally was a below average sales representative whose inability to schmooze the clientele and the artists we represent nearly cost me one of my best clients."

"Mars?"

Torquemada laughed. "Hardly. Poor Mars, a.k.a. Larry Gilman, is nothing but a wannabe."

"I have it on good authority that he has a record as a violent felon. That he may have committed murder," I replied.

"He was a co-defendant in an assault charge that was downgraded from manslaughter. Larry got into a bar fight with some Puerto Rican punk over a girl and the kid died later. Larry-the-murderer didn't even do hard time—just parole. Likes to play it up, though. Thinks it's good for his resume."

"Isn't it?"

"You have to have at least a modicum of talent," Torquemada replied. "*Mars* was strictly fan-boy. Japanese Manga meets Jackson Pollock. Really quite derivative. Sometimes I move his stuff to the Goths who can't afford to purchase the real thing."

"Like one of those fine clown paintings, you mean?"

"They may not be profound, Ms. Cosi, but they were

produced by a mind bold enough to grasp a much darker vision of the universe than Larry Gilman's. Or most definitely, yours."

Yes, most definitely, mine, I thought, *and thank goodness.*

"How would you characterize the relationship between Larry Gilman and Sahara McNeil?" I asked.

"A lapdog to its master. He worshiped her. She tolerated him. Sahara moved art for Larry. She even let him come over to the gallery for long, soulful chats." Torquemada examined his nails and sighed.

"Sahara probably liked the attention, but I doubt very much there was any more to it than that. She was ten years older than Larry in age—and light years ahead of him in education and sophistication. She had a degree in fine arts, Larry was a Jersey boy who'd dropped out of high school. What could she really find attractive about a crude post-adolescent no-talent?"

Torquemada moved to the leaning stacks of black leather portfolios and tossed one onto the desk.

"Mars came by earlier today, brought me these." He flipped open the leather folder.

Inside were pictures painted in acrylic. Ten of them. The same woman in every one. I recognized her flaming red hair and green eyes from Cappuccino Connection night.

"Sahara McNeil . . ."

The pictures were wonderful, luminous, highly idealized portraits. The kind of pictures a passionate young man would paint in the throes of heated infatuation.

"I can't even sell these," Torquemada said, his voice pained and regretful. More melancholy than irritated, he closed the portfolio. "They look like pictures of fairies or something. Who'd buy them?"

Who indeed? Obviously none who shopped for fine art at Death Row Gallery.

I studied Torquemada's resigned expression. One thing still bothered me. "You said Sahara McNeil almost cost you a high-end client. Who might that be?"

Torquemada moved behind his desk and sat. I tried to keep my eyes from straying to the skeleton hovering in the corner behind him, silver tray extended in an offering.

"Seth Martin Todd," he said as Matt and I took seats across from him.

"The name doesn't ring a bell," said Matteo.

"Yes, well, I'm not surprised," Torquemada replied, somewhat defensively, I thought.

"It just so happens that Seth Martin Todd is going to open a one-man exhibition at the Getty Museum in Los Angeles next week. His paintings now command huge sums of money. Money that generates commissions this gallery needs to survive. Sahara jeopardized my trusted relationship with Mr. Todd."

"How?"

"Todd accused her of underselling one of his works," Torquemada replied. "He blamed Sahara for a canceled appearance on *The Charlie Rose Show*, and also for mishandling an exhibition of his work at MoMa."

"Did Mr. Todd threaten Sahara?"

"On a number of occasions. But he threatens everyone," replied Torquemada with a wave of his puffy pink hand, "—even me."

"So he's just another wannabe? No danger at all?"

"I didn't say that, Ms. Cosi. Seth Martin Todd is the real deal. He murdered two people. One of them his wife."

Matteo leaned forward. "So he's in jail? Or still facing trial."

"The charges against him were dropped on a technicality. The murders occurred in Vermont and the small town sheriff who was the arresting officer botched the chain of evidence. A high-priced lawyer got all of the evidence against him thrown out in a pre-trial motion. Todd got off without even a trial, and the notoriety made his work highly sought after among a certain class of collectors."

"Does Mr. Todd live in New York City?" I asked.

Torquemada snorted. "If you call Queens New York City, then yes."

He opened a drawer, pulled out an index file, and drew out a business card. "Here's his address. Give him my regards, if he'll even see you."

Matteo's eyes narrowed. "Oh, he'll see us."

"He refused to meet with the representative of the World Trade Center Memorial Commission yesterday. I wanted to send the man over, but Todd said the representative wasn't morally or ethically fit to judge his work."

"Why not?" I asked.

"Todd has got a problem with men. A rooster complex. He's superficially charming around both sexes, but he truly prefers to deal with women. Especially if it has to do with his career. In my opinion, it's the secret of his success . . . his way with the ladies, I mean. My boy Seth has charmed his way to the top." Torquemada offered me a malevolent smile. "If you're very lucky, my dear Ms. Cosi, he'll work his magic on you."

Sitting next to me, Matteo shifted his weight and folded his arms tightly. I could hear the tension in his voice when he asked, "Does that magic include murder?"

"Seth has his personal ghosts to deal with," said Torquemada, his attention straying to the skeleton behind him for a moment. "We all do."

Then he looked at me. "If you think Seth murdered Sahara, you're wrong. He felt nothing but contempt for Sally and her bourgeois background. Seth's power as an artist comes from the knowledge that he destroyed something he loved. That the one person who meant more to him than life itself died at his hands."

The bald man's gaze strayed to the skeleton behind him again. "I understand Seth," he continued. "In a way, I know how he feels. I didn't kill my wife, but I stood by and watched her die."

He looked back to us, but his eyes were distant as he kept talking. "Madeline had a taste for the needle . . . heroin . . . That coupled with her inability to measure anything correctly caused her to have an overdose. But she's still here, with me."

Call me naïve, but it took me a few seconds to understand that he was referring to the skeleton. That medical school anatomy specimen standing behind his shoulder was the mortal remains of Torquemada's late wife.

Good god, I thought. *This place really is a horror show.*

"I can't forget her, you see," Torquemada said. "At least Mars was healthy enough to let go, to bring those pictures to me. To never look upon the dead face of Sahara McNeil again."

"Thank you for your time," I said, rising quickly. Matteo followed my lead. Before I turned to leave, however, I couldn't stop my eyes from straying morbidly to the contents of the tray clutched in the late Mrs. Torquemada's hands.

I saw a syringe, a spoon, a clear plastic bag of white powder, and a candle burnt down to the wick. There was also a shrunken object that looked like a turkey neck—whatever it was, it was definitely organic.

Matteo glanced at the tray, too, and I heard his breath catch in complete horror. "Jesus Christ, man!"

Matt's outburst set off Torquemada, who rose quickly and nearly pushed us out the door. "You'll never understand," he said angrily. "There are many ways to be faithful, to keep one's promises . . . I have been faithful, in my fashion."

Matteo grabbed my arm and the next thing I knew, we

were both out in the street, sucking in fresh, cold air like a pair of trapped miners resurrected.

"Thank goodness we're out of there," I said. Then I turned to Matt. He looked pale. That surprised me—frankly, his outburst surprised me, too.

"Since when have you been so squeamish?" I asked him. "You've seen bones before. And New York City creeps."

"It wasn't the bones that got me, or that creep Torquemada. It was the thing lying on that tray," Matteo said, hustling me along Thompson Street.

"The needle? The heroin? The turkey neck?"

Matteo shook his head. "That wasn't a turkey neck, Clare."

"Then what was it?"

"When I was in Africa some time ago, two men were convicted of rape. After their trial certain body parts were removed as punishment."

"My god," I choked, "then that was—?"

"You heard the man," said Matteo, nodding. "He remained 'faithful,' in his 'fashion' . . ."

Nineteen
∿∿∿∿∿∿∿∿∿∿∿∿∿∿∿∿∿∿∿

After we left Death Row Gallery, Matteo and I walked to the R line and boarded the uptown Broadway local—the train Valerie Lathem died trying to catch.

At Times Square we switched to the Queens-bound 7 train for the ride out to Long Island City. The 7 train travels underground from Times Square to Fifth Avenue, and on to the deepest level of Grand Central Station. Then it races through a tunnel under the East River and emerges to run along an elevated track across the middle of Queens to Flushing's Shea Stadium and the end of the line.

Among the 7 train's passengers, Hispanics and Asians dominated, along with East Indians and a smattering of florid-faced Irish newcomers who had migrated from the Emerald Isle to Woodside, Queens, to be among their fellow émigrés. Matteo and I would be getting off before we reached that tiny Irish enclave. We were heading to a far less pleasant place, a nominally industrial area of Queens known as Long Island City, which was in transition to residential zoning—in other words, we were going to an old factory district that spirited urbanites had begun to homestead.

Despite our wretched experience in the bowels of SoHo, or maybe because of it, I found the train's hypnotic underground motion sending me into a daydream—back to Bruce Bowman's unfinished house, where my skin still faintly tingled from the hours he spent touching me, our last coupling in his four-poster bed.

Until recently, the transit authority ran an older scarlet-painted train along this line, known as the redbird, with drafty, noisy old cars so loud on some sections of track it made conversation almost impossible. The new cars were sleek and quiet, but Matteo and I still chose not to converse. I remained in my reverie, and beside me on the hard, plastic orange seat, Matteo sat with arms folded, staring into the distance, looking as though he'd gone somewhere else, too.

I roused when the train emerged from its tunnel, the glaring light of late afternoon bursting through scratched windows. Then the track inclined and the 7 Local became elevated, crossing over a deserted railroad yard covered with puddles of mud and melting snow.

Despite long and extensive work on the tracks, and the new train, the 7 line still looked dismal and worn in places, like an impoverished cousin of the Manhattan lines, with their restored mosaic-tiled stations.

Century-old elevated 7 stations like the one at Queens Plaza were a throwback to the Industrial Revolution—no-frills steel-framed structures on tall iron stilts, with several levels of concrete platforms and wooden tracks. When the subway clattered into that station, it sounded to me like the old wooden roller coaster I used to ride at a local amusement park growing up.

We disembarked just after Queens Plaza, at the Thirty-third Street stop. From its narrow concrete platform, we had a magnificent view of the Empire State Building across the river, burnished by sunset's golden rays. We walked down three long flights of stairs to Queens Boulevard, one of the borough's two major thoroughfares. While we waited for the light to change, a tide of traffic flowed by in three crowded lanes. It was here, over the roar of the engines, that Matt and I began to argue.

"This is a bad idea, Clare," Matteo said. "Why confront Seth Martin Todd now? Today? We already know he's killed—twice. Why enter the predator's den?"

"You *know* why. It's something I have to do for my own peace of mind."

"We could let Quinn handle it. Police detectives *must* do more than eat Krispy Kremes and chase divorcees, right? Let that faded gumshoe earn his salary for once."

"You don't have to insult Quinn," I said. "He may be wrong about Bruce, but he's not a bad cop. And I do intend to let him handle it . . . I just need to give him an 'it' to handle. Come on, we've got a good lead here. You're usually up for a challenge."

Matteo's face was stone. "A challenge is one thing, Clare. But now you've got me escorting you to the home of a murderer, and I don't like it."

I sighed. "You don't want me to go alone, do you?"

"I don't want you to go at all."

"Well, I am. So it's your choice."

Matt rubbed the back of his neck, then shook his head. "Come on. Let's get it over with."

"It's really the perfect opportunity," I said, trying to sound encouraging as we crossed the busy street. "Torquemada said Todd blew off a member of the World Trade Center Commission, and that he runs on charm, right? So I'll pretend to be another person from the WTCC, and while he charms the heck out of me, I'll pump him for information."

"What am I supposed to do while you're, uh, pumping him?"

"You will wait outside. Torquemada said Todd had a problem with males in authority."

"No, Clare. That's *really* not a good idea."

"Of course it is. If I'm not back in a reasonable amount of time—say thirty minutes—you can call the cops. You can even call Quinn. This isn't his usual stomping grounds, but—" I threw Matt a look. "I'm sure there's a Krispy Kreme around here somewhere."

Matteo returned my look but said nothing.

The sun was touching the horizon now, and streetlights were flickering on as we moved north up Thirty-third, a largely commercial area of auto body shops, steel finishers, furniture makers, and garages—closing up now or closed already.

In the distance, there were several tall loft-type manufacturing buildings, and they appeared to be at least half vacant. This was not a residential neighborhood, and no one had bothered to clear away the snow. It lay on the street and sidewalks in dirty layers. There were no stores, or diners, supermarkets or newsstands, either. As far as city living went, this was certainly the proverbial "urban frontier."

As we moved past a vacant lot that some Hispanic teens were using as a ball field, I felt feral eyes watching us— and was suddenly regretting the decision to wear my brand new, thousand dollar, floor-length shearling. The chic coat was the perfect garment for garnering admiring glances in the streets of SoHo, but far from the smart thing to wear in Long Island City.

After the teens gave Matteo and me a second and third look, Matteo offered them a sneer of his own. They quickly returned to their game.

"In case you haven't noticed, Clare, this it not a great neighborhood," Matteo said evenly.

"If you can make a Jeep trip through bandit country to Jiga-Jiga, I think you can protect us both in the jungles of Long Island City."

"In Africa I carry a gun."

Twilight descended quickly as we turned right, into a narrow, dead-end alley between two tall manufacturing buildings. On our left, through three separate eight-foot, barbed-wire-topped chain link fences, a large black dog snarled at us. The building on our right—a six-story manu-facturing and warehouse structure that covered nearly the entire block—had the same address as the one printed on the business card Torquemada had handed me.

"Here we are," I announced brightly.

Matt grimly scanned the shadowy alley—still paved with its original cobblestones—and the dark windows on the buildings, through which no interior lights shone. "Yeah. Home sweet home."

We walked to the far end of the dead-end block, stop-ping before a windowless steel door, a bare unlit bulb above it. In the last dying light of the day, I read the sign.

"*Tod Studios*. This must be the place, but I wonder why he misspelled his own name. His business card spells it 'Todd' with two D's."

"It isn't a misspelling of his name," Matteo replied. "*Tod* is the German word for *death*."

"Oh." I took another look at the strange door on the stark building and shrugged. "Well, on that note, I'll say good-bye."

Matt tugged me back by the sleeve of my shearling. "Let's synchronize our watches. Thirty minutes," he said, fingering his Breitling.

"Got it. Now get out of sight."

From a hidden vantage point, Matteo watched as I

pressed the button beside the door. I heard a loud, warehouse-style bell echo through the massive, empty structure.

It took so long for anyone to respond that I thought I'd be spending my whole thirty minutes just standing there, in front of that door. After about ten minutes, I heard footsteps. The bare bulb above the door suddenly glared to life and, with a shrill metallic squeal, the door swung open.

A slight blonde man with tousled hair and sharp features stood in the doorway. Though tall, he was so slim I decided I probably outweighed him, and his complexion was pale and unhealthy looking. But there was both intelligence and energy behind his sky-blue eyes, and he seemed open and friendly. In fact, the only unsettling thing about Seth Todd was the fact that his hands and arms were stained with a wet, dark red liquid all the way up to the elbows.

"Gosh, I hope that's paint," I said.

To my surprise, the man laughed—and so did I.

"Can I help you?" he asked.

"You can if you're Seth Martin Todd."

He nodded. "At your service, and you are—?"

"Clare," I answered. "I understand you submitted a proposal to the World Trade Center Commission?"

"Pleased to meet you, Clare." Seth Todd thrust out his hand to shake mine. Then he noticed it was still covered in blood-red paint.

"Sorry," he said sheepishly. Then we both laughed again.

A perfect romantic comedy moment, I thought, *except for the fact that this guy murdered his wife.*

"Come in," Seth Todd said, using his scuffed Skechers to open the door wide enough to admit me.

With a quick, uneasy glance over my shoulder, my eyes found Matteo's silhouette, far down the alleyway, lurking in a doorway. I turned toward Todd and entered.

"Go on inside," he said, directing me to a large, open door with his elbow. "I'll join you after I clean up."

I crossed the threshold and found myself in a large, barren industrial space with oil-stained concrete floors, a high ceiling, and visible plumbing and heating ducts running up the plaster-free brick walls.

This area of the warehouse looked like it had once been a loading dock. Two huge garage doors in the wall faced Forty-third Avenue, and a cold draft leaked through the joints.

Though there were tall windows lining both sides of the room, strategically placed in the days before electricity to admit both the morning and afternoon sun, it was now getting downright dark outside, and much of the massive interior space was slipping into shadows.

Now that I was inside the building, I understood why there were no interior lights visible through the windows. Todd used only a tiny corner of the massive space for his work area, and only that part of the room was lit—by three naked light bulbs hanging on long cords from the ceiling.

There were several chairs—none of them matched—a few stools, and several easels with various paintings displayed. Some were abstract, but not all. There was an oil of an old Gothic church, and another of a farmhouse that reminded me of Andrew Wyeth's work.

Todd's current work in progress rested on a large easel in the center of the workspace, a six- by ten-foot canvas covered in various shades of scarlet—from the color of bright blood freshly spilled, to the dull crimson of a new scab, to the dark brown blot of an old bloodstain. Though abstract, the elements came together to evoke an emotional impact. The artist showed real genius in his selection and arrangement of the hues, shapes, and textures.

"Would you like some tea?" Seth Todd asked, appearing at my side with a steaming silver pot and two white ceramic cups.

"Thank you," I said as he set the cups on a low wooden table and poured.

"Please take off your coat. Sit down."

I slipped off the shearling and threw it across the back of an overstuffed armchair. He pulled over a battered chrome bar stool with a black cushioned seat and sat across from me. I sampled the tea and found it savory—a Darjeeling with a subtle fruity tang.

"I actually prefer coffee," Seth Todd said apologetically, his Skecher heels resting easily on the bottom cross bars of the stool like a teenager in an episode of *Leave it to Beaver*. "A good Kona, or a Blue Mountain would be great about now, but I've been having trouble sleeping, so no caffeine after six P.M. My friends say I should switch to decaf, but I'd just as soon skip my evening cup as resort to such desperate measures. The poet Dante forgot to write about that ring of hell reserved for those who oppose caffeine."

I laughed out loud. *My god,* I found myself thinking, *if I hadn't been told he was a killer, he'd be a man after my own heart.*

"My sentiments exactly," I told him. "I'm a bigger coffee afficionado than you could possibly imagine, but I have to admit that this tea is delightful."

"I bought it in Chinatown, a little store on Mott Street called Wen's Importing. I won't touch anything other than leaf."

I scanned Seth Todd's work area. It was, as far as I could see, a typical artist's studio. Tubes and jars of paint. Brushes. Pencils. Canvas and paper. There were some pen-and-ink and pencil sketches tacked to another easel. Human studies, mostly. Faces and figures, several portraits obviously drawn from life—none of them slashed or stabbed or brutalized in any way. But my eyes were constantly drawn back to the large red canvas that dominated the room.

"That's a powerful painting," I said.

"Thank you," he replied, his eyes watching me. "It was commissioned for the foyer of the Seattle-based software firm, Gordian Incorporated. Their brand new headquarters building was designed by Scott Musake and Darrel Sorensen. Really amazing."

He spoke about several other commissions—for the Tokyo headquarters of an electronics firm, a skyscraper in Sri Lanka, and the grand ballroom of a Paris hotel still under construction. He also managed to drop the fact that his work was displayed in several museums and galleries around the world.

Though he came on a little strong, I found Todd's enthusiasm for his art and the design work of others infectious. He was a serious painter, but one concerned with his own notoriety, too. Some would probably be bothered by his ambition, but I found it honest and refreshing—at least he wasn't hiding what he wanted out of life from anyone.

"So," he said at last. "You're here about my WTCC submission?"

I nodded, hoping my lie would hold up under scrutiny.

"I don't judge the submissions, of course," I said, playing for time. "I don't even get to see them. I merely conduct an interview. We try to screen every artist and designer who wishes to be involved in this important project."

"I was expecting a man," Todd said. "A fellow named Henderson. A critic who used to write for *Art Review*."

"Ah, yes. Well, we felt that Mr. Henderson had too heavy a hand to deal with certain artists, so I volunteered to fill in for him."

"I'm delighted you did, Clare," Todd said, his pale blue eyes staring into mine. "Henderson panned one of my shows, and I didn't think I would get a fair evaluation from the man."

This was not quite the tantrum Torquemada hinted had

occurred. It wasn't that Todd had something against men, it was more like he had something against this particular man. But, to be fair, it sounded more like Todd was just being protective of his own work and reputation, and he spoke about the issue with such genuine sincerity that I believed every word he said.

It was disturbing in a way, but it was hard for me to see this man as the same one Torquemada had described.

"So why do you want your work to be displayed in the new World Trade Center?" I asked.

"Because it's important," Todd replied. "Millions of people will eventually walk through the doors of that complex, once it is completed. This new World Trade Center will become the commercial capital of the world, and a showcase of art and design. Not since Cheops built the Great Pyramid has an architectural project received such widespread international attention. What better place to showcase my artistic creations?"

"I . . . see."

So far Seth Martin Todd sounded more like a huckster than a killer, and I was already convinced I'd reached another dead end in my quest to clear Bruce Bowman. Still, I pushed on.

"Your work has been sold through Death Row Gallery? By a Ms. McNeil. Sahara McNeil?"

Todd's eyes hardened. "Ms. McNeil sold one of my paintings to a Japanese conglomerate. Why do you ask?"

I set my cup down.

"I guess you heard about Ms. McNeil? The accident yesterday morning?"

Seth Todd blinked. "No."

"She was killed. Crushed under a sanitation truck in Greenwich Village."

"And this has what to do with the World Trade Commission?"

"We like our prospective artists to have clean backgrounds," I said as coolly as I could manage.

Todd leaned forward and set his own cup down.

"You already know about my background, or you wouldn't be here, asking questions about a dead woman."

"I know you were accused of murder."

Todd snorted.

"Accused? No. I *committed* murder. I went up to my cabin in Vermont and found my wife making love to another man. I felt betrayed. I went a little crazy. I killed them both. Do you understand how it feels to be betrayed?"

"Yes, as a matter of fact. I do."

"Then you understand."

We sat in silence for a time.

"So you're really here to see if I had anything to do with Sahara McNeil's death?" Todd said.

He stood up and walked to his canvas. He stared at it, his back to me. "Did Torquemada send you? Did he say I was angry at Sahara, that I threatened her?"

"Did you threaten her?"

I watched Seth Martin Todd's shoulders heave in a long sigh.

"I threaten a lot of people, Clare. I have a temper as you well know. People don't like me when I'm angry."

I stood up.

"I'm sorry to have bothered you, Mr. Todd," I said.

He turned and faced me again. He was smiling.

"Come on, Clare. Ask me. That's why you came here."

I shifted uncomfortably. "Did you kill her, Seth?"

"No," Todd said after a long pause. "I did not kill Sahara McNeil."

I channeled Quinn, knowing that I would have to tell him about Todd unless I heard the right answers.

"Can you account for your whereabouts yesterday morning, between seven and ten A.M.?"

"Yesterday?" He laughed and went over to his desk. He returned with a video cassette. He handed me the plastic case and tapped it.

"Read the label."

I did. It was the tape of an interview with Seth Martin Todd aired on *MetroNY Arts,* a cable access morning show. The interview was broadcast live from a Queens television studio at the time of Sahara McNeil's death.

"Sorry to disappoint you," he said. "Really."

"God, I'm so embarrassed," I found myself saying.

Seth Todd looked at me with wry amusement. "Don't be, Clare. I get these kinds of questions all the time."

"What? Someone asking you if you've killed again?"

"Okay," he said. "Maybe not *that* one."

I slipped back into my shearling. "You must know I'm not from the World Trade Center Commission," I confessed.

Todd nodded. "I figured that out."

"So don't you want to know why I really came here?"

"Not really . . . I like the suspense. Now, can I call you a car? No taxis come near here, but I have a car service I use regularly."

"No thanks," I said. "I have a . . . car waiting at the end of the alley."

"Well, it was pleasant meeting you, Clare. Drop by again—maybe next time you can critique my art—that gets me *really* angry."

I shot him a look, and he raised his hands in mock surrender.

"Just kidding . . ."

After escorting me to the door, Todd said good-night with an admonishment to be careful in this neighborhood.

"Don't worry," I told him. "My, uh . . . driver . . . once fought his way out of a Calcutta hellhole."

"Cool."

I walked down the dark cobblestones. At the far end of the alley, Matteo stepped out of the shadows.

"I was about three minutes away from calling Quinn on my cell," he said, suppressing a shiver. "So, how did it go?"

"Todd is another dead end—pardon the pun. But I did learn one important fact . . ."

"What's that?"

"You can't judge a novel by its dust jacket."

Matteo gave me a sour look. "That isn't very helpful."

"No, it isn't," I replied, thinking about how charming and erudite, educated, and intelligent Seth Martin Todd really was, despite being a double-murderer—and, unfortunately, how much he reminded me of Bruce Bowman.

The Genius could see the girl was pleased to be around him. Sharing a cozy table at her mother's coffeehouse, sipping cappuccinos, chatting easily. How nice. How very, very nice . . .

Yes, Joy, you have a pretty name and a pretty face. But it's your youth, your silly, bubbly youth that's the biggest attraction.

That ridiculous yellow parka of yours is clearly history now. I can see you love the new shearling that's taken its place. Charming how you don't want to take it off, even as you sit here at a table by the fire, enjoying your cappuccino.

But you don't really deserve that coat . . . because you are clearly too young to carry it off. And, my dear Joy, the truth is, you are just too carefree . . . and careless . . . and you don't understand when you take teasing too far, how your laughter cuts me in two.

Neither do you understand that I, the Genius, am the one with the power, not you.

You will learn it quickly enough, though, my dear Joy . . . and soon . . . because I'm just about ready to teach you . . .

Twenty

~~~~~~~~~~~~~~~~~~~~~~~~~~~~~~

"But nobody questions your morals,
And nobody asks for the rent,
There's no one to pry, if we're tight, you and I,
Or demand how our evenings are spent. . . ."

SOMEWHERE under the East River, Matt turned to me and recited those lines from "Life Among the Artists," a nearly century-old ditty written by journalist and radical John Reed, who'd lived for a time in New York.

"And?" I asked when he was done. "What are you getting at?"

"This town is the perfect place for people like Toddie the painter boy back there, people who want to escape their pasts. In New York, people may see you, but they don't know you. And they might even know you, but they don't *really* know you."

"Matt?"

"You're out of leads, Clare—"

"No, I'm not—"

"Listen to me. You admitted that Seth Todd was as charming as Bowman. He's probably sensitive and sweet, too, when he's not in a murderous rage. You may think you know Bowman, but he may turn out to be exactly like Todd. That may be the real reason Bruce moved to New York City, to escape other 'accidents' in his past. Certainly, your meeting with Todd should at least make you stop and consider it."

I shook my head.

"Consider it, Clare. I think you have to begin to acknowledge the possibility that Quinn was right."

I slumped back against the cold, orange plastic subway seat and wrapped my shearling tighter around me, trying to feel the warmth of Bruce again.

As we rumbled out from under the river and toward the first underground stop in Manhattan, we passed a slower train on a parallel track. The people appeared like ghosts in the darkness, their heads and torsos surreally floating by in the frame of the other train's windows. I thought of Valerie then. How her body had been mutilated on one section of these miles and miles of subway tracks, and despite the shearling, a shiver ran through me.

"Clare, come on. When you walked out of Todd's studio, you bluntly admitted to me that he surprised you. That you never would have guessed he was a murderer—"

"But I only just met Seth Todd. I haven't spent time getting to know him. I haven't snuck around his place and read his e-mails, and—"

"—you haven't *slept* with him."

Matt's raised voice drew some glances in the subway car. Two Hispanic teenage boys snickered then looked away. An old Filipino woman narrowed her eyes at us, then shook her head and went back to reading her paper.

"Let's table this discussion," I whispered, then slumped back in the hard, plastic seat and once again closed my eyes—trying to close out Matt's words with them. Instead of considering Bruce's guilt, I wanted to consider the facts.

Fact: Bruce was innocent. Okay, maybe it wasn't a fact yet to Quinn or Matt but it was to me. I knew it. I just had to prove it.

Once again, I thought about Valerie Lathem. But not the dead Valerie. The live one. The Valerie that had been dating Bruce for a short time.

Bruce had met Valerie through her job at a travel agency—and that simple fact was probably all Detective Quinn wanted to focus on right now.

Obviously, the detective had begun eyeing Bruce as a suspect when the evidence at Inga's crime scene had turned up a note signed with a *B*. So it made perfect sense for Quinn to stop asking questions about Valerie's love life once he discovered Bruce's basic connection to her.

But Bruce had revealed to me that it was Valerie who'd turned him on to the SinglesNYC site, which meant she had been using the same on-line dating service as Inga Berg. Maybe Quinn knew this already, or maybe he didn't. To me, however, it seemed like a significant connection to pursue.

Okay, I admit that Quinn wasn't wrong to focus on Bruce Bowman, the one man connecting Valerie and Inga (and Sahara, too, for that matter), but the detective wasn't convinced of Bruce's innocence, and I was. So there had to be another man connected to some or all of them.

If Valerie and Inga were killed by the same guy, chances were good that the guy who killed them probably met them both through that on-line dating site. All Matt and I really had to do was cross-check the site names. Whichever guy showed up on the dating lists for both of these women had to be a viable suspect.

And, frankly, if Sahara McNeil's name showed up as a registered user of the SinglesNYC dating site, too, I wouldn't be surprised. After all, Sahara had turned up at Cappuccino Connection night, which meant she'd been mate shopping—so it was highly possible that she may have tried SinglesNYC.

Bottom line: If I could find the one guy, other than Bruce, who was associated with all three women, I'd probably have my killer. And I'd happily serve him up to Quinn on a platter finer than Torquemada's.

"Yes. There is a new lead," I murmured, almost to myself, my eyes still closed. "SinglesNYC.com."

"What?"

"Matt, listen to me." I opened my eyes and turned to face him. "This isn't just about my being charmed or duped by Bruce. This is about me trusting my own judgment. It took me a long time to believe in myself, but I do. And I trust that I'm right on this. I have one more lead I need to check out. It's an important one. Can't you trust me, just a little longer?"

From a safe distance, the Genius followed the bubbly girl as she left the Village Blend. Her thousand dollar shearling was easy to spot in the crowd of Old Navy peacoats, leather jackets, and cheap synthetic parkas.

There was no plan here. None.

The Genius didn't care. Something could be improvised. The Genius was truly gifted with improvising, and this girl had just gone too far tonight, teasing him unmercifully, laughing and flirting with him for a solid hour before rising to go.

The girl walked east from Hudson, toward Seventh Avenue South.

Good, thought the Genius. Very good. Perfect.

The Saturday night streets were crowded with college

students and partygoers, straight and gay couples, uptown slummers, bridge-and-tunnel kids, night club groupies, drunks and drag queens. The carnival was nowhere thicker and louder and chaotic than Seventh Avenue South.

On a corner near a college bar, the crowd had over-flowed onto the sidewalk. The bus stop midway down the block was the perfect nexus.

Joy strode to the corner and waited for the light to change, ready to cross the wide boulevard. A blonde young man with a goatee said something to her. She turned and smiled.

Good, *thought the Genius,* go ahead and tease the boy. You like to tease, and you'll be just distracted enough for the improvised plan to work.

Here it comes, the Downtown M20, speeding right along, swerving toward the curb to get to the stop half a block down. Here it comes, your last stop, Joy Allegro.

The crowd was thick, and the shove was easy, no one could even tell who'd sent the girl off the curb and right into the path of the oncoming monster.

For the Genius, this final impact would be the sweetest, most satisfying of all . . .

Twenty-one

~~~~~~

MATTEO and I emerged from the subway at the 7 train's last stop in Manhattan, Forty-second Street and Broadway.

We ascended the stairs to street level, pushed through the subway station's doors, and hit the raucous Saturday night wall of Times Square crowds. Hundreds of bodies were jostling for space on the packed sidewalk. Matt guided me to a relatively sane spot near the doorway of an office building, and by the light of a million neon bulbs, he pulled out his PDA. A quick cellular connection got us the SinglesNYC web site and its FAQs got us the address of its main office and some bad news.

"The office is closed already," said Matt. "And they'll stay closed until Monday morning. No Sunday hours."

"Let me see. Maybe if the site lists the proprietors' names we can look up their home addresses in the phone listings. One of them might be listed publicly."

I took the PDA and jumped around the site a little. "Bingo!"

"You get some names?"

"No. Even better. Look, a seminar is being held to-night." I glanced at my watch. "It's starting now. We have to get downtown. If we grab a cab, we can walk right in."

"A seminar? What sort of seminar?" Matt called. I was already moving through the crowd and into the street, rais-ing my right arm high.

"Some sort of dating guru seminar thing," I yelled over my shoulder. "It's held once a month at the big auditorium at the New School. Taxi!"

We caught a cab and drove down to the corner of the Ave-nue of the Americas and Twelfth Street, then walked half a block to the New School of Social Research at 66 West Twelfth.

As we talked over our final plans, we walked by a build-ing under renovation. Matteo stopped dead in front of a shocking poster plastered to a plywood construction barri-cade.

The huge poster displayed an image of a woman's naked torso, her breasts shaded by the discrete placement of an arm. Bold black lines had been drawn all over her flesh as if she were a cow, the lines delineating various cuts of meat—shoulder, loin, ribs, chops, shank, etc.

"Jesus, I hope this isn't an advertisement for the dating seminar we're going to," said Matteo. "I heard it was a meat market out there, but I never took the term quite so literally."

"Very funny."

I glanced at the poster and saw it had nothing to do with the SinglesNYC site seminar. It was advertising a Meat No More charity lingerie show at the Puck Building later to-night. I shuddered, remembering Brooks Newman and his "genius" scheme as the new director of fundraising for that vegan group. It looked like he'd pulled it off.

I wasn't sharing my recognition with Matt, however, because I wasn't all that keen on conveying how Newman had turned our innocent little Cappuccino Night playgroup into a play*grope*.

"Let's go," I said.

The foyer to the New School's main building was busy and brightly lit. I approached the information desk, where a bored student tried to study his notes despite constant interruptions.

"Excuse me," I said. "I'm looking for—"

"SinglesNYC? End of the hall, turn right, and go to the tables for registration. Look for the 'Pull the Plug' sign."

Did I look that desperate? Or was it simply assumed that every single woman in New York City was man-hungry and on the make?

The seminar was already underway, so there were no lines at the registration table. On a stand was a large placard that read PULL THE PLUG with a cartoon of a trendy couples kissing over a computer tossed into a garbage can.

"Are you a registered member of SinglesNYC? If you are, there's a thirty percent discount to hear Trent and Granger," said a perky young woman wearing muddy brown lipstick and a short matching dress with a neckline even lower than the one I'd worn for Bruce.

"No," said Matteo. "We're not registered members."

"Yes, actually," I admitted.

Matteo looked at me in stunned surprise. "You *have* been busy while I was away."

I ignored Matteo and gave the woman my e-mail address and she cross-checked it on a laptop. I felt like grabbing the computer and fleeing into the night, certain that all the information I needed was imprinted inside of that little machine's drive. But nothing in life is that easy, and I'd probably get caught halfway down the block with the heels I was wearing.

"Clare Cosi? Welcome to 'Pull the Plug: Freeing Yourself from the Mouse,'" she said, handing me a brochure.
"That will be forty dollars."

I sighed.

Here I stood in the hallways of the New School, a haven
for academics and literati since World War I, the 1930s East
Coast nexus for intellectuals and scientists fleeing the Nazis.
Within this school's sphere, luminaries such as William Sty-
ron, Edward Albee, Robert Frost, Arthur Miller, and Joyce
Carol Oates had taught or lectured, along with cranky, con-
troversial iconoclasts like psychologist Wilhelm Reich and
psychedelic guru Timothy Leary.

And what amazing lecture was I about to hear? "Trent"
and "Granger" talking about how to pick up the opposite
sex without the crutch of a Web site.

I paid cash.

Low-neckline Girl turned to Matteo and asked if he
wanted to register as well. My ex didn't answer immediately—the woman's cleavage and full lips had momentarily distracted him.

Luckily, my elbow to his ribs solved this dilemma.

The auditorium was large enough for a thousand people,
but less than two hundred were crowded together in the
first ten or twelve rows, over two-thirds of them female. Almost all the audience members looked to be over thirty and
under fifty.

As we found seats close to the stage, Matteo complained incessantly that he had to pay sixty dollars to gain
admission.

"You could feed a Kenyan family for six months on
sixty bucks."

"Hush and you might learn something."

He shot me a look that said "I doubt it," but he shut up
for the moment.

On stage was a tall man with dark, floppy, Hugh Grant

hair and thin lips. He wore a tight black shirt, open at the neck, black slacks, and a charcoal gray Italian silk jacket. He moved with confidence, and as he spoke he drifted back and forth across the stage, addressing audience members as if they were the focus of his lecture.

"So far we've covered the rules of engagement and how important they are," he said into a microphone. "And how those vitally important rules get trashed in most on-line hook-ups. Now we all remember rule number one, right?"

The man next to him—shorter and a little stout, with tiny dark-rimmed glasses and a round face—hit the button on his power pointer and a phrase appeared on a large blank screen behind them. On cue, the audience read along like it was karaoke night.

"Not all of the Creator's children are beautiful," the audience chanted.

"And rule number two?" Matteo whispered. "These guys are total grifters."

"So how do you know if they're hot or not," continued the man on stage, "if you don't meet them in the flesh? Is she a Monica or a Hillary? Is he Prince Andrew or Homer Simpson? The dirty little secret is that you'll never know if you meet them in a chat room. But you *will* know if you meet them *in the flesh*."

He emphasized the last words with what he thought was an erotic thrust of his pelvis—but this guy was no Elvis. Beside me, Matteo let out a disgusted sigh.

"That's why I'm here. My name's Trent. And this money dude right next to me is Granger. Granger and I have sacrificed our Saturday night to provide you with a guaranteed map through the minefield of real-time, face-to-face hook-ups."

Trent stepped closer to the edge of the stage and lowered his voice an octave.

"Ladies and gentlemen, we call it dating without the

Net—it's real, it's risky, but the rewards are well worth the hassles. I'm asking you to try, at least for a little while, pulling the plug on that computer. Douse that mouse. Be the player with all the right cards in your hand and you'll come up a winner every time—and find a better love life than you ever dreamed possible."

"I can't believe this," Matteo complained in my ear. "They're teaching supposedly urbane, sophisticated, well-educated New Yorkers how to hook up with the opposite sex? Some of us figured that one out in high school."

"You figured it out in the sixth grade," I whispered.

Matteo frowned. "I told you about Maggie?"

A thirty-something woman in the row in front of us turned, and I'm pretty sure she intended to shush us. But when she laid eyes on my ex, her resolve seemed to weaken—as well as her knees. She glanced flirtatiously at Matt, then gave me a nasty look.

"He's all yours, honey," I murmured.

Matt glanced at me, and we both laughed.

"In the next hour, we're going to look at the right places to find a perfect match," purred Trent. "It's like The Donald says—location, location, location—and you'd be amazed at how many people get it wrong.

"Are you looking for a disco diva? Don't try to score at the Natural History Museum. Got a clandestine office romance going? Don't take her to the boss's country club for dinner. Looking for hot, delicious, no-commitment sex? Don't cruise church groups! Remember rule number seven."

Granger activated the power pointer and the audience chanted along.

"When looking for a love location, *destination is destiny.*"

"I'm going to puke," Matteo groaned in my ear.

"Just don't do it on me," I warned him.

"We're going to take a twenty-minute break before part two of this seminar begins," Trent announced. "Don't forget to take a brochure, and I suggest all you latecomers chat up a few of the early birds to catch up on what you missed—and you might even make a connection . . ."

The stage went dark and the audience rose and stretched, murmuring among themselves.

"Let's go," said Matt, grabbing my hand. He practically dragged me down the aisle, rudely pushing his way through the crowd as we moved against the flow of traffic. I apologized to the folks my ex shoved aside, until the way to the stage was finally clear.

"Matt, what's gotten into you?"

Matteo's face was set in harsh lines as he surged forward.

"Quiet," he said. "Just getting into character."

One of the stage hands moved to block our path, but he was just a slender college kid with a backward baseball cap. Matteo pushed right past him and charged onto the stage. Trent and Granger were sitting there, fiddling with the power pointer. Matt walked right up to them and roared in a suitably angry and combative voice.

"My underage daughter registered with your site and has dated a number of middle-aged men. Some of her friends did the same thing. She's just a teenager! She's in junior high for God's sake! I want to know the names of the men she and her friends have gone out with or I'm going to the police."

Granger shrank back fearfully as Matteo's tanned and muscular form stood over him, fists clenched, a vein throbbing in his temple.

Trent, on the other hand, remained cool. I watched him glance out at the auditorium, where heads turned and necks craned to hear more.

Frankly, I had to hand it to Trent. Matteo was always a

pretty intimidating presence, but when he was angry, he was a force of nature—a lot of men would have become sniveling idiots in the face of Matt's fury, calling for security or running. But Trent didn't.

He faced Matteo and, with a forced smile, gamely tried to handle him, and the situation, professionally. "Listen, calm down, Mr.—?"

"Allegro."

"Mr. Allegro, this isn't the time or place. Come to my office Monday and—"

"My daughter and her friends are out on dates right now. By Monday I'll have you arrested for facilitating the corruption of a minor!" yelled Matteo.

More heads turned. People who had started wandering toward the auditorium's exit doors for a smoke or restroom break suddenly decided to loiter in the aisle, eavesdropping.

"Come with me," said Trent, leading Matteo and me to a small waiting room behind the stage. On his way out, Trent ordered Granger to fetch one of the laptops from the registration desk.

Pay dirt!

We sat down in steel folding chairs while Trent apologized repeatedly.

"We've never had this happen before," he said. "We're proud of our screening process and will cooperate with you and your wife in any way we can."

Granger arrived with Low-neckline Girl in tow. She carried the black laptop like a serving tray. I tried not to remember Torquemada's offerings.

"Our entire database can be accessed by this wireless remote system," Trent began. He keyed in a password and looked up at Matteo.

"So what do you need to know?"

Matt gestured to me. "My wife will tell you."

"Let's start with my daughter's best friend, Valerie

Lathem," I lied. "She was sharing names with my daughter, we understand."

Trent typed in Valerie's name.

"This account isn't very active. Valerie hasn't visited our site since October. She made a total of six dates through our registry."

"Who?" I'd already pulled out a small notepad and had my pencil poised.

"Jack Wormser, Parnell Jefferson, Raymond Silverman, Dr. Anthony Fazio, Julio Jones, and Brooks Newman."

Brooks Newman? I thought. That was interesting.

"Nobody named Bowman?" Matteo asked.

Trent shook his head.

Of course, Bruce wasn't going to be there—I knew that. Valerie had met Bruce through her job, not through this site.

"Our daughter's other friend is Inga Berg," I quickly continued.

Trent's fingers flew across the keyboard.

"Ms. Berg has been busy . . . very busy. There are dozens of dates here since August." He looked up at Matt. "Here's the name you mentioned, though: Bowman. Bruce Bowman of Leroy Street in the Village. He definitely dated Inga."

"We're looking for the names of the men she last—uh, most recently dated," I said. "The last two weeks you have on file for her should do."

"Inga's account hasn't been active lately, either. Her latest hook-ups were Bowman, and also Eric Snyder, Ivan Petravich, Gerome Walker, Raj Vaswani, and Brooks Newman."

I blinked. *Brooks Newman.* Mr. No Way. Mr. Three Days Vegan. Mr. Meat No More Lingerie Show. Mr. Serial Seducer with a Peter Pan Syndrome.

Yes, I could believe he was a serial killer of women, too.

Newman's attitude toward the opposite sex was close to misogyny—although if you asked him, Brooks would probably proclaim that he absolutely adored women, for their bodies, anyway.

"Mr. Newman is one of the men who's been leaving messages for our daughter," I lied. "Any other hook-ups on file for him?"

Trent glanced at the screen.

"Nothing in the last ten days . . . guess he's been busy at work. But Mr. Newman has put two client profiles in his personal basket—that's a cyber space for members to store the profiles of people they are interested in hooking up with in the future."

"Who are they?" I asked.

"Ms. Sahara McNeil, and Ms. Joy Allegro, that's your daughter, right?"

The confirmation that Brooks had put Sahara in his basket was less of an impact on me than the mention of my daughter's name. I closed my eyes. "Oh, my god, Joy!"

Suddenly, a number of unconnected facts linked up in my brain to form a blood-red flag. It waved in front of me now in dire warning.

"Come with me!" I cried, grabbing Matteo's hand.

"But—"

"Come on!"

Matteo got up, leaving Granger and Trent totally confused.

"Hey, what's going on?" Trent demanded.

"You'll . . . you'll hear from our lawyer," Matteo cried, still in character, as I dragged him away.

I practically ran down the aisle, past the registration desk, and outside. Matteo hurried to catch up to me.

"Clare, what's the matter?"

I ran down the block, until I reached the boarded-up building.

"Oh god," I cried when I looked again at the Meat No More poster.

"Clare, talk to me!" Matt demanded.

"It's Brooks Newman!" I cried. "He's the one who's been killing these women. I'm sure of it now. He dated Valerie, he dated Inga, and he'd obviously hooked up with Sahara at Cappuccino Connection night—her on-line profile in his web basket just confirms his interest in her . . . And now he's after Joy."

"Don't worry," said Matteo. "He'll never get near our daughter."

"She's with him right now!"

"What?"

"The poster." I slapped the board. "This is advertising the Meat No More Lingerie Show, it's at the Puck Building tonight—it's starting right now!"

"So?"

"So Joy told me she's catering a vegetarian party at the Puck Building tonight. This is it, Matt. She's there. Our daughter is with Brooks Newman right now!"

Twenty-two

~~~~~~

"Hi! You've reached Joy Allegro. I can't pick up my cell right now. I'm either in class or trying to keep a French sauce from separating. Either way, leave a message!"

Sitting next to Matt in the back of the cab, I exhaled in frustration. Waited for the beep.

"Joy, this is Mom, call my cell the second you get this message. I don't want to alarm you, but I want you to make sure you stay away from Brooks Newman. If he should bother you in any way, go to your teacher at once. Don't get caught alone anywhere, stay with your teacher. Be careful and just wait at the Puck Building for me and your dad. We're coming to pick you up and make sure you get home okay. I'm not kidding, Joy. Call me as soon as you get this message and I'll try to—"

Beep!

"Shit!"

"Take it easy, Clare, it won't help Joy to go bananas. Keep a cool head."

"I know. Okay. I'll try."

I hated this feeling, and it wasn't just the fact that Brooks Newman had killed at least three women and had targeted Joy, I couldn't shake the feeling that Joy was in danger. Call it a mother's intuition, but this nagging dark feeling that my daughter needed me had been running through me since we'd entered the New School auditorium.

I tried Joy's apartment, but I'd just gotten her home machine. Not even her roommate was around tonight to answer.

"Try the coffeehouse," suggested Matt.

The phone picked up after five rings.

"Village Blend. Hello." It was Esther Best's voice.

"Esther, this is Clare—"

"It's Clare!" called Esther, obviously yelling it to someone nearby.

"Esther!" I yelled. "Esther!"

A second later, Esther came back on. "Are you coming back anytime tonight? That's what Tucker wants to know. It's pretty busy here."

"Esther, listen to me, you two will have to hold down the fort a little longer, okay? I'm calling because I need to find Joy as soon as possible. It's an emergency."

"Oh, wow. Well, she's not here. She was. But she left with some guy."

"What guy?"

"He was an NYU student. Hot, too. Had short blonde hair and a goatee. I actually think I've seen him around school. Buffed dude with combat pants and a peacoat. She said he saved her life on Seventh Avenue South."

"What! What do you mean he saved Joy's life?"

"What!" cried Matt beside me. "Clare, what's going on?"

"Shhhh! Stay calm," I told my ex-husband. "Esther, what happened?"

"Oh, Joy said there was this big drunken crowd in front of a bar on Seventh Avenue and she got shoved off the curb in front of an oncoming bus."

"Jesus." I closed my eyes.

"She's okay, though," Esther continued, "because this NYU guy sort of flirted with her for a second before it happened, so he was watching her when she went over the curb. He lunged forward and grabbed her by the hood of her new coat. Nice coat, too. That hood and that dude really saved her life. But she was pretty freaked out about it, so he brought her back here, and she told me and Tucker about it. Then they had some coffee and were laughing, and then she said the guy was gonna make sure she got to the Puck Building for her catering thing okay, and they left. That's all I know."

I nodded, my eyes meeting Matteo's. I put my hand over the cell's mouthpiece.

"It's okay. Joy's okay. Some boy escorted her to the Puck Building."

"*What* boy?" Matt's jaw clenched.

"A nice college kid, according to Esther. Take it easy."

But he didn't. Instead, he leaned forward, poked his head through the plastic partition in the cab, and yelled, "Get this damn cab moving faster. Now!"

The cabbie threw a disgusted look over his shoulder at Matt, muttered something in Russian, then returned his attention to the road, without increasing his leisurely speed one iota.

I sighed. Sometimes Matt didn't act like he remembered a thing about living in New York City.

"There's an extra ten in it for you," I called sweetly.

The cabbie immediately put the pedal to the metal. As we zoomed down Broadway, I punched a stored number on my speed dial.

"Who are you calling now?" asked Matt.

"Mike Quinn's cell." But he didn't answer. I got his voice mail. "Mike, this is Clare," I said the second I heard the beep. "Meet me as soon as you possibly can at the Puck Building. It's an emergency. I'm certain I've found the killer of Valerie Lathem, Inga Berg, and Sahara McNeil, and right now I'm worried he's after Joy—"

The beep blared in one ear as a curse sounded in the other. Matteo was reacting to the jam just up ahead. After turning onto West Houston, the cab had slowed to a crawl, then came to a dead stop.

"Matt, I don't think we have to worry. It's not like Brooks is going to do anything to Joy right there, in public. She's okay, I'm sure of it," I lied. Matt was steaming, and I didn't want him to blow.

The cab lurched forward, then stopped again. The traffic signal had suddenly turned red. Matteo cursed.

Traffic in New York can be as dicey as a freak storm, and, like unpredictable weather patterns, New York traffic has a way of changing when you least expect it—and, for me, usually at the least opportune moment.

"Sum-zing iz goin on," grunted our middle-aged Russian driver.

Indeed there was. The intersection of Houston and Lafayette, where West Houston becomes East Houston, was a roach nest of crawling black limousines all trying to scurry to the same place at the same time.

"Do you think those limos are going to the Puck Building?" I asked.

"I don't think they're flocking to the sale at Dean and DeLuca," Matt replied.

"At eight fifty for a jar of pasta sauce, I doubt there's ever a sale at Dean and DeLuca."

"My point exactly."

We waited as the traffic light went from green to yellow to red. The cab never moved. Matt's leg began pumping like a piston, and I knew from experience that the explosion was coming.

"Come on," I said, popping the door to release the pressure. "It's only two blocks away."

Matt climbed out and I tossed the driver my last twenty.

As we walked down West Houston we got a better look at the passengers of all those limousines.

"This thing is black tie, and invitation only," I said. "How are we going to get inside there and find Joy?"

"The same way we saw Trent and Granger," said Matt, striding forward.

"No, Matt, listen—" I tugged his arm. "This isn't a public seminar. We can't just walk in. Since 9/11, security at these sorts of things is tighter than ever, especially when celebrities, politicians, and media people are attending. We could give any song and dance we wanted to the people at the door about Joy or anything else, but unless we have real credentials, or an official invitation, they'll call security and boot us out."

"What do we do then? I'm not waiting around for that flatfoot."

"I could try Mike's cell again, but if he isn't picking up it's probably because he's in the middle of something. And Joy's cell is probably in her bag, which is in a locker or back room while she's working."

"Well, if you're out of ideas, I'm going to take my chances with shouting my way into this thing."

"Matt, it won't work."

Just then, I heard a young woman's voice, loud and vacuous, and right in front of us.

"Oh," she giggled on the sidewalk to a passerby. "It's not an *F* at all. It's really a *P!* I *thought* that was a funny name for a building."

I turned to see a tall, reed-thin blonde with long straight hair and enough black eyeliner to please an Egyptian pharaoh wobbling on super high heels. Though she was wearing an overcoat, her naked legs and strappy shoes looked totally inappropriate for a cold late autumn night.

The passerby, a Hispanic man in a delivery uniform, eyed her with a mixture of interest and bemusement. Then her wide blue eyes met mine and I smiled sweetly.

"Do you need help?" I asked. She looked at me and Matteo at my side and nodded enthusiastically.

"I just got out of a cab and walked two blocks. I'm looking for the Puck Building," she said breathlessly.

"That's where we're going. It's just up the street," said Matteo. "Are you a model?"

"Yeah," the girl said, pushing hair away from her face and offering us a profile.

"Him, too," I decided.

Surprised, Matt opened his mouth to speak. I elbowed him before he could utter a sound.

"Yes," I continued. "Brooks Newman hired Fuego here to model some skimpy little thing."

"Fuego!" Matt cried.

I elbowed him again. "I'm Fuego's agent. My name is Clare."

"Pleased to meet you, Clare. And you too, Fuego," said the woman. "I'm Tandi Page. That's Tandi, with an *I*. My agent told me to make sure people always got my name right."

"Did Brooks get your name right?" I asked.

"Hah! I don't think he even noticed my *name*."

We reached Lafayette and the Puck Building loomed over us. I always thought of this place as a sort of whimsical structure, and not just because of its origins. Named after an irreverent satirical magazine that had its headquarters here, the building still boasted glided statues of Shakespeare's Puck, the weaver of dreams from the play *A Midsummer Night's Dream,* complete with top hat.

The Puck's architectural style actually felt whimsical, too. It was a Chicago School steel-framed structure with horizontal bands of arched windows that admitted a vast amount of sunlight. Its skillful use of a cheerful thin-line red brick combined with sober green trim presented a delightful combination of impressions—not unlike reading the comedies of Shakespeare. While on the one hand you could see the lightness and the grace of its simplicity, on the other you could feel its underlying strength and permanence.

Originally, the entrance to the building was on Houston, but a century ago, *Puck*'s editors so angered the corrupt politicians of Tammany Hall that they zoned part of the building out of existence to create Lafayette Street. After the partial demolition, the building grew like a phoenix from its fractioned ashes, sprouting additional floors and an opulent new entrance foyer on Lafayette.

At the moment, I was standing outside that foyer, looking up at a gilded, top-hatted Puck who seemed to be laughing at the foolish mortals entering his building—men in evening suits and women in opulent gowns, all of them impatiently jamming the doorway, their limousines clogging the streets around them. The building itself, a city block large, was ablaze with light, its tall windows casting a golden glow on Houston, Lafayette, Mulberry, and Jersey Streets.

Tandi drew a letter from her tiny purse. "I think we're supposed to go to the Jersey Street employee entrance."

We dodged the crowd and circled the building. There was also something of a crowd at the Jersey Street entrance, which was lorded over by a portly man in a black suit, black shirt, red bowtie, and conspicuous bright red socks.

"Hi, Trevor," Tandi warbled.

"Tandi, you made it," the man cried. "The other girls are already inside. Go dish, girl."

Tandi waved goodbye.

"Good luck, Fuego," she squeaked. Then she catwalked through the door and out of sight.

"Can I help you?" the man asked, batting his eyes.

"We're here to model," I said.

He examined me and his eyebrow went up. "Surely not."

"Not *me,* my client, Fuego." I pushed Matteo forward like an offering.

"Not bad," the man said appraisingly. "Where's your contract and letter?"

"My what?"

He thrust his hand out. There was a ring on each finger, but tastefully he'd skipped his thumb.

"Your contract?"

"Brooks Newman said he would send it over by messenger but it never arrived," I lied, impressing myself with how good I was getting at dissembling. "Brooks only saw Fuego a few days ago. Said he'd be perfect for tonight's event."

"So Brooks is shopping for rough trade these days?"

He looked Matteo up and down as if he were a racehorse.

"A little long in the tooth but not bad," the man snorted. Then he folded his arms.

"But you have to have a letter to get in here, sweetie. I've got J. Lo in there. I can't just let every Tom, Dick, and . . . Fuego in, you know."

"Brooks *did* give me his card," I said, fumbling through my wallet, praying I hadn't thrown it away since our dinner at Coffee Shop.

"Here it is!" I thrust it into the man's hand.

"Okay," he relented. "But you're lucky we have more thongs than the buns to fill them or I'd send Fuego back to the meat packing district."

He stood aside and Matteo and I stepped forward. Then his hand shot out and stopped me.

"Where are you going, sister?"

"With my client, I—"

"He's modeling. You're not."

"But Fuego . . . He doesn't speak a word of English," I stammered. "He's very obedient. Does whatever I tell him. But I have to tell him what to do because . . . well, just between you and I, Fuego is pretty but a little dense."

The man's round face broke into a grin.

"Oh, I love that in a man! Go on then, honey, and good luck."

"A little dense," Matteo hissed after we got inside.

"I also said you were pretty."

Just then, a lean, muscular young man with no visible body hair strode by wearing a leather codpiece and a string holding it up—and nothing else.

"You'd better be pretty, if you want to compete with that." Matteo snorted.

"The dressing room is this way," cried a scrawny man. He held a hair dryer and was waving us forward with it. Behind him, the room was full of nubile young bodies in various states of undress. There was no privacy, and models of both sexes were changing into their outfits together.

"This might not be so bad after all," said Matteo, grinning.

"Break a leg. Once you're changed, you should be able to move around freely and look for Joy. I'm going to try to find the kitchen."

It took me ten minutes to locate the damn thing. Between banks of steel refrigerators and an expansive range, dozens of cooks in white coats were preparing trays of elaborate canapés—all vegan.

"Excuse me," I said to a man who was checking the trays as they left the kitchen. "I'm looking for a young woman working with one of the caterers. Joy Allegro? I was supposed to meet her here."

"Not here, upstairs," the man replied. "We're the Puck

caterers. The private caterers are working the Skylight Room upstairs. Are you one of the wait staff?"

"Why . . . uh . . . Yes."

Since I wasn't dressed as a guest for a formal function, I figured it was the only answer I could give. Telling him anything else might have just gotten me thrown out—and I couldn't risk it. Besides, the Skylight Room sounded exclusive, but posing as a waitress would certainly get me right in.

"Thank goodness!" he said. "The boss told me if one or two of the no-shows didn't get here soon I'd have to send one of my own staff up there to fill in."

"Well, here I am!" I chirped. This was perfect. I'd worked for a caterer part-time in Jersey, so this act was sure to be a breeze.

"Yeah, none of my girls wanted to wear the outfits."

My blood froze. "Outfits?"

"You can change in here, but hurry," the man said, opening a locker room. "Victoria's Secret contributed this stuff for the event, so you'll probably find something that fits. Let me know when you're done and I'll take you upstairs."

I hesitated and I guess he saw the dread on my face. "Oh, don't worry. It's not underwear you'll be wearing."

"Thank goodness."

"More like a flimsy nightgown kind of thing."

Twenty-Three

∽∿∽∿∽∿∽∿∽∿∽∿∽∿∽∿∽∿∽∿∽∿∽∿∽∿∽∿∽

I emerged from the dressing room ten minutes later wearing red mules and a silky floor-length nightgown with a low but not grossly immodest neckline. The design was a pink floral pattern with tiny red roses sewn around the neckline, and the material itself was clingy, accenting my curves. Still, it was awfully thin material and downright drafty. Okay, I admit, it looked quite elegant, and I might have loved wearing it, too, if I were at *home,* in my *bedroom.*

The chef returned. I suppressed the urge to cover myself.

"The service elevator is taking more cases of beverages upstairs. It'll take some time, so just go through the main ballroom and use the elevator up front."

"What? Through the main ballroom? Like this?"

"You've got nothing to be ashamed of—"

Oh, good god.

"Besides, compared to the women out there serving drinks, you're dressed modestly. Anyway, there are two hundred people in the Skylight Room who are going to see you in that getup, so you might as well get used to it. There are a lot of celebrities upstairs, too, so don't lose your cool."

He pushed the kitchen door open. "Right through the middle of the room to the door on your right, then up the elevator to the top. Speak to Ellie at the bar up there, and she'll get you a serving tray."

I didn't want to do it, but it was the only way to get to Joy. So, after a deep breath, I took the plunge.

The floor of the brilliantly illuminated main ballroom was jammed with elegant partygoers drifting gracefully between the columns to the strains of harp music, the men in black tie, the women in floor-length gowns or skimpy haute couture. Jewels dripped from throats and sparkled on ears and fingers. Even the lingerie models who drifted across the hardwood floor serving refreshments looked somehow in character with the décor, like delicately flitting fairies in a Victorian painting.

Only two things ruined the picture perfection of the scene.

Hanging from the main ballroom's sixteen-foot ceilings were huge, bloody sides of beef, shanks of lamb, whole, gutted suckling pigs, and hundreds of dead chickens. Though it didn't take me long to figure out that, mercifully, all the animals and animal parts were fake—rubber chickens, luridly painted plaster of Paris shanks, etc.—the message was far from subtle.

"A little much, don't you think, Brooks?" I muttered, frowning at the collection of fake dead fowl.

The second disturbing element was the beautiful couple posing on pedestals near the ballroom entrance across the room. They were two of the most perfect physical specimens I'd ever seen. The man wore nothing more than a Speedo, the woman a thong and skimpy bikini top. Their muscles were toned and tight, their flesh smooth and healthy—and divided by bold black ink into their various cuts of meat, just like the poster for this event.

I got about halfway across the ballroom when I heard a woman's voice slurring a familiar name.

"Oh, Maah-Teyyy-Oooooh."

I turned to find Matteo, wearing velvet slippers, silk boxers, a look of stunned terror—and nothing else. He was obviously rushing to get my attention when an older woman had intercepted him, her spidery arm locking itself around my ex-husband's bicep.

I recognized her at once. It was Daphne Devonshire.

Well, well, well, Daphne, whaddya know.

The last time I saw Madame's friend, she was a well-preserved glamour queen who had gotten into the habit of luring my husband to a seaside love nest in Jamaica. But that was almost fifteen years ago and those years had not been kind. Daphne's once classic features now appeared frozen in a plastic surgery and Botox-induced death mask. Her skin, once tanned and healthy, took on the sallow look of a heavy drinker and excessive smoker. Worst of all, her lycra, strapless number was far from figure flattering. Daphne still looked shapely, but that gown was made for a twenty-five-year-old built like Pamela Anderson—not a woman in her late sixties.

"Matteo, darling! It's so wonderful to see you," Daphne cried, air kissing him. Her arm never loosed its iron lock around his bicep. As she talked she spilled some of her drink. "Remember what I used to sing to you down in Jamaica, *mahn?*"

Now she was affecting a Jamaican accent, a really bad Jamaican accent.

"Maah-Teyyy-Oooooh, Maah-tey-eh-eh-Oooooh. Daylight's gone and you're comin' to me home . . ."

Matt looked at me with desperation. His eyes were imploring.

"Joy's upstairs," I told him. "I'll see you up there." Then I blew him a kiss and moved on, leaving Matteo to extract himself from his ex-lovebird's death grip all by his little old self.

I hadn't gone far when I heard a familiar female voice call my name.

"Clare, my dear, that's quite a daring outfit, though I must admit you carry it off well."

I turned to find Madame, my ex-mother-in-law and owner of the Blend, standing in front of me. She was arm in elegant arm with a "special friend" she'd met a few months ago, Dr. Grey Temples—a.k.a. oncologist Gary McTavish.

Standing there, feeling half naked, I think I may have blushed.

"You remember Dr. McTavish," Madame said, deftly covering my discomfort.

He smiled and took my hand. "You look stunning, my dear."

"Yes, she does," said Madame critically. "Though a little jewelry would have made her seem a little less . . . naked."

Madame gazed past me, searching. "Are you here with anyone in particular?"

I bit my tongue about the murders and Brooks Newman and my trying to get to Joy. I'd sound like a raving lunatic blurting it all out for one thing, and it would just waste more time for another. Neither was this the time or place to give Madame a heart attack over the safety of her granddaughter. I just needed to extract myself politely and get my drafty rear upstairs.

"Matteo," I replied quickly. "I'm here with Matt."

Madame's eyes lit up.

"That boy of mine," she said. "He's been back from Africa for days and hasn't visited me yet. Where is he?"

I glanced over my shoulder. "Well, I . . ."

Madame frowned when she looked around the room and found her son, still trapped with her old friend, Daphne Devonshire. (Really, an *ex*-friend ever since her fling with Matteo.)

"Oh, god, Clare," Madame said with a sad sigh. "Why did he ever get involved with *that* woman?"

"We weren't getting along. It was the early nineties. Rap was eclipsing New Wave . . ."

"He was using drugs!"

"That too."

Madame shook her head. "Cocaine is a terrible thing."

"Perhaps you should rescue him," I suggested, ready to bolt.

"Perhaps we should let him lie in the maid he's bedded. Perhaps—"

But Dr. McTavish took Madame's hand. "Perhaps we shall," he said, then led her across the floor and toward her son.

I reached the elevator to the Skylight Room without further incident. As I expected, the security person guarding the door saw my outfit and nodded, assuming I was part of the staff, and waved me on. I boarded the empty elevator and rode it upstairs.

When the doors slid open a handsome young sandy-haired man in black tie was standing in the hallway. He looked very familiar.

"Have a nice evening," he said as I stepped out of the elevator and he stepped in. The deep, resonant voice triggered my memory, and I realized I had just passed Pat Kiernan, Esther's and Joy's favorite morning anchor for New York's basic cable Channel 1.

I turned, but the doors had already closed. "Well, I sort of met him," I murmured, plowing ahead. "I'm sure Esther and Joy will be impressed."

Up ahead, loud voices and bursts of laughter poured through the wide open doors to the Skylight Room. I moved quickly into the throng and toward the bar. Someone was taking so many pictures that the flashes made it impossible to make out many faces.

"Ms. Cosi! Is that you?"

The shocked voice belonged to a young man standing near the bar, a classmate of Joy's named Ray Harding. He'd been by the Blend several times with Joy, so he knew me well, but poor Ray was used to seeing his classmate's mother in a giant blue apron, not a Victoria's Secret nightgown. He appeared embarrassed. *Well, kid, join the club.*

"Have you seen Joy?" I asked.

He nodded. "Come with me."

Ray led me out of the crush of people and into a back area that looked like a very large closet stacked with chairs and tables.

"I'm sorry to tell you that Joy had a really bad night."

"Is she okay? What happened?"

"She's fine. But she left. I understand that creep Brooks Newman made a pretty obnoxious pass at her. Pawed her up and everything. Amber told me all about it. She said Joy didn't want to cause any trouble for our teacher, so she just pretended she wasn't feeling well and left."

My fists clenched. "Where is she?"

"On her way to the Blend. She left twenty minutes ago."

"Where's Brooks Newman now?"

Ray frowned. "Back there, in the Skylight Room, sucking up to the high-end celebrity donors and sucking down vodka and tonics—a lot. I've been helping at the bar, and I've served him five so far."

Good, I thought. *That means he's not out on the street stalking Joy. All I had to do now was find Matteo and get back to the Blend—and never let Joy out of our sight until Quinn arrested Brooks Newman for murder.*

"How can I get out of here fast?"

"Not the guest elevators," said Ray. "Too many people using them. Folks have been complaining all night. Go through the kitchen and use the service elevator—" He pointed. "We just finished unloading some cases, and it's free right now. Should come right up for you."

Ray went back to the main room and I ducked into the kitchen. I pressed the button and waited for the service elevator to arrive. I heard a door open behind me and turned.

Brooks Newman was standing not ten feet away, and a little unsteadily.

"Hey, babe," he called, waving to me. "Need some help with a group. Come with me."

I turned my back on him, pretending I didn't hear.

Heavy footsteps fell behind me, then a strong hand gripped my arm.

"Hey, didn't you hear me? I said I need a waitress," Brooks said, pulling me around. His eyes took a second to focus. "Clare?"

"Let me go," I said.

But Newman was awake now. "You helping out your daughter again?"

"I said let me go."

Thank goodness, he did. But he didn't go away. "Nice outfit. You look hot, Clare. Really hot."

I heard the elevator rumbling in the shaft behind me. When was it going to arrive?

"Why don't you join me fer a drink?" he said, slurring his words a little.

"I've got to go," I said, backing away. "My date's downstairs, waiting."

"Let him wait," Brooks said, cornering me.

Whoever said vodka is undetectable is full of crap, because I could smell the alcohol on Brooks Newman's breath. Maybe I should have been afraid, but I wasn't. Unlike Joy, I knew what Brooks Newman was, so I wouldn't be such an easy victim.

The elevator gears squeaked as the car rolled even with the door.

"Don't go yet, Clare. Let's hook up for the night. I'll be done here in a little while."

"No, sorry," I said in a neutral voice.

That's when he lunged at me. His move was so sudden it had to have been uncalculated. Like a clumsy bear he pawed at me. I fought him off and lurched out of his grip just as the elevator doors slid open.

I got away on cue. Part of my gown didn't. With a tear, a considerable section of the flimsy material ripped away.

I screamed, trying to cover myself as a massive form shot out of the elevator, nearly bowling me over.

Then came a howl of pain, and a metallic clink.

Holding my gown in place, I turned to find Mike Quinn, legs braced. He held Brooks Newman in his grip. Newman's arms had been handcuffed behind his back and Quinn was bending them in such a way as to force Brooks to his knees.

"Are you okay?" Quinn asked over Brooks's outraged cries.

"Arrest him," I said levelly. "Brooks Newman killed those women. He met them through SinglesNYC. He slept with them, or tried to sleep with them, and then he murdered them."

"What?" Brooks Newman squealed. "I never killed anybody."

"Shut your mouth," Quinn warned.

Brooks Newman whimpered.

Suddenly Matteo burst into the kitchen.

"Clare!" he cried, racing to my side. "Are you all right? Where's Joy?"

"She's safe. She's on her way back to the Blend."

"Then she may not be safe," said Quinn.

"But you have the killer right there."

"Sorry, Clare. Brooks Newman is innocent. I came here because of your call, but I know Newman isn't guilty—not of murder anyway. I investigated him early on. He had a rock-solid alibi for the time of all three murders. But more importantly, I know who the killer is."

"Please, not Bruce Bowman," I said. "Not your theory about Bruce again."

"Not Bruce. His ex-wife, Maxine Bowman. When you called, I was on my way back from Westchester. I'd been interviewing a police detective up there as part of my background on Bruce Bowman. The detective was absolutely convinced Maxine Bowman had killed a young intern in Bruce's office about a year ago. He just couldn't prove it to the District Attorney's satisfaction.

"Seems one night this female intern went up to the roof of Bowman's building, where she worked, and subsequently plunged to her death. It was publicly ruled a suicide, but the detective discovered that the intern recently had begun dating Bruce Bowman, who had just separated from his wife. The victim's roommate claimed Maxine had started harassing and stalking the intern.

"Unfortunately, Maxine Bowman hired the best lawyers in Westchester County. They provided an alibi for Maxine, challenged the veracity of the roommate, who had a record of drug use, and privately pressured the DA into agreeing there wasn't enough evidence for a solid case. This detective still disagrees with that conclusion, but his hands were tied. As of now, the Westchester authorities have lost track of Maxine. We know she moved to New York City and is using another name. But she can't just vanish. We'll find her."

"Bruce's ex-wife." I closed my eyes. It did make sense, and the truth was, seeing all those raging e-mails from Vintage86 in Bruce's computer had disturbed me. But something in me just couldn't equate a woman spurned with serial murder. After all, I'd been spurned myself, I'd felt that consuming rage, that devastating pain, but I'd never acted on it, never tried to physically hurt anyone. I'd assumed Bruce's ex-wife wouldn't, either. Maxine must have gone off the deep end.

"I knew Bruce was the key in some way, Clare," said Quinn. "Even if it wasn't Bruce Bowman himself, then it had to be someone close to him."

I shook my head. "I thought you were trying to get Bruce."

"I don't try to get anyone. I try to get evidence. And I thought he was a strong suspect."

"I'm not a suspect," Brooks said. "I didn't do anything!"

"We're not talking about you," barked Quinn.

"Then let me go," Brooks cried.

"I'm booking you for sexual assault," said Quinn.

"Against who?" Matteo demanded.

"Against me," I said, still holding together my torn nightgown.

Matteo seemed to notice this for the first time. Not too surprising, since there wasn't a whole lot to this nightgown in the first place. He turned to Brooks. "You son of a bitch. If you weren't in cuffs I'd punch you in the face."

"Matt, you don't know the half of it. He made a pass at Joy, too."

"I'll kill him."

"Calm down, Pool Boy," Quinn said, blocking Matt's reach. "We have other issues. I talked to Esther Best back at your store and she told me about Joy's little shove off the curb and into the path of an M20 bus. I doubt very much that what happened was an accident—Maxine Bowman is a pusher. I'm betting she tried to kill Joy."

"Try your cell!" I told Matteo.

He spread out his arms. "Like I have a place to carry a cell phone."

"Here," said Quinn. "Use mine."

I dialed the Blend. Esther answered. "Esther! Is Joy there?"

"She just got here."

"Don't let her out of your sight! Tell her to stay put. We'll be right there!"

"What's the meaning of this!" an outraged voice bellowed.

A portly bald man in evening clothes hurried across the kitchen. "What are you doing to my client?"

"Jerry, thank God!" Brooks Newman cried. "Get me out of this. Now!"

Quinn flashed his badge and the portly man calmed a little.

"I'm Jerry Benjamin, Mr. Newman's attorney. Are you going to charge my client with a crime?"

Quinn looked at me.

"We don't have time for this," I said.

Quinn shook his head. Then he stood Brooks Newman up and unlocked the handcuffs.

"That's better," Brooks said, rubbing his wrists. "Why I ought to charge you with police brutality!"

He was so angry at Mike Quinn that he never even saw Matteo's fist coming.

Twenty-Four
〜〜〜〜〜〜〜〜〜〜〜〜〜〜〜〜〜〜〜〜〜〜

BACK at the Village Blend, we found Joy safe and sound. After a round of hugs, Joy said she was really tired and wanted to go back to her apartment. I asked her to please consider staying over in the duplex upstairs, but she flatly refused.

She said her roommate was home now and she was eager to check her home machine and see if the young man she'd met earlier had called—they had a "date to talk" after she finished her work. I pointed out she could call him from upstairs, but she wanted her privacy—either that or the date was for the young man to stop by, too, and not just call. *Ah, youth.*

Well, I couldn't stop her from going, but it gave me a substantial amount of relief to watch her walk out the Village Blend's front door in the company of her father. If there was one thing Matteo Allegro could do without fault, it was protect his daughter.

And if there was one thing Mike Quinn could do, it was cuff a guilty party. He had identified the murderer, now all he had to do was locate her. After we parted at the Puck Building, he said he was off and running in an attempt to locate and arrest Bruce's wife.

I knew Maxine Bowman wouldn't be that hard to find— with driver's licenses, credit cards, social security numbers and the like, nobody could hide for long in this day and age, even if she was going by another name. And, of course, Bruce could help locate her, too. Even if he didn't know the woman's exact address, he could probably help Quinn set up some sort of trap.

A few feet away from me, behind the coffee bar counter, Tucker looked completely exhausted. After pulling a double shift, I hated asking him to stay a little longer but I didn't want to be here alone, and Matt said he was coming right back.

When the store's phone rang behind me, I quickly picked it up.

"Village Blend."

"Clare? Clare, is that you? Thank God." It was Bruce. His deep, warm voice resonated in my ear, feeling more like a touch than a sound.

"I am so happy to hear your voice," I told him. It felt like a year had passed since I'd last seen him. "It's been one crazy day."

"Has it? I stopped in earlier and saw Joy but nobody seemed to know where you'd gone or when you'd be back. I was really starting to get worried."

"You don't have to worry. Everything's okay."

"I'm in lower Manhattan, in my SUV. I'll be there in ten minutes tops. Don't move."

Since he was on his way, I didn't bother trying to explain anything that had happened over the last two days. I'd probably need hours to do that anyway. Quinn would also need to be updated. I intended to call the detective after Bruce got here—and we had a few minutes privacy to say hello. Whether Bruce knew the location of his ex-wife or not, I was sure Quinn would want to question him.

"Don't worry," I told Bruce. "I'm about to close, and I'm not going anywhere. If you don't see me and the door is locked, I'm probably upstairs. Just call my cell and I'll come down."

I hung up and smiled brightly at Tucker, my energy renewed.

"Why are you so happy?" he asked.

"Bruce is the most amazing man, and I've fallen in love with him."

Tucker gave me a tired smile. "I'm glad for you, honey. Really glad."

"He's on his way up."

Tucker nodded. "I'll stay till he comes."

But I felt terrible making him wait. He looked ready to collapse. "You don't have to. I can see you're exhausted. Just help me shoo the last customers out and lock up. What can happen in less than ten minutes with me locked in here?"

Tucker nodded. "I am about ready to fall off my feet. You're sure?"

"Of course." And to be honest, I suddenly knew how my daughter felt, rushing back to her place for privacy with a new beau. I couldn't wait to be alone with Bruce again, so I could wrap my arms around his neck and just hold on.

In the next two minutes, Tucker and I politely shooed the last five customers out of the place. Then Tucker gathered his things and headed toward the front door.

"Are you sure, you're sure I should leave?" Tucker asked again.

"Positive!"

"Thanks, Clare. Good-night."

I locked the door and quickly began to clear the marble-topped tables of any stray debris, mostly crumpled napkins, crumbs, and paper cups. When I got to a table by the fireplace, I noticed a closed laptop computer.

"What a thing to leave behind . . ."

Curious, I flipped up the top. The machine's screen was blank. I hit the spacebar and it sprang to life. There were files on the desktop.

"Okay, who do you belong to?" I murmured, trying to find a name. I clicked on a folder that read "E-mail Back-ups." Inside were two more folders. Before I could read the folder names, I heard an insistent tapping at the front door.

"Winnie?" I called as I approached the door. It was Winnie Winslet, the Shearling Lady. "Can you open the door, Clare?" she called. "I'm so stupid—I left my laptop."

"Oh! So it's your laptop. I was wondering. Just a second."

The key was still in the lock, waiting for Bruce to arrive so I could easily turn it and let him in. I turned it now, for Winnie.

"Come on in."

I closed the door and led her back to the computer. As I approached the laptop, I was ready to apologize for snooping. My eyes strayed to the screen, ready to point and explain when I saw the names on the "E-mail Backups" folders: *Vintage86 Sent* and *Maxine's Incoming*.

I looked into Winnie's face.

"Is that your screen name?" I asked as steadily as I could manage. "Vintage86?"

"Yes. It is," she said.

"Winslet's your maiden name, isn't it?"

"Yes."

"And your married name was Bowman, wasn't it?"

The gun was drawn quickly. She'd been ready. The laptop was clearly a ploy to get back into the closed Blend.

"You're kidding yourself if you think Bruce cares about you," she said. "He doesn't. He's playing a sick little game behind your back, by the way—your daughter spent the night with him. I bet you don't know that."

"I spent the night with him, Maxine."

Winnie's superior, condescending mask momentarily fell. "What? You're lying. I saw Joy go in."

"You saw Joy's coat go in. That was me. What is 'Winnie' then, your cover? Did you change your name?"

"It's an old nickname, bitch, not that it's any of your business. Now let's get this over with fast. Turn around."

"No."

"Turn around. We're taking a walk." She cocked the gun. I looked into her eyes. She was ready to fire and we both knew it.

Bruce was coming. He'd be here very soon. Matteo was coming back, too. If I could just stall her . . .

"Okay," I said. "Okay . . . where do you want to go?"

"First to the front door. . . ."

She told me to lock the door. I turned the key back and forth, but I didn't actually lock the door. I locked and unlocked it. Clearly, she thought I had obeyed her.

"Let's go. To the stairs."

I tried to walk slowly, but she jammed the gun into my ribs and pushed. We climbed past the second floor and third, past my duplex door and all the way up to the highest landing of the service staircase. Before us stood the door to the roof.

On the way up I'd been careful to push each door all the way open. I had told Bruce I'd be upstairs, so if these stair doors were left open and my duplex door was locked, I prayed he'd follow the obvious lead and come up to the roof, which was clearly where we were headed.

"Unbolt the door."

I turned the heavy lock at the center of the roof door, retracting the thick bolts backward from the wall.

"Let's go," she barked, and we were out on the snowy roof, the door standing wide open behind us.

The wind was whipping off the river and it lashed my body with icy blasts. I shivered in the dark, stepped forward, and slipped, going down to my hands and knees. It wasn't an accident. I wanted to be down here. My hands closed on the layer of snow still there from the night before.

"You're going over, Clare. Let's go." She grabbed me by my hair and tugged.

"No!"

She pulled harder, forcing me toward the edge.

"You have two choices. Jump, and you might survive the four-story fall. Or I will shoot you dead and make it look like a smash-and-grab robbery. These idiot police won't do a thing. Believe me, there are no geniuses in law enforcement these days."

"Don't be too sure, Maxine," I said, shivering with pain and fear and cold and still trying to stall. "Detective Quinn already knows about the intern in Westchester."

Once again, Maxine's beautiful, confident face fell. "What? What does he *think* he knows? What? Tell me?"

"He knows you pushed that girl to her death. That it wasn't a suicide. He knows you pushed Valerie Lathem, too, at the Union Square subway. He knows you lured Inga Berg to the roof and somehow made her jump or pushed her off. He knows about Sahara McNeil. He knows about Joy, too, and for that I hope they light you up like a fireworks display—"

That's when I let her have it. I sent the icy snowball right into her face and stumbled to my feet. The snowball landed hard, smack on the plastic surgery perfect nose, between the high cheekbones, above the collagen lips.

"You bitch!" she screamed, but I was already lunging away from her and the edge of the roof.

She dove for my legs and I went down. Now we were both in the snow and struggling near the roof's edge. I felt her get on top of me, straddle me. I was kicking and screaming, then somewhere in the struggle I heard Bruce's cry—

"My God! No!"

He ran toward us, and then I felt the gun at the back of my head.

"I'll kill her," rasped Maxine, her voice high-pitched and crazed. "I'll shoot her, Bruce. I will. Then your little precious Clare's brains will be all over the nice white snow."

"No! Don't hurt her, Maxi. Don't. It's *me* you want to hurt. You know that. Come on, Maxine. Hurt *me*."

The gun moved away from my head for a moment. My god, I thought, what was she doing? Was she going to shoot Bruce?

"No!" I cried.

And then the gun was back, the cold barrel pressing against the base of my skull, and I knew I was dead.

A second later, I heard the explosion. The gun going off was like a cannon at my ear, but I wasn't shot. My ears were ringing painfully now, but the bullet had missed, and I could no longer feel Maxine's body straddling mine.

I was alone on the roof, and I realized Bruce had thrown his body at Maxi, knocking her off. The body slam had knocked the gun away from my head, but the momentum had carried them both a few feet beyond the edge of the roof.

I was very close to the edge myself. I looked down, into the alley behind the Blend, then closed my eyes. The image was one I'd have to live with for the rest of my life.

Bruce and Maxi were laying four stories down on the concrete, their still bodies in a terrible, twisted embrace.

Twenty-Five

MAXINE died almost instantly, her neck broken.

Bruce had survived with injuries to his spine and internal bleeding. He was rushed to St. Vincent's and, I was told, regained consciousness.

My friend, Dr. John Foo, a resident and a regular at the Blend, had been on duty in the emergency room when they'd rushed Bruce in. I remained in the waiting room, pacing. Matteo was there with me, sitting nearby. He stood up the moment Dr. Foo came out of the OR.

"How is he?" I asked.

Dr. Foo hesitated. "When Mr. Bowman regained consciousness, he asked the attending if you were okay. We told him you were fine and a short time after that we lost him . . . I'm sorry, Clare. We did what we could, but he let go. I'm so sorry. He's gone."

It's a terrible feeling to lose someone. Losing someone you had just fallen in love with—there aren't any words for that. None. I just felt myself falling—a hole, black and empty, was swallowing me up.

And then I was caught.

I don't remember much after that, just feeling Matt's arms around me, and hearing his voice saying over and over—

"I've got you, Clare. I've got you."

THE next day, I swore out my statement for the police. Quinn was very patient and more than kind. Within a week, he came by the Blend to spend some time with me, talking over the case at length.

Tucker brought a ten-cup thermos of Mocha Java to my office, then closed the door as he left and Quinn and I sat down.

He began by telling me that their search of Maxine's apartment revealed some expensive surveillance equipment, high-powered binoculars, and the same printer and personal stationery used to write the note to Inga. Her laptop revealed evidence that she'd hacked into Bruce's e-mail account. The police also found a folder on her laptop containing an extensive personal journal.

"The entries were rambling and full of wild rants. It was clear she'd been enraged by Bowman's decision to divorce her. She believed he'd been nothing before her and now that she'd 'molded' him into a man worth having around, some other woman was going to benefit and she couldn't let that happen. The first murder, the intern at Bowman's Westchester offices, had apparently been an escalation of a confrontation. When the push led to the woman's death, and the police ruled it a suicide, Maxine began the pattern, thinking herself a genius who was smarter than the 'idiot' police. You get the picture."

"I don't think I do, Mike . . . It's so hard to equate that

attractive, together woman with someone so out of control."

Quinn took a long sip of coffee. "The Right Man."

A shiver went through me, remembering what I'd labeled Bruce when I'd first met him. Was Quinn reverting to gallows humor? If he was, I wasn't laughing.

"Excuse me?" I said stiffly. "Do you mean 'Mr. Right'?"

"No, Clare. The Right Man is the term for a syndrome. It's a way of explaining, for example, what happens in domestic violence cases. A man sees himself as always right. He can seem completely charming to the world, and be totally in control in most every aspect of his life, but he'll choose to be out of control in one aspect—toward a wife, for example, beating her severely if he perceives she's made a fool of him in some way or disobeyed him or cheated, any one of which could be a fantasy perception on his part."

"You're saying Maxine had this syndrome?"

"I'd say it looks that way from everything we've learned. She was the Right Woman—a goddess of her world, dominant in the marriage, likely spoiled as a child, always right, used to having her way, yet, ironically, at the heart of it she harbored deep insecurities. That was clear from the writings in her laptop's journal, as well."

"Where did Bruce fit in then?"

"From what you've told us, Bruce looked up to her for years. And Right Men and Right Women often look for mates who are submissive and admiring because it fills them with a sense of self-worth. Deep down, Maxine thought she was a failure. There were ramblings about her father and hurtful things he'd said to her and about the people at the law firms who fired her. But Right Men and Women don't necessarily have to be failures. They can be worldly successes, too. What's critical is whether or not they're harboring a deep-seated sense of inferiority. And, it's fairly clear that Maxine did."

"Insecurity is one thing . . . but all those murders?"

"Yeah . . . I know . . . but you have to understand that remaining in control to the rest of the world is a hallmark of this syndrome. To function in the world, everyone learns self-control. The Right Man or Right Woman does, too, and he or she will maintain this self-control with every other person in his or her life, but one. Around this one person, the Right Man or Woman will decide that self-control is not necessary—be it a lover, wife, child, or parent. For Maxine Bowman, it was her husband, Bruce. With him, she made the decision to be out of control, to explode at will, venting rage, even violence, if she wished. It's a decision, Clare, a conscious decision to be out of control."

"So you're telling me when Bruce left, Maxine's escape valve left, too?"

"Yes. No more man around to look up to her no matter how she treated him. No more reassurance that her father was wrong . . . that she wasn't an aging princess who'd failed to make anything of herself. No more special place to release her inner demons, to be out of control. Worse than that, in her mind, the guy was now betraying her with other women and these women were going to benefit from what she perceived as her property—a piece of real estate she felt was hers by virtue of the effort she put in to making it valuable."

"Sweat equity," I murmured, remembering the way Bruce had talked about his own efforts in turning the Westchester house he and Maxine had shared into a property worth twice its purchase price. "It must have been a shock to Maxine to find Bruce stubbornly fighting back in the divorce for his fair share of everything."

"Yet another tangible example that she'd lost control of him, that he had finally become his own man, a man who was now tossing her away. And when he began to see other women—"

"She killed them."

"Yes. She obviously didn't want to destroy what she'd put so much effort into building, so instead she killed any woman who dared to attempt ownership of it."

"But what was her end game? What did she think she'd gain from it? Did she really think Bruce would go back to her once all these women were dead?"

Quinn shook his head. "Crimes of passion are a base transfer of rage. There's no logic to it, Clare. Only violence and pain . . ."

"And tears."

Quinn was frowning. I was crying.

"I'm sorry," I said softly, wiping away the wet.

"I went to see Valerie Lathem's mother and grand-mother," he said softly.

I closed my eyes, shuddering with the memory of those front page photos, thanking god I hadn't seen Joy's name in the headlines.

"They're a religious family . . . so knowing that Valerie didn't take her own life . . . it meant something to them."

I nodded.

"Listen, I'm worried about you. Are you going to be okay?"

"Yes . . ." I swallowed, sniffled, and nodded again. With a deep breath, I looked up, into my friend's wind-burned face, so full of concern, his blue eyes intense, waiting. For his benefit, I managed a small smile. "Thanks, Mike."

He let out a fairly substantial exhale. "Kid, I'm just glad you're still here."

So was Joy. So was Matt.

"So am I."

FOR a long time, I avoided routes through St. Luke's Place and its curving extension just beyond the historic district's boundary. I tried my best to forget the snowy night I'd gone to that house on Leroy, the night I'd crossed the line. One chilly spring day, however, I wasn't paying attention to the direction of a stroll, and Joy led me back to that site.

Unexpectedly, I found myself standing once more in front of that simple yet refined house of Bruce Bowman's. The house that had never become a home.

"Mom? Is anything wrong?" Joy had asked.

"No, honey . . . just memories."

In the end, I tried not to become bitter over the tragedy of what happened, the horrible waste of it. I wanted to find a better way of remembering Bruce . . . so I tried to remember the early snowfall in the Village that Friday evening. Beautiful but transitory, disappearing by Sunday's sunrise.

Bruce was like that to me, I decided. My lovely afternoon, my gorgeous evening. Not lasting, but remembered, and with something more than fondness. If only Maxine could have learned how to let go, I often found myself thinking, she would still be alive herself . . .

Thomas Paine, that fiery soul who'd died two centuries ago in Greenwich Village, once said, "We have it in our power to begin the world over again."

Maybe some of us do. But some of us don't.

For Bruce it was too late. For Maxine, too.

It wasn't too late for me, though. I had started over more than once in my life and I would do it again. The pain, I knew, would eventually recede . . . melting in time as inevitably as an early snow.

Recipes & Tips
From the Village Blend

The Village Blend's
Café Mocha
(A chocolate latte)

Pour a generous helping of chocolate syrup into the bottom of the cup. Add a shot of espresso. Add steamed milk. Stir the liquid, lifting from the bottom to bring up the syrup. Top with sweetened whipped cream and ground cocoa.

The Village Blend's Café Nocciuola
(A hazelnut latte)

Cover the bottom of a cup with hazelnut syrup. Add a shot of espresso. Add steamed milk. Stir the liquid, lifting from the bottom to bring up the syrup. Top with foamed milk.

Clare's Café Frangelico
(A hazelnut-liqueur latte)

Pour a shot of Frengelico (a hazelnut liqueur) into a cup, add a shot of espresso. Add steamed milk. Stir the liquid, lifting from the bottom to bring up the syrup. Top with foamed milk or whipped cream.

Matteo's Coffee-Hazelnut Cocktail
(Hold the espresso!)

¾ ounce Kahlúa (a coffee-flavored liqueur)
2-½ teaspoons Frangelico (a hazelnut-flavored liqueur)
¾ ounce vodka
3 ounces crushed ice

Combine Kahlúa, Frangelico, and vodka. Stir well. Pour over ice and serve in old-fashioned glass.

Coffee Marinated Steak with Garlic Mashed Potatoes and Hearty Coffee Gravy

COFFEE MARINATED STEAK

Place two to four of your favorite steaks (T-bone, Rib Eye, Sirloin, etc.) in a large flat pan and add enough strongly brewed coffee to cover. (A slightly acidic bean is recommended, but any Latin American blend will do. It's the acidity that does the tenderizing.)

Marinate at least 8 hours. Overnight is best. Cook in a cast-iron skillet, or under the broiler.

GARLIC MASHED POTATOES

Peel three to six large Russet or Yukon Gold potatoes. Cut up into same-size pieces. Peel one clove of garlic per potato (more or less to taste).

Add potatoes and garlic to three quarts of salted water. Bring to a rolling boil. Cook until potatoes are soft. Add two to three tablespoons of butter, and a fourth cup (12 ounces) milk or cream to hot potatoes. Mash, then whip. Serve hot.

HEARTY COFFEE GRAVY

5 tablespoons butter
¼ cup flour
1 cup (8 ounces) beef broth or stock
¼ cup (4 ounces) freshly brewed coffee
2 or 3 tablespoons pan drippings (optional)

Melt five tablespoons of butter in saucepan. When melted, whisk in one-fourth cup flour, eight ounces of broth, and two or three tablespoons of pan drippings (if available). Whisk together with one-fourth cup fresh brewed coffee. Heat slowly until it just boils. Serve hot.

The Village Blend's Coffee Storage Tips

1) Do keep your beans away from excessive air, moisture, heat, and light (and in that order) so you can preserve the fresh-roast flavor as long as possible.

2) Do not freeze or refrigerate your daily supply of coffee! Contact with moisture will destroy the flavor.

3) Do store your coffee in an air-tight container and keep it in a dark and cool location. Remember that a cabinet near the oven is often too warm, as is a shelf near the heat of a strong summer sun!

4) Do purchase coffee in amounts that make sense for how quickly you will use it. The fresh smell and taste of coffee begin to decline almost immediately after roasting, so DO buy freshly roasted coffee often, and buy only what you will use in the next week or two.

**Don't Miss the Next
Coffeehouse Mystery**
LATTE TROUBLE

Clare Cosi was never under the impression that one could wear a latte. Of course, her ex-husband once had—courtesy of Clare herself—on the morning after one of Matteo's "extra-curricular" romps. But this was different. This was fashion. Lottie Harmon, longtime Village Blend customer and once-famous fashion designer, has created an exclusive line of pricey, coffee-inspired jewelry and accessories. Now the Village Blend becomes a *fashionista* showplace— a stage for Lottie's debut, and for murder. Suddenly, Clare is caught up in another mystery, because when somebody poisons one of the Blend's famous coffee drinks, death returns to the coffeehouse door, bringing with it a latte trouble!